THE STARS ARE MY SALVATION

BOOK 1
THE REASON

THE STARS ARE MY SALVATION

BOOK 1
THE REASON

Stephen Langford

STYGIAN
P R E S S
PITTSBURGH, PENNSYLVANIA

Book Design and Formatting by Craig Hines
using stock content under license from Adobe Stock and Envato.
Book Cover Design by Ebook Launch

Edited by Hannah Ryan, Colette Freedman, and Charlie Knight

PUBLISHER'S CATALOGING-IN-PUBLICATION DATA
Names: Langford, Stephen, author.
Title: The stars are my salvation : the reason / Stephen Langford.
Series: The Stars Are My Salvation
Description: Pittsburgh, PA: Stygian Press, 2023.
Identifiers: LCCN: 2022913619 | ISBN: 978-1-958268-00-1 (hardcover)
| 978-1-958268-01-8 (paperback) | 978-1-958268-02-5 (ebook)
Subjects: LCSH Interstellar travel--Fiction. | Interplanetary voyages-
-Fiction. | Human-alien encounters--Fiction. | Science fiction. |
BISAC FICTION / Science Fiction / Space Opera | FICTION /
Science Fiction / Action & Adventure | FICTION / Science Fiction
/ Space Exploration | FICTION / Science Fiction / Alien Contact
Classification: LCC PS3612 .A582 S83 2022 | DDC 813.6--dc23

First Paperback Edition
ISBN: 978-1-958268-01-8

Published by Stygian Press
www.StygianPress.com

25 24 23   LSI   0 9 8 7 6 5 4 3 2 1

Content Advisory

This novel contains some brief scenes, content, and dialogue
that may be objectionable to some readers. For more detailed
information, please visit the publisher's website.

For my wife, Sandy,
who set me on this new journey.

Part One

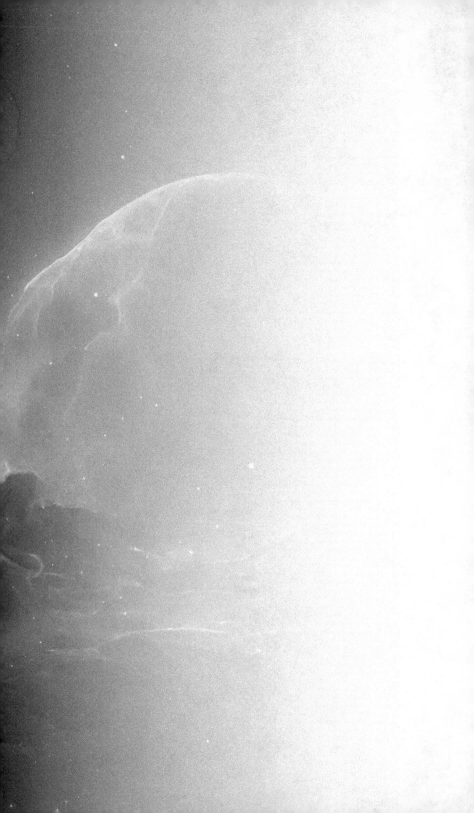

PROLOGUE

2176

As Commander Kris Galloway gazed out at the star Sirius from a sick bay porthole, his mind was consumed by one word: mutiny. His eyes dropped to a transport cruiser filled with gold miners that were slipping under his ship. He was envious of the miners passing beneath him. They were getting out of harm's way. They would live to see tomorrow.

They jumped into hyperspace in a brilliant green flash, which deposited a swirling light show of tiny green particles that rolled and scattered to the right.

Mutiny had been on his mind for the last ten days as the war raged on across the great expanse. It was a week ago when he began to hatch his plot.

Kris turned away from the porthole and ran his hand through his wavy brown hair. It was a habit when he was nervous. He sat down a little too hard on a stool. His legs were weak. He'd been up for thirty hours or so, and the Lasta pills were wearing off.

Kris' ship, the Concord, was the last starship left in orbit around Sirius. There were twenty other fleet vessels posted nearby, but his ship was the furthest one out. The ship closest to the war.

They were to be the next wave. The last wave.

Kris stared in the mirror at his bloodshot hazel eyes, seeing a weary young man who didn't look that young anymore. He was twenty-eight and felt forty. He looked around the sick bay and recalled how much he disliked the sterile smell. The rest of the ship was outfitted with sniffers that produced pleasant or familiar scents. He was especially partial to deck B as it smelled like grass-covered hills. It reminded him of growing up in Wyoming and the endless stretches of green.

"Time," Kris said to the room, and the computer voice answered. "10:20."

Kris had been in the treatment room for twenty minutes. He didn't like to wait and was relieved when the door slid open and Dr. Rourke bounded in. Rourke was in his forties with an unruly mop of blonde hair and scrubs that were overdue for a wash. He was an energetic man due to a dedication to exercise and eight cups of coffee a day. He talked a little too fast, which gave Kris pause as his life was in his hands.

"How does it look out there?" Rourke asked while eyeballing the melanoma on Kris' hand.

"Grim." Kris winced as Dr. Rourke poked around the cancer with his gloves. Dr. Rourke glanced down at a scan-pad and saw the diagnosis pop up. It was several pages long, and the commander waited anxiously while the doctor scanned through the charts and digital images. Even he could see how deep the cancer went.

"Stage four." Dr. Rourke shook his head as if admonishing a child. "Why'd you let it get this far?"

"Slipped my mind."

"That's really gotta be painful. How'd you let that slip your mind?"

"War."

When Kris started out, he had a bit of a mouth on him. He was more knowledgeable than most and made sure everyone else knew it. He once corrected his commander, Willie Stone, and, as a result, Stone posted him to a planet called Galox, which had a weak atmosphere that allowed an abnormal amount of radiation to seep through. Kris had been overexposed during his tour. He consequently had several melanomas in the years since.

He cursed Commander Stone before recalling that Stone's ship was blown apart in the first wave of attacks. A shot from a Citari cruiser landed on the flight deck, vaporizing Commander Stone and his crew. Kris couldn't be that vindictive. He wouldn't wish that on his worst enemy. There was only death beyond the star he was circling.

He winced again as the doctor squeezed the discolored area. "Does that hurt?"

"Of course, it does," Kris said, raising his voice a little. "Why do you do that? You know it's going to hurt."

"It's a reminder to take care of your health."

Dr. Rourke retrieved a device with a snout-like end, placed it over the melanoma, and punched in a few numbers. The device vibrated and made a soft clicking sound as it sucked away the infected tissue and replaced it with new skin. Kris felt a strong pinch but nothing more. The melanoma disappeared in a matter of seconds. Kris gripped his hand, mostly out of instinct, pain free.

Rourke pulled out a nose spray. "Chemo."

Kris took a hit of the spray. He shook a little as he felt the chemicals coursing through his bloodstream, and he felt a slight burning sensation that went away after a minute. Kris felt a little dizzy and gripped a nearby desk to steady himself. It quickly faded away.

Kris got to his feet to face a grinning Dr. Rourke, who clapped him on the shoulder.

"You should be cancer-free by lunchtime tomorrow."

"Thanks, Doc."

"Oh, and Galloway?"

"Yeah, Doc?"

"Try not to get us killed."

"Nobody's dying today," Kris assured him.

"Have they come to their senses?" Rourke asked hopefully.

The question went unanswered as Kris headed out of the treatment room with the doctor's words ringing in his mind. He had to make the right moves. It was a matter of precision. He had rehearsed the plan every evening after his shifts. Kris hadn't slept last night. He was preparing. He was saving his species from annihilation.

He was a mere ten years out of high school and billions of lives were in his hands. This was the most singular moment in human history. No man had ever faced a challenge of this magnitude. He had to extinguish the madness and save humanity.

Kris was filled with self-doubt since his demotion. He had to temper his low self-esteem. It could engulf his soul and Kris knew he couldn't allow this frailty to consume him. His mind had to remain keen. Earth was depending on his mutiny.

Kris stepped onto the flight deck and covered his eyes to shield from the glare of Sirius. He squinted and blinked. It was too bright.

He looked to the science officer, Delilah Court, a thirty-five year old with jet black hair and an eternal pout planted on her face.

Hearing the door open, Court turned and stared at Kris, un-impressed. Kris shrugged it off. He knew she didn't care for him. She should have had his job. He'd been demoted to what should have been her promised promotion. She'd played the good soldier the best she could, so, to Delilah, Kris was an insult. Whenever he was around, her jaw went tight, and her eyes went icy cold.

Kris could feel her hostility, but he remained indifferent. Delilah wasn't on his mind. Saving the human race was.

"Court."

"Sir."

"Increase filter by twenty-five percent," Kris ordered.

"Aye. Hurting your eyes, sir?" she said with a little sting in her voice.

Kris felt guilty. She had every right to needle him at every opportunity. He shouldn't be here. He should have resigned in protest and gone back to his parents' house in Wyoming. He could have stayed in their log cabin near Jackson Hole and fished carp. He could have drenched himself in fresh air and cool beer and completely checked out. But something kept him on the Concord.

He remembered the first time he put on his flight suit. He was in a locker room in front of a mirror and realized for the first time that he, Kris Galloway, had an identity. He wasn't anonymous when he walked down the street in uniform. People knew what he did, and strangers shook his hand for doing it. He didn't join NASA to find something that set him apart from others, but when he became aware of that feeling within him, Kris realized it was something he needed. Kris wondered if this was a flaw in his character, a bit of narcissism that needed to be fed. It gave him a great sense of unease, for he knew, deep in his heart, he craved it.

Court took her time increasing the filter, just to irritate him. Finally, after finishing some procedures at her station, she decreased the intensity. Kris shifted his weight a little as the room became darker. He even felt his breathing become more measured. He considered that she had turned the brightness up just to get under his skin. She'd do that from time to time.

"Thank you," Kris said.

Court didn't acknowledge him as she stared straight ahead at her station.

Kris watched the helmsman, Hernandez, a Hispanic man with wide brown eyes and a tiny frame, punch commands to turn the ship out toward empty space. Kris stepped down to the command chair and stood by it, resting his hand on one of the arms. He regarded the chair with a slight sense of regret. The arms were brown leather and a little worn. He could see a stain where the captain had spilled some coffee. It had once been his chair. He was the youngest captain in the fleet, the boy destined to become admiral by thirty. But, due to circumstances aided by his honesty and boldness, Kris' life would divert on a course he couldn't begin to imagine.

He had started to turn away when there was a flash in the corner of his eyes that he first assumed was a side effect of the chemo, but then it happened two more times in rapid succession. He pivoted around and couldn't help but let his jaw drop a little before he caught himself.

As Kris stepped forward, walking past Court to the side of the helmsman, he could see the war raging sixty million miles out in the void. He sighed. This shouldn't be happening. He had warned them. There was no question of the outcome.

Kris told the helmsman to increase the magnification on the screen, then instantly wished he hadn't. His instinct was to turn off the screen altogether, but that would make him look weak to the crew. He had to accept the alternative: watching the Earth's battle fleet exploding across the great expanse.

Kris was watching his friends die.

He directed his attention to the science panel. He was dodging the view still, but not as obviously. He didn't want to think about the myriad of faces, of friends out there, frozen in the harshness of space, their last memories of war, knowing their lives were over.

Kris pictured others either vaporized or dying slowly in the hulks of starships with no hope of rescue. They would only have time to think about death from either radiation exposure or dwindling oxygen. They were friends, mentors, lovers, and enemies, all dying for a folly.

He came out of his fog and realized it was time. Time for mutiny. A mutiny of one with no accomplices.

He had the flight deck. It was his moment to come out of the shadows and be bold again.

"Where's the skipper?" Kris demanded.

"Torpedo room. You told him to confer with the weapons officer. Remember? Before we go in," the helmsman reported, his eyes filled with fear.

"Right. Right."

Kris plopped into the command chair. He was offered a coffee by an ensign, and he grabbed it and gulped it down. The cream and sugar felt good sliding down his throat. The ensign lingered.

"What? Something on your mind?" Kris asked.

"You wrote the Keifer Report."

"Yeah, that's me. And by the looks of it, I was pretty accurate."

"Why didn't they listen?"

The Keifer Report was a detailed analysis of the Council, the leadership of the most powerful aliens in the galaxy: the Citaris. Using intelligence analysis, the report determined that war with the Council was futile. It explained how Earth needed to reform its ways or else face destruction. Yet the warnings were not heeded, and hubris reigned.

In return for writing the report, Kris had been relieved of his command as captain of the Monmouth and was demoted to commander, then reassigned to the Concord.

Kris gazed in horror at the deep blue flashes in the distance, but soon noticed they were becoming less and less frequent. A few minutes later, there were none. All they could see was the stark blackness and the stars. In his gut, he knew they'd just lost the war.

Kris shifted in his seat, his jaw tightening. "Communications, what's the chatter level?"

The communications officer slowly turned to him, stifling back tears, her voice trembling. "None of ours. Only Citari."

The ensign stared at Kris with fear in his eyes. The whole flight deck fell silent, save for the pulsing and beeping systems that ran the ship. The Concord had been one of the backbenchers in the war, but it was quickly apparent to everyone on the deck that they were the new front line.

"Captain still in the torpedo room?" Kris asked.

"He's on his way up," Court said.

Kris knew that the captain was itching for battle, but he had no sense for tactics. He was at the bottom of the barrel in the fleet. He got his command because he'd been in the game so long, they had to finally give him a ship. Kris was assigned to be his babysitter.

But Kris was done. He had resolved he was going to protect Earth from itself.

Taking decisive action, Kris flipped open a panel on the command chair. He could see the captain's beacon, indicating he was on an elevator. He quickly went to a second panel and shut down that elevator, cutting off its communications. This was the first step in his silent mutiny. No one would know. It would read as a failure in a relay and nothing more.

Kris was going to put an end to all the madness.

"Helm, release buoy. Five, seven, five."

"A buoy, sir?"

"I didn't ask for questions. Move!"

The ensign released the buoy and it floated past their viewscreen.

Court turned around to Kris curiously.

"Engage drive. Set course for Earth. Seventy-five lights," Kris said sternly.

"The captain? Are these his orders?" Court questioned.

"The Directorate. It's above your paygrade," he retorted.

Court stood up and stared him directly in his eyes. Kris didn't flinch. Court walked up to him in her panther-like way. She eyed him suspiciously as the rest of the crew damned her silently for questioning his orders. Kris watched her approach, not believing she was pulling this now. He could see the other crew members shooting daggers at her from around the flight deck.

"The Directorate?" Court echoed.

"Lieutenant, return to your station," Kris said firmly.

"I'd like a confirmation," Court insisted.

"If you're willing to wait in the brig for it," Kris said coolly. Court unclenched her fists and turned away, defeated. She glowered at him, turned away, and sat at her post. Kris opened a panel on his chair and punched in a code. It was the recall code for the other ships scattered in the quadrant. He was supposed to tell the communications officers to send it, but he had rewired the module the night before. No one on the deck would know what had happened.

The code went out to the last ships in the fleet. The cruisers, without question, turned around and headed back to Earth.

The Concord jumped into hyperspace and headed home, too. The Council ships arrived five minutes later. Theirs were larger, outfitted with turret guns that swung on the buoy, but they didn't fire. The guns still glowed white hot from the battle they'd just won.

Kris' eyes were on a scanner, watching the Citari ships hold their positions. The Citaris by now could hear the song in their native language being broadcast from the buoy as it blared into the speakers of all the Citari flight decks. Kris knew the melody would be familiar to all onboard the Citari starships. It was ancient, dating back to the twelfth mellen of the Citari race. It was "The Song of Salaya." The song of surrender, one that the Citaris had accepted as the end of hostilities for thousands of years. Kris knew when he broadcast the song it would be seen as a sign of respect from the Earthers. When those haunting words were sung, Kris was certain the Citaris would accept that they were victorious. They had made their point. Over four hundred Earth ships were destroyed or missing. They had boxed in the Earthers. As "The Song of Salaya" repeated chorus after chorus, the Citaris stood down. The conflict was over. Kris eyed the message that the Citaris had accepted. The surrender came with terms that the Earthers could travel no further than the DMZ, which was four light years past Proxima Centauri.

Kris felt satisfied seeing that the remains of the fleet, twenty ships, were hyper-spacing back to Earth, so this was all done with one vote. His vote. The vote of Commander Kris Galloway, the secret mutineer.

By the time the Concord arrived in Earth's orbit, Kris learned the Council had notified Earth that the boundaries were set, and they were not to cross them. Ever. Congress revolted against the hard-liners who had promised Earth would become the leaders of a great galactic empire. They told lies to get a war vote. There was an earthquake in Washington, D.C.

The president and vice president resigned instead of facing certain impeachment. The Speaker of the House, Helen Swope, rose to the presidency that day and accepted the terms. Internally, countless heads rolled in the government. Swope promised that there would never be hostilities between Earth and Citari again.

Kris sat in his quarters, looking down at Earth, and knew it was safe. It was the year 2176, and he had made sure there was going to be a 2177. He wondered if anyone would uncover his mutiny. He didn't care if they did and threw him in jail. With no one else willing, he had to stop the madness.

Kris gazed at the blue world below, dotted with white puffs of clouds. He smiled, knowing it would be his home again. Forever, he hoped.

Kris slipped into his bed and pulled the sheets tight. He wanted to feel secure. He fell asleep and dreamed of fishing striped bass at Bighorn Lake in Wyoming.

CHAPTER ONE

Ninety years ago: 2086

The orbital insertion burn shook the Falcon spacecraft and its crew for six minutes. They had been traveling at three hundred thousand miles an hour across the solar system, and had been firing a series of breaking retroburns in the past twenty-four hours to decrease the ship's velocity. The Falcon engaged its final burn as it slipped into Pluto's orbit.

Pluto was the last body in the solar system that hadn't been explored. It had been twenty years since the last venture to one of the moons of Neptune, Triton. Pluto was three billion miles away from Earth. It was simply out of reach until a breakthrough on a new fusion propulsion system in 2081. After the revolutionary advance, work began on a manned Pluto landing with a touchdown scheduled for 2086, and the Falcon was chosen as the spacecraft to make the historic journey.

Captain Jedidiah Fitzhugh was short in stature with a broad chest and sandy brown hair. He clung to a porthole staring out at Pluto, floating. He stared down at the northern hemisphere. It was a mixture of white and red with a patch of black. He was alone in his quarters, and that's the way he liked it. Fitzhugh didn't want the crew to witness his boyish glee. He'd always dreamed of being immortalized in the history books. Soon, he would be the first man on Pluto. His name would be mentioned alongside the greats: Gagarin, Glenn, Armstrong, Fuentes, Delton, Scott, Akido and now, finally, Fitzhugh.

The lander, the Cyclops, was online and ready. The landing sequence would commence in a mere five hours. The mission was staying within parameters... until the burping started. He had Mexican food for dinner and quickly surmised it wasn't agreeing with him. The burping became more intense. He tried soda, then gas tabs, then finally sonic antacids, but nothing seemed to work. Fitzhugh went to the zero g toilet, and that's when the fever started. He went to sick bay and saw Dr. Kyle, who quickly concluded that he needed his gallbladder removed. Fitzhugh was beside himself, insisting the doctor was wrong. His temperature was rising, as was his anger. The doctor had to forcibly sedate the captain to take him into surgery.

Fitzhugh's second in command, Mariah Chen, lurked by the sick bay, clinging to a handle as she floated. Dr. Kyle turned toward Mariah and informed her the captain was incapacitated, and she was now in command. It was her task to pilot the Cyclops for its imminent flight down to the surface of Pluto. She pressed her face against the window. She stared down at Pluto. It was all on her now. She'd been thrust into history by a gallbladder attack. Mariah would be the first person to step on the surface of Pluto.

Mariah was five foot five, toned, with jet black hair that slanted to the left. She was assigned to be the copilot, but that had all changed in a matter of half an hour. She was now in command and had to make the critical go or no-go decision. Mariah checked the time and realized the landing window was rapidly approaching. Communications with Earth took four and a half hours each way. That meant missing two landing opportunities if she aborted.

They had a finite amount of time on Pluto. The tight schedule was jammed packed with science and exploration. With only a brief launch window for their return to Earth, she had to make a decision.

Mariah floated down a corridor packed with bulky equipment and netting. She grabbed at the netting and thrust herself forward, then used her boot to bounce herself off a wall, which sent her sailing into her quarters. She sealed the door and glanced around at walls that were lined with pictures of her family and a boyfriend she had disappointed due to her devotion to the mission. It was either Frank or going to Pluto. It was a hard decision for her when she chose to go to Pluto.

She peered at the ship's clock. They had twenty minutes to finish the preflight checklist. Her chest heaved at the responsibility. She closed her eyes and meditated, calming herself. This is what she had trained for. The remote possibility of her taking command on account of Fitzhugh being incapacitated had been one of the training scenarios.

Mariah picked up a photograph of her mom, Casey. She taught her how to be a strong woman and not shrink in the face of great responsibility. Mariah stared at her picture as she floated sideways and gripped more netting to steady herself. She had never been in command before. Fitzhugh didn't delegate. He was a self-admitted control freak. She sighed loudly, wondering if she was up to it. She had only commanded simulated flights in Houston. Mariah questioned if she could find that perfect balance of focus and compassion that makes a great leader. She reasoned she would just have to. She only hoped the crew would sense this and support her. Mariah opened the door and floated back to the flight deck. All eyes were on her.

Mariah surveyed her crewmates' faces. These were the people with whom she had trained for four years and spent the last three months in space. They were family, and she realized she was their leader now. She shot her hand up and pushed herself down to a standing position on the ship's grated floor.

"Alright, let's finish the Cyclops' checklist. Pluto deorbit in 21:20. Hop to it, people." Mariah noticed the crew seemed uneasy. She couldn't reveal she was uneasy too. So, she grinned broadly.

"Take it easy, everybody. We trained for this. Sobisky, you're my copilot now. You've done the simulations. You can do this."

Sobisky's pale face brightened. A plum-shaped guy with a beard and a few patches of hair left on his bald head, he was a quiet man, but very skilled at what he did. He was third in command and didn't relish being the new Number One, but he stepped up, nevertheless.

"You heard her, people. Move." Sobisky nodded to Mariah. He had her back.

As the crew jumped into action, Mariah let out an infectious whoop.

"We're landing on Pluto and we are the first!"

Mariah kicked herself forward toward the lander hatch. She gripped a blue handle and pumped it twice, then punched in the code on a panel of square green buttons. The locks released with a loud metallic click. The hatch opened, and Mariah dove in. Sobisky floated in after her. They steadied themselves in the lander, sliding their boots into slots that locked their feet into a standing position. They both began their preflight checklist and finished powering up the lander.

Members of the landing party took their positions. Evan, the youngest crew member at 27 years old, floated by the lander hatch waiting for the signal to close it. Sobisky nodded to Mariah that he was ready. Mariah gave Evan the thumbs up. He sealed the hatch and worked his way down to his seat, where he punched in a series of commands.

"We're green and go for undocking," Evan said.

Mariah pulsed the reaction jets and backed the ship away from the Falcon, gently puffing the reaction jet with her grip handle. She made a flip maneuver that turned the ship on its back, facing away from Pluto. Mariah watched the Falcon getting smaller in her window. She couldn't fathom she was going to be the first human being to set foot on Pluto, but she couldn't let that cloud her thoughts. She had a job to do.

Mariah stared straight ahead, calling out the ship's status. She knew that by the time NASA learned of Fitzhugh's condition, she'd have already landed the Cyclops. Because of the distance from Earth, all go, or no-go decisions were up to her and her only. She called out that the landing was green and go.

The crew's confidence in Mariah grew swiftly, and she could sense it. She was meant to be here. Her assuredness was unwavering. She may have been a rookie, but she was a natural commanding figure, and the crew could feel it.

Mariah went through the flight command sequence like it was her tenth landing on a planet, though it was only her first. "T-minus twenty seconds to deorbit burn," she said calmly as she gripped a controller handle, lightly tugging on it and lining up the ship to the navigation target pulsing a light green on the flight panel.

The Cyclops twisted on its axis ever so slightly. The computer indicated she had a green light for the deorbit burn. Mariah tapped the code that told the A.I. to take over, then checked the pair of landing straps that held her in place. She was no longer the pilot; the A.I. was flying now. The cabin went silent. Mariah remained stoic. Twenty seconds later, the engine fired and they dropped down to Pluto.

The Cyclops hovered for a few minutes, searching for the perfect terrain for landing. They were floating about one hundred feet above the icy surface. The engines were stirring up ice and rock below the Cyclops, creating Plutonian dust devils, possibly the first ever to adorn this ancient world. Mariah checked the fuel gauge. It was getting low. She spotted where she wanted to land, a flat, open space, and disengaged the A.I. She grabbed the lander grip controller and became the pilot once again.

"There's a nice sexy spot." She grinned and eased the lander to a soft landing. As they settled on the surface, the Cyclops pushed ice and rock out of the way as the landing pads settled in. She shut down the engines, keyed her mic, and calmly said, "Houston, the Cyclops has landed. We are on Pluto."

The message sailed through space at light speed.

Mariah undid her landing straps and turned around to the crew with her hands on her hips, beaming. "Suit up everybody. It's time to make history." The crew crowded by the window, stoked to be the first humans to gaze at the surface of Pluto.

The crew donned their spacesuits, which took a little over ten minutes. They checked their seals and oxygen supplies, and then Mariah rechecked each one of them herself, giving each a thumbs up as she approved. Sobisky turned on the camera drones that would film them outside. The drones disconnected from the lander floating outside as their tiny micro-pulse jets fired, supporting them.

"Ready anytime you are, Skipper," Sobisky said.

It was the first time anyone had called her skipper after her sudden ascension to commander of the mission. It touched her, and she pulled Sobisky into a hug. She didn't mind showing her emotions to the crew. Overwhelmed, Sobisky hugged her back.

"Start decompression," ordered Mariah.

Mariah reached for the hatch handle, pumped it three times, and opened it. Then she turned herself around and backed out the hatch. Her first sight outside the ship was the Cyclops itself. She saw Evan waving to her through the window. Mariah waved back. She saw a shadow overhead and realized it was one of the drones filming the historic moment. Mariah gripped the ladder and put her boot in the first rung. She eased down to the pad as she felt something she hadn't felt in a while: gravity. It was one-fifteenth of Earth's, but it was gravity, nonetheless. She climbed down to the pad and landed with a bounce. She could see Dr. Fitter on his way down the ladder after her.

"Hey, Doc, you're gonna love the view," Mariah said, still lingering at the bottom of the ladder.

"I will if you get moving," he responded. Mariah stepped back out of the way as he descended.

Mariah twisted around and saw the digi-drones locking their cameras on her. They were lining up in preparation. Her eyes drifted across Pluto's landscape. It was grey, icy, and alien. Words escaped her. Nothing profound formed in her mind. But then it came to her.

She stepped off the pad and whooped and hollered, dancing a jig. Ice chips and pebbles kicked up, floating around her before settling to the ground. Dr. Fitter was now on the landing pad, smiling at her antics.

After that impromptu display of euphoria, Mariah Chen, the green-eyed Chinese American cowgirl from Plano, Texas, became an instant sensation on Earth... with a four-point-five-hour delay.

"Look at me, I'm a Plutonian!" she said, doing a back flip. Mariah was always an outsized personality. She was vivacious and boisterous. Whenever there was a party, she was the life of it. Only now, she had an audience: Earth, Mars, and a few moons. She was funny, charming, and hardworking—and the world loved her for it.

Millions of t-shirts were sold with that phrase. Her broadcasts from Pluto were the most watched digital event in history. People couldn't get enough of her unadulterated joy in science. Mariah would start each broadcast saying, "Let's start exploring, everybody!"

For over five days, the crew of the Falcon explored the region called Tellen Terra. The discoveries were boundless, but unfortunately no one was aware of the deadly secret of Hadley Ridge. Beneath it was an active ice volcano. It had been brewing for over fifty years. The survey equipment detected it too late. By the time the data arrived warning of impending eruption, it had blown during a live broadcast while Mariah and Dr. Fitter were examining a rock. The screen went white, then finally cleared to reveal two eerie, frozen statues: Mariah and Dr. Fitter.

People were shattered. The world mourned their loss. It was a tragedy that affected the solar system as a whole. The vivacious Mariah was gone. She had been an inspiration to countless viewers. The mission to Pluto had devolved into a tragedy. Mariah's optimism had touched millions. Her five days on Pluto had filled people with hope. She allowed them to dream that anything was possible.

Sobisky had descended down to the surface and openly wept in his pressure suit as he gazed at Mariah, eternally frozen in time. He turned away and headed back to the Cyclops, climbing the ladder and sealing the hatch behind him. He took off his suit as Brenda, a mousey geologist, stepped forward, kneading her hands nervously.

"What about Mariah and Dr. Fitter?" she asked.

"They should be a monument," Sobisky declared, his jaw firm.

"You mean leave them?"

"If we touch them, they might shatter. This way, they'll always be here," he said with reverence.

Sobisky told the crew to get into their positions. Mission rules were certain. If there was a loss of any crew, that called for an immediate abort. He was in command now, a position he'd never desired, but Mariah gave him strength he didn't think he had. Sobisky had to be that person for Mariah and her memory. He fired the ascent engine and the Cyclops rose back into orbit, docked with the Falcon, and headed home.

The site would be considered sacred. Mariah did end up in the history books. She was the first human on Pluto. But her chapter ended in tragedy.

CHAPTER TWO

Kris had imprisoned his captain in an elevator so he could execute his mutiny. When he released him, the captain was furious. He was supposed to be leading the fleet into war. Kris just shrugged and showed him the acknowledgement from the Earth Directorate that affirmed the war was over. The captain didn't understand how the hostilities had ceased, and Kris had no intention of explaining. Kris returned to his quarters and slept on the way home.

When Kris woke up, he propped himself up on his bed and thought back to how they had arrived at this point in history. He was a voracious reader on the subject. He had a book on his shelf concerning how the growing conflict had begun, which he picked up to thumb through again. It all started with Sirius Minor.

The star caused excitement and wild speculation. A planet that seemed as though it could support life! But probes voyaged out and discovered the blue world wasn't viable. It was lifeless.

They discovered life, as it turns out, closer to home. It was a little blue planet in the Goldilocks Zone. It was far closer to Earth, orbiting Proxima Centauri B, only 4.24 light years away. It could become the second Earth, as it was uninhabited with smaller mammal-like creatures and aquatic life forms. The planet was showered with probes as Mars had been in the twentieth and twenty-first centuries. They named the planet after the space hero, Mariah.

The landing parties followed, and within ten years human presence in space began and ushered in what was called "The Great Expansion." Humans were finally becoming a star-faring species.

The planet Mariah's discovery became the motivating force in finalizing the Alcubierre Drive. It had been in development for thirty years, and Congress had finally grown weary of funding what they felt was a boondoggle. The contractors kept saying they had almost cracked it, but Congress had heard enough; the project was scuttled.

But then a probe launched twenty years earlier using lasers and wind sails arrived at Mariah, six months after the drive was abandoned. Humanity didn't know what information was racing to them at the speed of light, but when it did finally arrive, it told the tale that there was another planet near them that supported life. The Alcubierre Drive was revived.

The drive allowed travel over vast distances of space by folding it, to move greater distances in a shorter amount of time. It was the dream of the long-dead Mexican theoretical physicist Miguel Alcubierre. The day the drive was completed, he gained the only immortality a person can attain. His name became eternal.

The Orion, the first starship, came together and journeyed to Proxima B. The drive made it a short trip. By the time the public gasped at the broadcast of the first astronaut stepping onto an Earth-like world, the ship had already returned. The astronauts beat the signal back by four years. The signal traveled at the speed of light, but man could now travel faster.

The stars were finally in Earth's grasp, and what happened next was swift.

Colonization.

In a matter of ten years, the population grew to one hundred and ten thousand. Mariah was a boom planet. Cities popped up and it became a vacation destination spot, as commerce invested in Earth's new sister world.

The desire to move beyond Mariah grew rapidly. The Earth Directorate was formed by the United States to manage Earth's expansion into the galaxy. They decided to venture out further, seeking more opportunities for colonization. A collective feeling had grown that the stars were theirs to conquer.

Starships became faster and more sophisticated. The first missions were filled with a sense of wonder. Most of the planets they found were inhabited by primitive civilizations. That's when the hubris began. Human history started to repeat itself. Governments were stretched too thin to reach light years and, consequently, corporations made their own laws. Humans built empires and class systems driven by their technological superiority over hundreds of other planets. The humans looked down on other, lesser sentients. Earth's leaders deemed that humanity's destiny was to rule over the galaxy.

As humanity expanded, their arrogance didn't go unnoticed by the Citari Council. The Citaris had originally dreamt of plundering the Milky Way. But as the Citari evolved, they realized that conquering weaker neighbors would be a folly. Though they had great power, they also had great wisdom. The Citari history was not an easy one. It had been filled with conflicts that had threatened their extinction. When the stars beckoned, they understood that they had to follow a path of grace. Mathematicians guided the Citaris by predicting outcomes. Their conclusion was that the inhabitants of the Milky Way needed to abide by the same rules.

While the humans from Earth wanted an empire, the Citaris merely wanted alliance. The Citaris would protect planets and ask for nothing in return. Then Earth began to encroach on those protected planets. The Citaris politely told the Earthers to cease their ways. But the Earthers ignored them. War was brewing.

Kris laid down the book. He picked a copy up of the surrender document the Citaris had sent. The Earthers' boundaries would be pushed back to within eight light years of Earth. Kris closed the document and remembered that, at one time, Earth held influence over nearly three hundred light years' worth of the expanse. But that was all over, and Kris was fine with it. Humanity wasn't ready to be a player in the galaxy. Earthers had proven their goals were anything but pure.

CHAPTER THREE

Kris was appointed captain of the Concord again after the war ended. The reason was simple. The war had been such a failure that the Keifer Report was published after lawyers pressed for its release through The Freedom of Information Act. Kris was a gifted spokesman on camera, and in demand—the world had questions and it seemed he had the answers. Interviewers asked him why no one had heeded his warnings. Kris would often blame himself, taking responsibility for humanity's actions. He thought he hadn't been forceful enough. He hadn't fought adequately to be heard. Perhaps if he had, they wouldn't have lost so many to war. Kris frequently ended his interviews with, "We went out to the stars, but maybe we went too far. Maybe we've gone far enough right now."

A billionaire named Haven Soares debated him in the press. He believed they should have continued to fight on, but his voice was drowned out by the support for Kris. Kris was the man of the hour; Haven Soares was the past. The war for the stars was no longer in fashion. Haven became a ridiculed sideshow act and, in the end, left the public stage.

Kris retired from NASA a few years later and moved to Modesto. It was about this time a clever hacker named Cleaven Holt broke into the Concord's records and revealed Kris' one-man mutiny to stop the war.

Kris was not vilified—rather, the public declared him a hero. Soon publishers were knocking on his door to tell his story. The offers were generous. He wrote four books on the war with the Council, all bestsellers. He then went on the speaking circuit and earned more money than he knew what to do with, but he grew weary of the topic as his bank account got fatter.

The idea of being anonymous became his soul ambition in life, and he went all in to achieve it.

———————

Two years later, he met Mindy Cyrus. She was a beautiful and charming doe-eyed blonde. She reminded him of a Disney Princess gifted with a biting sense of humor. The courtship was short, as they both yearned for the same thing. They wanted to be a quiet couple with a few kids and a modest business—he was financially secure and didn't have to work, but uncomfortable being idle.

One day, he saw a commercial on the digi selling Toyota jet cycles. They were racing hypercycles children could fly. They were safe, with a canopy, and used an electric form of jet propulsion. Kris bought some bikes and started a weekend kiddie party business, turning an old skating rink into a Cyclorama. He launched it successfully just in time for the birth of their first child.

Kris had settled into the calmness he'd craved. He had everything he wanted. He was in a new chapter of his life. The stars didn't beckon him anymore.

Kris was content as he stood over his son's crib. The baby was asleep and fidgeting around under his blanket, probably dreaming. Mindy came to Kris' side, and he tucked his arm around her waist. She gave him a peck on the cheek.

"We have to decide on a name," Mindy said.

"I know."

"I thought you were the guy who made all the big decisions." She gazed up at him lovingly.

"Pass. I'm out of the big decision business. It's your call, honey." He kissed her on the top of her head as she stared at a list of names on her digi-pad."

Kids were still racing on hypercycles at Kris' Cyclorama. The party they were hosting for a seven-year-old had gone late. Kris sent his family home as he waited for the last drunk parents to stumble and fall into their hovering vehicles. He watched as an A.I. driver shuttled the last guests home. Kris locked up the Cyclorama with his A.I. helper, Zooney. He barked out orders as he sat, his legs heavy from exhaustion. The gates were sealed and Zooney turned off the lights. Kris rose from his chair and trudged to his levitator pack, struggling to strap it on. He was dog-tired as he set his destination for home. Kris chose some old music for the ride: Tony Bennett. With a growing hum, Kris rose above the ground and in no time went limp with sleep, while Tony Bennett belted "I Left My Heart in San Francisco." When he arrived at his house, the levitator woke him up with three strong pings.

Kris woke up but was still wiped from exhaustion. The levitator lowered him softly. Within minutes, he slipped in beside Mindy and immediately fell into a deep sleep. He fell asleep so quickly, he didn't notice that the comm on his wrist was ringing silently.

CHAPTER FOUR

Kris woke up and found the house empty. He forgot Mindy was taking the kids to a playdate over at the Hennesseys'. He strode into the kitchen and decided to forgo having Zeke, his house A.I., make coffee. He opted to hit up Jack's Cava Café, one of his favorite coffee joints, located in Modesto's town center.

Kris walked through the living room and into the garage. He glanced at his hopper then, feeling too lazy to drive, turned to a glass cabinet where he stored the levitator packs. He loved the anti-gravs and had four of them; he used them more often than his hopper car. His favorite one was green with white trim.

"Green levitator."

The glass door slid open and the levitator rose with a quiet hum. Kris grabbed it out of the air and strapped it on with greater ease than he had the night before. He turned and faced the garage door.

"Garage."

The garage opened and across the street he could see his neighbor, Farley Kurtz, washing his gunmetal grey hopper. Kris noticed he had new license plates that read "ME HORNY." Farley was single with greasy hair and built like a dragon fruit. Kris guessed, correctly, it would take a lot more than a new hopper for Farley to get a good woman.

Kris told the levitator pack to take him to Jack's Cava café in downtown Modesto. With a woosh, he was flying down the street and then up twenty feet and off to his destination.

Kris arrived, handed his pack to a valet, and strode up the stairs. He entered and surveyed the café. It was empty, as it was early, and he guessed most people were sleeping in this morning. He was thankful he didn't have to wait in line. The kiddie party had knocked him on his ass. He needed to wake up for the day. Jack's Cava was his favorite coffee haunt.

Jack's was three stories up and had a dazzling view of the Pacific. The interior was designed with a dull pewter theme that was splashed throughout. The smell of freshly baked muffins piqued Kris' interest as he peered at the goods in the display case.

Kris approached the barista, Nan. She was six feet tall with bleached white hair, olive skin, purple lipstick, and ample bosom. She looked at Kris while tossing a used infuser in the trash. Her lips turned up slightly in a knowing smile.

"What are you having, Galloway?"

"MJ infusion, please, Nan."

"Coming right up. Take the blue seat. That'll be forty dollars."

Kris waved his hand, then heard a soft click from the register. He forced his eyes away from Nan and turned to the chairs, each a different color. He liked it when he was given an easy chair. Blue. If it were crowded, he would have had to figure out which color was burnt peach. Kris headed to the blue chair and eased himself in. A panel lit up on the chair showing his order was coming.

"Neck pillow. Six point five."

A neck pillow inflated and he rested back on it, getting comfortable. He reached for the silver hood and had to stretch to pull it down. The aerosol infusion of mocha java wafted by his nose, and he relaxed and breathed it in.

He pulled the hood down. Kris was focused on his own experience, until he got a hint of a vanilla flavor mixing with his. He was annoyed at first but tried to ignore it for the sake of peace, until the vanilla smell grew overwhelming. Kris became annoyed, to the point that he raised the hood.

"You mind turning on your fans?" he requested of the woman in a red chair next to him.

"Sure, Kris."

Kris couldn't place the voice, and it threw him. It had been a long time since he was recognized. His eyes swung over to the red chair, where he found a thirty-something Latina woman with startling black hair peeking over the side. Kris had no idea who she was.

"My apologies," she said, never taking her gaze from him.

Kris realized she knew exactly who he was. The silver pin in her lapel featured two I's. That's when he realized that their meeting had been deliberate. She sat up in the chair, her high heels hitting the floor with a double clack. She eyed him for a few seconds and Kris felt a wave of nervousness like he hadn't in years.

He had family, he had money, he had everything he needed. The troubling times were long behind him. He was no longer in the game of split-second decisions. He didn't have to face life or death situations. He was just private citizen Kris Galloway of 424 Helton Court Road, Modesto, California.

"I.I.," Kris said.

"Yes. I'm Agent C."

She stood confidently, offered her slender hand, and eyed him. She cracked a Mona Lisa-like smile that made Kris recoil. He knew she was trouble for him, and he wanted no part of it. She stepped forward and nodded for him to join her at a more secluded table in the back.

Kris knew what it meant when an Intergalactic Intelligence agent introduced themself, so he rose from his chair and walked toward her table, certain he was headed into a trap. I.I. had eyes everywhere. The Keifer Report had made him a cause célèbre, but before the war it nearly ruined him. I.I. were the big players back in the days of the surge into the galaxy. They were the architects of discrediting the Keifer Report. They made Kris look like an ill-equipped, bumbling fool, spouting nonsense. He had lost friends because of it. Friends who would later lose their lives, sixty million miles from Sirius Minor, thinking of Kris in their last moments.

Kris walked over to the agent and took a seat. She crossed her long legs and let her heel dangle. Kris never took his eyes off her, as he knew this wasn't a friendly encounter.

"Kris Galloway. You are quite famous."

"Correction: I was famous."

"Fame never really goes away."

"I'm doing pretty well at trying to make it. It's my life's mission now," Kris said. "Look, I'm gonna cut to the chase. You've obviously been following me. So why don't you just tell me what this is about, Agent C?"

"Right to business. I like that. I agree. Why bother with all the endless banter back and forth, right? Okay, I'll get to it. Kris, did you know we still listen to chatter beyond the DMZ? We've got some pretty sophisticated probes out there as our ears," C told him.

"Why? We're out of that business."

"We are, but we made a lot of enemies. Good to be prepared, right?" Agent C said.

"Sure. But what does this have to do with me?" Kris shifted in his seat. He wished he'd stayed in bed. His Sunday was turning into shit. He just wanted to hail his levitator pack for a quick return home.

Agent C opened her palm, revealing a tiny projection that was lit up. He could see a visual soundwave crackling over her hand, dancing in a pale blue light against a black background. She turned up the sound until the voice came through, still faint but clearer. Surprised, Kris sprung to his feet. He hadn't heard Citari voices in years. He could translate only a few words. He was out of practice.

Citari was spoken throughout the Milky Way, but Kris never got the hang of it. It was a guttural language, harsh to the human ear. It was tough to master it, so those who did ended up with massive houses and fat pensions.

Kris got distracted by the sound of an infusion machine warming up as someone prepared an order for a customer. It drowned out the recording until the barista finished. Then Kris turned his attention back to Agent C and stared into her palm. He listened to the scratchy Citari voice, crackling with interference. Again, he translated random words in his head. And then, in the middle of a sentence, an alien voice said a word he understood clearly: "Galloway."

Kris' eyes widened and he stepped back, his mouth hanging slightly open. Agent C leaned in and grinned. "You look like you just saw me in a bikini," she said with a wink.

He waved his hand, indicating for her to play it again. Agent C leaned further over the table and then complied. Kris listened intently, again hearing his name in that scratchy-sounding Citari accent. He went pale, wondering how this could possibly be. How could his name be uttered so far away?

"What's going on? Why are they talking about me?" Kris eyed her, seeking an explanation.

"That's what I was hoping you could answer. A Citari Council head sends a transmission saying your name. After all these years since the war. Why is that?" she inquired suspiciously.

"I have no idea," Kris replied, a little frantic.

"You sure?" C asked pointedly, looking for something in his eyes that indicated deception.

"Look, I saw the coded date of the transmission. It was over a month ago. Meaning you've been watching me like a hawk for at least that long. And after being bored by my quiet, happy life, you decided to confront me because you were out of options. Am I close?" Kris guessed.

Agent C eased back in her chair and looked at him slyly.

"You're telling the truth."

Nan brought over a couple of coffees Agent C had ordered. Kris drank his without thinking.

"Dead on," Agent C continued. "It's not often Earthers are referenced in forbidden space."

"It's not possible. Why would I be talked about?"

"We aren't sure. We were hoping you had done something stupid like contact them, but that doesn't seem to be the case." C stared at him, waiting for an answer.

"How could I talk to them?" Kris wondered.

"There are underground ways."

"I'm not aware of them," he insisted.

Agent C sipped her coffee. She reached for some sugar and cream and then more sugar. She stirred, then drank it in a gulp. Kris could see she was forming a thought, but couldn't guess where she was going. She glanced at her sharp green nails. Then her eyes went up to Kris. She reached for her scan-pad without looking.

"You're going to Mariah?" Agent C inquired while pocketing the pad.

"Next week to visit my wife's parents, but clearly you know that." Kris admitted.

"Look, if anything pops up... you know about this. Give me a call."

She touched his hand, and her number was instantly added to his comm. Agent C stood up and sauntered out of the Cava, swaying her hips confidently. She glanced back at him with another Mona Lisa smile. She must have known about his past. His first failed marriage and how his will power had limitations. She was testing him. Kris had conquered his issues, but Agent C was someone who would do anything necessary to complete a mission. The very thought that he was a subject of an investigation sent a shiver through his body.

Kris never finished his infusion. He ran past Nan without saying goodbye and headed to the valet, who handed him his levitator. He raced home, pale as a ghost, forgetting to tip.

The winds were coming from the southwest, a storm brewing on the horizon. Mindy had always loved the rain. She waited on the porch for it. Their youngest, Annie, was playing on a swing. She was five and singing to herself. Mindy turned her eyes skyward. The clouds had grown murkier. She saw a flash of lightning and moved toward Annie.

"Annie, get in the house. A storm's coming."

"I don't want to."

"Annie!"

"I just got out here."

Mindy had been through these arguments before and knew it was best just to act. She ran down to the swing, scooped Annie up, and they headed back into the house. She glimpsed her ten-year-old son, Justin, who was walking outside with a baseball bat. She set Annie down and called Justin back inside.

Mindy could hear the levitator pack whining, and it was coming in fast. Too fast. She stepped forward as Kris raced up and landed. The levitator dropped him off and he ran to a stop. He had to grab onto the house to steady himself. Kris fell into the rocking chair on the porch and exhaled loudly.

"What's wrong?" she said softly.

"An agent visited me." he explained breathlessly.

"From where?"

"I.I."

"What did they want from you?"

Kris recounted the meeting and the curious recording. Mindy was grateful he was telling her what was going on. They had no secrets, that was their understanding, but what she was hearing was frightening her. They had simple lives. Her sister married a millionaire who was an alcoholic and had multiple affairs. He got her best friend pregnant, which led to an ugly divorce that left her bitter about life. Mindy had seen so many of her friends and family ending up heartbroken. But she had found intimacy with Kris, and he had found it with her. She didn't want anything to get in the way of the deep connection they felt for one another.

"Do you think they'll contact you again?"

"Why? I'm a nobody. I've been out of that game for twelve years; I have a kiddie party business now," Kris sputtered.

"But there must be a reason," Mindy insisted.

"I can't imagine why they'd be talking about me."

Mindy cuddled Kris. The tension eased in his back, and he calmed down. Kris inched his eyes up to hers and rested his head on her shoulder. He'd had a rush of anxiety at Jack's Cava. He hadn't felt that way since his days among the stars. He didn't want to experience it again.

"Time on Mariah will do you some good," Mindy suggested.

"Yeah, a little Yaya fishing couldn't hurt," Kris admitted.

"You and my dad always have a good time." She smiled at him. "Maybe it's nothing."

"Maybe. Maybe it was a Citari historian. I could be just a reference, maybe."

"Yeah, it's gotta be something like that."

There was a bright flash followed by deep rolling thunder. They could feel the sound waves enter and exit their bodies as they raced inside. The storm had arrived.

Before Kris made it home, Agent C boarded a thruster ship that was rocketing to Washington, D.C. After she arrived, she headed to I.I. headquarters to update Severen, the Director of I.I., on her interaction with Kris Galloway. A receptionist directed her to wait in his office. She entered the dark and dignified space. It was a long room with a glass conference table with numerous computers and screens. It smelled of Severen's sweat, as he often slept on the couch during the week.

Severen entered behind her and crossed to his desk. He was in his fifties, bearded and a little paunchy. He'd been working long hours, and the bags under his eyes were the proof.

Severen moved himself around in his chair to allow his gut to resettle. He let out a long sigh and peered up at Agent C. Severen had been reading a classified report on his pad and set it down on the desk. He folded his hands over his belly and leaned back in the chair.

"What did he say?" Severen asked.

Agent C turned and sat down, putting her high heels up on his desk. She was taking her time, and she savored it. It would annoy Severen. She scooped some snacks out of a bowl at the edge of his desk and silently picked at them, occasionally glancing up at an irritated Severen.

"He was as shocked as we were," Agent C stated blandly.

"So, he had no idea?" he said with disappointment.

"No, he's just a working Joe. Seems like he's blocked out the past. And I don't blame him. He had a shit deal. You ruined his name back in the day. He's left it all behind. He's got a babe for a wife, some kids, a house, and a dog. This guy's out," Agent C insisted.

"He understand it?" Severen questioned.

"Doesn't speak Citari."

Severen was frustrated. He'd been working on a puzzle for weeks and hoped Galloway would unlock the truth and reveal why his name was being bandied about light years away from Earth. He threw down his pencil angrily. It bounced off the side of the desk and landed on the floor.

Agent C sat up and leaned in toward Severen. "Look, I can't help you if I'm kept in the dark," she said.

"You did your job. You found out he wasn't complicit. That's all you needed to do," Severen replied.

"Complicit in what? I know there's more chatter, but you blanked me out on the rest."

"It's too sensitive."

"After today, I know my job isn't done," Agent C stated. "I can't work or come up with solutions unless you let me in. I know you can selectively declassify. You're G-1. What does it say, Severen?"

Severen stood, turning his back on her.

"Look, I've been on this thing for a month. I think I should know what's got a bug up your ass and the asses of everybody above you. I'm due at least that," C reasoned.

Severen sighed, closed the door, and turned on the deafening box to protect them from any audio or sensory probing in the room. It made a pulsing sound that would eventually give you a headache, so discussions of this nature were short and to the point. Agent C stood, crossed her arms, and waited.

"Must be pretty big."

"It is."

"Then what does it say?" she demanded.

"The message said, 'We need Galloway. How can we contact him?'" Severen responded gravely.

"What?"

"The Citari Council needs him for something," Severen repeated, tapping his hand on the desk.

"For what?"

"I don't know, C, but the sensory computer indicated that there was desperation in their cadence."

"Desperation? How does a guy running a kiddie business solve a desperate need for the Council?"

"The Keifer Report." Severen sighed again. "He was the author. He knew we were headed for catastrophe if we took on the Citaris. He got punished for it; he left the service after the war and never looked back. He was the lone sane voice."

"And do they know that?" C asked.

"The debates were digied all over the globe. We may listen to Citaris, but they also listen to us," Severen assured.

"I thought we're out of the star faring business. Save for Proxima B."

"Currently. But…"

"But what?" she pressed.

"We're looking for a way back in," he admitted.

Agent C sat down, realizing now that this wasn't a simple op. She liked simple ops. The oversized ones could get you killed, and it was obvious now she had drawn the short straw. All because she had to know.

She had gotten herself into the inner circle but, in doing so, she had inadvertently taken a blood oath. She silently cursed herself, as anything to do with the Council and the Citaris was trouble. It meant this was far from an op where she seduced hot guys and uploaded secret data from their comms. She always volunteered for those.

"I don't understand why we want to tangle with those guys again. They could come down on this planet and leave nothing behind," C warned.

"We're just trying to accommodate them, C. And if we find an opportunity to smooth things over with the Citaris, we must grab it!"

Severen pointed his stubby finger at Agent C. "I want you on the star transporter to Mariah with Kris. Make yourself scarce. He doesn't need to know you're there."

"What do you want me to do?" she asked.

"If they are going to make contact with Kris, they'd sooner do it on Mariah," Severen explained.

"They won't know Kris is there. I mean, thousands go every day."

"Normally. But there's been a request for an author signing in New Boston for one of his old books," Severen revealed.

"So?"

"There hasn't been a request in five years. Most of his books are out of print. We suspect it's a lure."

"By the Citaris?"

"By someone working with them."

"Human?" she clarified.

"Likely, but we'll want to advertise it to make sure. We'll send out a message that might get to the Council's ears. It'll be a press release from his publisher. Only we'll write it," Severen said slyly.

"And if they show up?"

"Get the Citaris what they want."

"Galloway?" C asked.

"Just make sure things don't blow up, and keep us in the loop," Severen demanded.

Severen handed her a red card. Agent C was impressed. She'd never been handed the red card. The card empowered an I.I. agent to facilitate any need required. The card could move mountains and buy anything. She grinned and clutched it to her chest.

"Red card?"

"There's a great deal of power in your hand. Use it wisely."

"Can I stay at the Montebelle? All the men I want?"

"Whatever. You don't have any receipts to worry about because this card doesn't exist. Just get the job done," Severen instructed coldly.

After she left Severen's office, Agent C went upstairs to Travel and booked a room on Kris' transport. She made sure she upgraded to a suite. After all, she had to be incognito, and that meant she'd have to stay in her room for the week-long journey. It was an opportunity to get drunk, kick back, party and ravage as many men as she could get her hands on. She reasoned it made up for the danger involved.

She loved her job.

CHAPTER FIVE

The transporter to Mariah punctured through the atmosphere and made its elegant descent down to the spaceport in New Boston. The leviathan-like vehicle landed on pad ninety-eight, its retractable legs extending as the engines throttled up, making a crackling and popping sound as the shuttle slowed. The thrust became deafening while sending dust and particles flying, swallowing the transporter in a cloud and obscuring the vehicle from view. As the dust settled, the ground crew and the transporter were revealed once more.

Kris, Mindy, Annie, and Justin were the first off and were greeted by Mindy's parents, Robert and Jessica Cyrus. Robert and Jessica squeezed their grandchildren with delight. Robert rushed over to Mindy, hugging her tightly, too. Kris stood off to side. Then Robert pulled him into a bear hug. It had been two years. Mindy had missed them and wished her parents could have seen more of their grandchildren, but they were on a fixed income and life on Mariah was considerably less expensive than on Earth.

The family walked toward gate fifty-seven as drones scanned them and logged them in. Once they were in the terminal of Logan Spaceport, they heard the pre-recorded greeting of Neal Dooler, the

Mayor of New Boston. "Welcome to Mariah and welcome to New Boston. Enjoy your stay. Visit our wineries and our theme parks."

———————

Yael Stein was still on board the transporter. She was taking her last looks with Cassie, a new star attendant on her first flight. Yael examined each suite, pleased that everything seemed to be in order. Cassie followed her, listening and taking notes as Yael ran down her routine.

"I always do a walk-through at the end."

"Why?" Cassie asked.

"Got a lengthy memo from United once that rooms had been damaged, and they hadn't been reportedly immediately. Now I always check. If you don't check, you have to fill out forms. Lots and lots of forms." Satisfied, she headed back to the lounge and was about to bring her comm to her mouth when she heard something behind her. She spun back around.

"What's that?" Cassie whispered.

"Suite fifty-seven," Yael replied suspiciously.

Yael inched past some seats in the bar and lounge and noticed the happy hour food hadn't been cleaned up. She pursed her lips. Rachel was supposed to tend to that, and she was already off the ship. She made a mental note to have a word with Rachel the minute she saw her at Hotel Luxo.

Yael continued past the lounge and reached for the door panel to suite fifty-seven. When she slid it open, she found an obviously exhausted man lying naked on the bed while a Latina woman was tying up her boot on a lounge chair. C found her I.I. pin lying on a table and snatched it up. Cassie darted back into the hallway, red-faced.

Agent C glanced up and smiled, unashamed. She grabbed her bag, got up, and left the room. Yael's eyes were drawn to the stirring man. He opened his eyes and instantly closed them again. Yael crossed her arms, waiting. Finally, he peeked at her with one eye. He grabbed for a sheet to cover himself, but it was out of reach, so he just laid flat, giving up.

"Yael."

"Captain. Shouldn't you have been in the cockpit?"

"Time got away from me. Besides, Sean kept harping on how I never let him land."

"Looks like you both landed."

The captain got up and grabbed his clothes, which were scattered all over the suite. He lost his footing while putting on his pants and tumbled to the floor. The captain struggled back up and finally got his pants on and then his shirt. He started toward the door, disheveled.

Yael stopped him, putting her arm across the exit. He finished dressing while Yael watched him, with a smile planted on her face. The captain walked out sternly. Yael shook her head and smiled as she followed him out and sealed the door. She looked to the pad outside suite fifty-seven and recorded that the suite needed super-cleaning.

Agent C's bright smile crumbled as she disembarked the transporter, the hangover deepening. She stood still for a moment, taking in the fresh smell of Mariah. There was a higher concentration of oxygen than on Earth. No pollution either. Her hair rippled as a fresh wind whipped off the Armstrong Sea. Agent C gazed across the vast ocean. Its surface was topped with white caps that went beyond the curve of the horizon; it looked like a storm was brewing from the east.

C was queasy. She had overdone it with Titan martinis, her favorite. She dug through her bag and found a bottle of Xylon AD. It was an antacid she always had when she knew she'd be carousing. As she swallowed the pill, she resolved that she'd have to dial down her antics. At least until tomorrow.

She headed into the terminal and picked up her checked items. The mayor's voice boomed through speakers, which only exacerbated her hangover. She'd never been to Mariah, but realized she'd have to wait until after her blinding headache cleared to appreciate it.

C stepped out of the terminal and checked her comm. Her hopper indicated it was waiting for her, but she couldn't tell where it was located. The terminal was thick with roaming hoppers. She spoke into her comm, "Identify."

The hopper assigned to her lit up bright green. She squeezed through a crowd of passengers and towards the ride that was swooping down to meet her. It landed and a door snapped open. Agent C stumbled in and landed, sprawled, face first into the back seat of the hopper.

"The Montebelle. Get me there before I vomit."

———————

Kris hadn't been to Mariah in two years. It had grown. The number of skyscrapers had doubled, and housing had tripled. There were no homeless, and mental illness had all but been cured eighty years back.

Kris held his youngest, Annie, as the hopper glided past the skyline of New Boston. It headed out of the city limits, skimming over a deep green, never-ending forest that arced over tall, lush hills. There were few roads down below, but since most transportation was made by hopper, one didn't need them. It was the unblemished version of Earth. Maybe he'd retire here when the time came.

When they landed and the door opened, Annie and Justin ran with their grandparents to the yellow clapboard house and disappeared into it. Kris took Mindy's hand. He could feel a few raindrops hitting.

"Bring bags inside," Kris spoke into his comm. The suitcases blinked yellow as the message was received. The suitcases levitated out of the trunk and followed Kris and Mindy into the house as the rain came down harder.

Kris felt relaxed for the first time in days. He didn't feel like Agent C was breathing down his neck and had hope that maybe, just maybe, this Citari business would not be his problem. Maybe it was a reminder that he should be thankful for what he had, because it could change in an instant.

The next morning, Kris woke up in his in-laws' house and saw Mindy wasn't in the bed. She was already up. He had gotten a good night's sleep, his first in a week. Kris got out of bed, opened the shades, and stared out at an alien sky. It was greenish blue with two oddly shaped moons hanging faintly to the north and to the west. He got dressed and headed toward the kitchen where he could hear conversations and children giggling. Everyone was around the breakfast table, and Jessica scurried to get him a plate.

"Good morning," Robert greeted him. "Mindy said you haven't been sleeping, so we figured we'd let you sleep in."

The smell of sizzling ham and eggs wafted toward Kris, and he smiled. He nodded thanks as he grabbed a fork. Kris was hungry and the homemade food was far better than what United offered on their transport.

"So, you have a book signing, I understand," continued Robert while poking at his food, trying to pick the right home fry.

"Yeah, out of the blue, really. I don't write anymore."

"When did you write this book? It was a while back, wasn't it?'" Robert asked.

"About six years ago," Mindy offered. "He's very talented."

"Never wanted to do it again, Kris?" Robert mused, pouring himself a cup of coffee.

"Don't need the attention. Besides, I did well with them," Kris admitted.

"So why now? The book signing?"

"Guess they found out we were coming here. Turns out they still sell a lot on Mariah. Fifteenth printing I'm told. It's out of print on Earth," Kris revealed.

"Must have been rough. All those people lost." Robert shook his head sadly.

"War is a fool's choice. I tried to warn them, but they said I had the wrong perspective. That's what I was told when they demoted me and put me on a ship in the backlines. My captain was always pissed at me. He couldn't get in the thick of action because of me. Though truth was, his posting wasn't my fault. Everyone knew he was a lousy skipper. But I gotta say, I ran into him years later and he thanked me. He knows he would have been dead fighting for the Directorate." Kris let the painful words hang in the air as he ate his breakfast.

Kris and his family arrived at the book signing to see the line to get into the Amazon store went around the block. The family stayed for Kris' reading, but the kids were sleepy by the time the signing began. Kris suggested they take a hopper home and he'd join them when he was done.

Kris was genuinely stunned by the attendance. He had been anonymous for so long; he couldn't figure out why there was so much interest. The overriding public opinion was that Mariah was the next target of the Citari fleet and they were saved because of his final act before he sent the Concord racing away from Sirius Minor. Kris Galloway had saved a beautiful, utopian world, and the residents wanted to shake his hand.

He took a few moments to admire the cover of the book. It was a painting of the buoy he launched with the black lettered title: "The Song of Salaya."

There were still humans beyond the buoy, but they weren't affiliated with the Directorate and were cut off from returning. There were a few who owned whole planets, but they didn't dare cross the DMZ. The Council would have them destroyed on the spot. You had to have the emblem to pass through, and no one had ever gotten it.

The emblem was the size of a comm. It could fit in your hand. It was made of a crystal substance that emitted a Council signal which granted its holder safe passage across. The Council broadcast this fact to the Earthers as a deterrent. A cheap one, but very effective. No one had even tried to approach the DMZ. In fact, the Directorate had ships patrolling to make certain some company ship didn't try to make a run for it and slip through. No one wanted a war again.

A South Asian man put his copy forward.

"What's your name?"

"Dr. Chopra."

"Oh, what kind of doctor are you?"

"Artificial Intelligence Sciences."

Kris wrote a personal note to him as he spoke. "You live here?"

"No, I'm due back on Mars in a week."

"Good luck to you."

Dr. Chopra stepped away. Kris glanced up at the long line and realized he needed to half his chat time. He signed the rest of the books quickly. With the fans coming in a steady stream, Kris barely had time to look up. But toward the end of the evening, a different book was put in his hand: The Keifer Report.

He glanced up at its owner and locked eyes with the chief doctor from the Concord, Dr. Ed Weiss. He'd aged a bit and looked every one of the seventy years.

"Can I have a word afterwards?" Weiss asked.

"Sure."

"Across the street. Nick's." Weiss suggested.

"Right," Kris nodded.

Dr. Weiss snatched up his book and tucked it under his arm. Kris watched him walk away and felt a slight tinge of nervousness. He kept furiously signing for the next hour until the line finally dwindled.

It was raining as Kris ran across the street to Nick's. He noticed a woman dashing behind a building. For a second, he thought it was Agent C. But he quickly discounted the notion. It was a quiet bar made to look like one of the quaint Boston bars from the twentieth century. Kris stepped into the establishment and immediately noticed it was empty save for Dr. Weiss sitting alone.

"This place does crappy business," Kris observed.

"Actually, they're not open today. It's a holiday."

Kris ran his fingers through his hair and noticed some cramping in his hand from all the signing. He shook it off. Kris knew this wasn't just about a pair of old crewmates getting together for a friendly drink.

He looked around and saw nothing out of place.

"Ed."

"Kris."

"How've you been?" Kris asked.

"Alive, thanks to you."

"I get that a lot."

"You should," Weiss said smiling.

"If you don't mind me asking..." Kris pointed to the dog-eared copy of the Keifer Report.

Weiss smoothed his hand over the cover. He looked at it affectionately as he placed it on the bar. Then he walked around behind the counter and poured two beers for them. Kris grabbed a beer and took a solid gulp.

Weiss' eyes dropped to the book again and then back to Kris. He clinked glasses with him. They both drank another round. Kris wasn't sure what this was about. He wondered why he'd brought the Keifer report with him.

"Very few men that were right get to put it down in words," Weiss pointed out.

"Yeah, that doesn't make me feel better."

"You're very popular here. You could have a political career on Mariah," Weiss suggested.

"The public eye and I, well... we hate each other," Kris smiled and admitted.

Weiss laughed and then became a little somber. He knew what had happened. He'd been a witness over the years. He saw how the Directorate degraded the Earth's reputation.

"Those days were hell. So many mistakes," Weiss said with remorse.

"I'll drink to that," Kris agreed. He filled himself up another mug, but he stayed seated behind the counter. None of this felt right to him, and he feared the wonderful silence he had thrived in with his family was about to be broken. He needed to numb the thought. He started to take another swig when Dr. Weiss reached out and grabbed his arm, stopping him.

"What if you could change the story?" Dr. Weiss asked.

"The past is the past, Ed," Kris sighed.

"I'm talking about the future. Beyond the DMZ."

"What's this about?" Kris felt the hairs on the back of his neck stand up. He knew something was wrong. He put down his mug. Something was very wrong.

"I need you to meet someone," Weiss pronounced.

"In here?" Kris responded, confused.

"Yes. I was contacted."

"By whom?"

"By me," came a voice from the corner of the room.

Kris whipped around, recognizing the scratchy accent. It was a Citari. He was yellowish and wore a black cloak. He moved forward gingerly; he was obviously advanced in age. The Citaris always seemed calm and non-threatening, but Kris recognized it as an intentional deception. He knew precisely how dangerous they could be.

The Citari picked up the Keifer Report from the counter and flipped through it "Wise words. Your words," the Citari declared, waving the book and putting it back down.

Kris' anxiety rose and he stumbled back, nearly knocking the bottles off the bar shelf. He steadied them, then his eyes landed on Ed.

"What is this?" Kris snapped.

"A gesture." The Citari offered his hand.

Kris looked to Ed, who urged him to shake it. Kris reluctantly did so and felt the coldness of the alien's delicate hand. Kris quickly recoiled as he thought of all the laws he might be breaking.

"I'm Vichon. Legion of the Council."

"How'd you get here?" Kris questioned.

"I was what you would call teleported. We have that technology now," Vichon replied in his scratchy voice.

"Good for you. You coming after us again?" Kris demanded.

"No, far from that."

"Ed, what are you doing with this guy?" Kris suddenly had no idea who his old friend had become.

"Just sit down and listen," Weiss assured calmly.

Kris realized he was standing now, out of reflex. He came around the bar, sat down heavily and stared into the eyes of the enemy. Vichon took a seat with him and rested his withered elbow on the counter. He signaled for the shades to be drawn.

That's when Kris saw the other Citari, taller and younger. He closed the shades and stepped into a dark corner. Kris' eyes were drawn back to Vichon by his voice.

"I took great risk coming here," Vichon started.

"You did, and I'm taking a big risk even talking to you," Kris countered.

"Your people would not be happy to have a Citari in their presence, would they?"

"It'd be messy, that's for sure."

"But what if I gave you a road map to the future?" Vichon teased.

"What kind of future?" Kris was curious.

"A healing one."

"Between the Directorate and the Council? Come on. You must be juiced on Tykon ale."

"We need you, Galloway," Vichon insisted.

The playback that Agent C showed him rang in his head. But why? After all these years, why did they need him? He was the man who was wrong until the deaths of thousands proved he was right.

The meeting made him dizzy. He shouldn't be here. He thought he should make a mad dash out, but a comforting hand landed on his knee. It was Vichon.

"You're respected on both sides," Vichon said firmly. "It can only be you."

"Be me for what?"

Vichon opened his palm, revealing a small crystal object that was unmistakably the emblem. Safe passage. Vichon put it in Kris' trembling hand. A power he never desired was lying in his palm.

Kris turned to Ed, shaking his head. "Ed. I can't."

"Just hear him out."

"You humans have something we need," Vichon acknowledged plainly.

"What?"

"Medical knowledge. We, the Council, are charged with protecting every planet from harm. We have a case that we simply can't handle."

"I'm not a doctor," Kris mumbled.

"We know that. We want you to bring a cure," Vichon explained.

"Cure? For whom?"

"The Genusians in Genus Major. There is a fast-spreading disease there. It is devastating the planet. The occupants are much like humans in physiology and appearance. The disease... what do you Earthers call it, Doctor?"

"Measles."

"Measles?" Kris was dumbfounded. "This is all about measles?"

"You've cured it. The final refinement stops it completely. We need you to go with a medical team to Genus Major and save the Genusians," Vichon urged.

Weiss jumped in. "Don't you see? We do a kind act, and the Council sees us in a different light."

"Ed, we would need a ship. I don't have a ship. I don't have a crew. How am I supposed to do this?"

"The Council agreed that only you could command a ship in Council space. It's up to you to save the Genusians," Vichon pronounced, straightening up.

"We've got the medical know-how to save the planet," Ed piped in.

"Look at it as a first step," Vichon added.

"I don't know how to do this," Kris stammered, overwhelmed.

"Think it over, something will come to mind. But time is of the essence," Vichon warned as he rose. He disappeared into the kitchen with an aide at his side.

Kris was breathless. "Ed, my biggest decision in a day is whether to buy new batteries for the hypercycles. This is way out of my league."

"You're built for this. You've just been dormant."

"I have responsibilities. My wife, my kids. I can't go off on some adventure. And, like I said, I don't have a ship, and I don't think one is just going to show up."

"You still know people," Weiss insisted.

"No, no, I don't. I'm an anonymous man," Kris protested.

Severen turned off the digi in his office and turned to the I.I. officials who were murmuring amongst themselves. He could sense the palpable anxiety in the room. I.I. used to be invincible—until the Council handed them their asses. Severen felt they had been limping ever since.

Severen rose from his chair. He paced around the room, thinking about the transmission he had just witnessed between the Citari and Kris Galloway. A lower level I.I. analyst awkwardly broke the silence and asked, "What do you think, Severen?"

"I'd say we have an opportunity," Severen answered. He looked to the communications officer, Derek, a fresh-faced twenty-five year old with a shaved head who stood nearby. "What's the chatter say?"

"The problems on Genusia are real. Heavy chatter, sir."

Severen pondered as he strode the length of the room and then turned back, following the same path. He stopped, rocking on his heels.

"We've got a man with the emblem in his hand, which means he can make peace with the Citaris."

"The Council isn't going to just roll over because we saved one planet," an agent sneered.

"This Vichon could be rogue," another officer speculated.

Severen slammed his knuckles onto the conference room table. "He has the emblem! That's no mistake. You can't get it without Council approval. Agent C authenticated it. We've got ten billion humans shaking in their boots because the Council might just say they're sick of us and swat us like a fly. Like Vichon said, it's a gesture."

"What's the Directorate say?"

"Do whatever is necessary to repair relations with the Council," Severen stated.

"They killed thousands."

"They could have killed billions," Severen snapped. "Kris Gallo-way saved all of us. But we are still under the thumb of the Citaris. That won't change, but if we can come to a new understanding, we might be able to expand again past the DMZ. We must show the Citaris that they misunderstand humanity. We'll show them we can play nice. I'm going to have Agent C expedite it. She'll go with Galloway on the mission to Genus Major. That way we have eyes and ears. Agreed?"

There was no vote. There didn't need to be. It was all Severen's decision. He sent a faster-than-light message to C, who received it while getting a massage from a broad-shouldered masseur at the Hotel Luxo.

She groaned, knowing she had to get back to work.

CHAPTER SIX

The first sound Kris heard was the familiar whine of jetpacks flying in unison. It was followed by a swishing sound as they took their positions. Kris glanced down at Justin. He was excited to see his first flyball tournament in person. Kris' hand landed on his gleeful son's shoulder. Justin smiled back at Kris, who hugged him. *This is what life is about,* Kris thought. The four of them. It's all he needed. They made him feel content. But today his nerves were on edge from the evening before. He had to smile through his anxiety and keep up a brave front.

Kris, Mindy, Annie, and Justin walked up the concrete stairs to the stadium. They had missed the first round, as Justin couldn't find his favorite shoes at his grandparents' house. He made quite a scene. They had the same number on them as his favorite player: Cody Barrett. Annie didn't help the matter by calling him a baby throughout his tantrum. Kris saved the day, finding the boy's shoes in his bag. Justin calmed down, threw on his trainers and headed out, the Nikes on his feet.

Kris held Annie tightly as they forged their way through the crowd. There was a wind tunnel effect in the stairway; Annie was shivering, and her cheeks were turning pink. Kris wrapped her in his coat to keep her warm. They reached their level, found their seats, and soon the kids were cheering on the men flying on jetpacks at high speeds, trying to dunk a glowing ball before their hands were singed from holding it too long.

The arena was filled with palpable excitement. It was New Boston against Grand Washington, rivals playing for the world championship. But Kris was there only physically. The cheers and the puttering engines of the jetpacks and the fireworks that went off at every score were muffled. Background noise. His mind was still in that quaint New England bar, Nick's. He was still behind the counter, still staring at a Citari and considering the possibility he'd drunk too much.

The game was engaging, so no one noticed the glazed look in his eyes. The players swirled through the stadium, mimicking a flock of geese bound together while they made wide turns, pirouetting across the sky. Even that didn't draw Kris out of his haze.

Kris had experienced two different lives. He lived a life of peril amongst the stars, and then he led a life of peace. The quiet existence had replaced the memories of space and war with a sense of calm. But now, Kris was frightened it all might slip away. He feared that the tranquility he enjoyed may become a dream once again if he was lured back to the stars.

New Boston recovered the glower ball and made a surprise score. Mindy jumped up to cheer. She landed in her seat and glanced over at Kris, who hadn't moved. She reached out for him and grabbed his shoulder, gently shaking him. "What's wrong?"

"Hmm?" Kris responded, lazily turning his head.

"I know something is wrong," Mindy prodded, deep concern etched into her features.

Kris didn't know how to tell her. He couldn't quite believe it himself. He needed to get it clear in his mind before he told her.

"Uh... the Citari recording. The one where I was mentioned. It really involves... me," Kris revealed.

"What?"

Kris looked at Mindy, helpless. "I met a Citari last night after the book signing."

"What? How?" Mindy leaned into him.

"He smuggled himself in."

"Why?" Mindy asked.

"They need help with an outbreak," Kris explained.

"You're not a doctor."

"They've reached out to doctors already. They need someone who can get them there."

"But you can't do that. You can't cross the DMZ," Mindy said.

Kris reached into his pocket and pulled out the emblem. Mindy's eyes widened at the sight of it. She made him put it back in his coat the moment she got a gander, and spun her head around, hoping no one had seen it. They hadn't, because New Boston had scored once more.

"What are you going to do?" Mindy whispered.

"I can't get us in trouble. I'm not an official. I don't have access to a ship."

Mindy looked at him sweetly and pulled him in, holding him tight. She kissed his cheek and ran her hands through his hair. He managed a smile. She could see he was tense.

"Maybe you should get a Chuggo in the bar."

"Yeah, maybe." Deciding it couldn't hurt, Kris rose and made his way toward the stairs. The yelling and thunderous stamping of feet became muffled behind him. He descended down the steps toward the concession stand. There was no one in line. The game had reached a fever pitch. Kris relaxed as he left the cacophony of cheering behind him.

He headed up to the bar and waited a minute while the bartender changed out a keg of beer. Kris' shadow stretched over the bartender. He hopped up, facing Kris.

"Sorry, sir. What can I get you?"

"Chuggo, silver."

"Coming right up."

He poured the beer and, before Kris could pay, a long slender hand reached in and waved over the pay scanner. Kris turned slightly, and his shoulders slumped when he found Agent C standing beside him.

"Guys are usually excited to see me," C said with a faux pout.

"You followed me here?"

"Of course, I did."

"We don't have anything to talk about." Kris stepped away from her.

"Gotta say, Kris, we've got a lot to talk about. Nick's bar. Have a seat," C ordered.

Kris grumbled to himself, walked to a nearby seat, and sat down. Agent C grabbed a chair, spun it around and sat, leaning on the back. Kris assumed she knew everything, so he was preparing a defense. He wasn't guilty of anything. He didn't arrange the meeting with the Citaris. Kris was about to throw Dr. Weiss under the hopper when Agent C smiled.

"I know you didn't put the meet and greet together. I.I. knows that, too."

"Uh, well... that's good."

"Kris, let me lay it out for you. The Directorate doesn't want bad blood between Earth and the Council anymore."

Kris rose quickly and stepped away from Agent C. He shook his head, taking it all in. He shifted his body and ran his hand through his hair. There was a long, awkward silence. Kris slowly turned around and faced her. Agent C was stone faced, waiting for an answer. Kris bit his lip and then a wry smile escaped. He landed back in his chair.

"So, you're here because they want me to help the Citaris?"

"You'll be one hundred percent backed. It's a first step."

"I don't have a ship," Kris reminded her.

"The Concord will be here in twenty-four hours. It's on full light drive, has a full crew complement and quadruple the medical staff, and all the medicine that's needed," Agent C answered calmly.

Kris hesitated. She had answers for every problem, except one. He looked her in the eyes and said with more vulnerability than he meant to reveal, "I don't want this."

"Kris, we got off to a rocky start. I came on a little strong. That's my way. We don't have trust between us, and I get that. But concentrate on this: the Citaris asked us nicely to back off from our plundering. We didn't listen, and all hell broke loose. They are now asking us nicely to help them with a problem. We need to show them that we learned, and we've changed our ways. We'll be the good guys again. You have the emblem. Only you. There's no backing out, Kris."

Agent C leaned towards him and lowered her voice. "Look, he transported here. Transported on a beam. That means they could be on our doorstep in a blink of an eye if they wanted to. How do we fight that? We can't. You need to make nice. You're the man that was right all along. We know it. They know it. Besides, you'll finally command in all your glory."

"I don't need glory."

"You studied the Citaris. You know their rituals and customs. Ask yourself honestly, what would happen if we turned them down?"

Kris knew what they could do. He knew all too well. Theirs were a complicated culture. Refusal to provide aid could be seen as an insult. Kris was truly stuck.

Agent C got up quickly and disappeared down the steps to the lower decks. Kris sucked down his beer, rose and headed to Mindy to deliver the news. His hands gripped the rails of the narrow staircase, and he trudged up the steps like a man headed to the gallows.

Kris came back up to the stands and sat next to Mindy quietly. Mindy studied his face as Kris gazed past her. Then their eyes met. Mindy finally said the words for him.

"You have to do it, don't you?"

"Yeah, I think I do."

"Will it take long?"

"It's still early days."

"Then we'll stay here on Mariah 'til you get back. You're doing a good thing. You'll make us all safer."

They took a hopper home after the game, flying at treetop level. Kris just stared out the window at trees, mostly silent on the ride. His mind was drifting as the foliage rushed beneath him. He was back in the thick of it again. All because he had put words to paper so long ago. Words that created trust with a race he feared and certainly didn't fully understand. He had put himself in the position of an expert in the field. Sure, he was more informed about the Citaris than the average person, but he couldn't claim to be a true scholar.

But he had to try. Maybe he could ease the tensions. Maybe he could show the kinder side of humans. He just hoped that this time, humans didn't muck it up.

CHAPTER SEVEN

Kris was given three days to pack, prepare, and say goodbye before he boarded the Concord. Half a day into hyperspace, Kris noticed some changes since star travel back in his time. The Alcubierre Drive made a soothing, rhythmic sound that helped crew members sleep. That always wasn't the case. The drive cores used to be loud and overwhelming until they built dampeners into the ships that turned the noise into a soft, almost melodic thump.

Kris bumped his head on the ceiling of his quarters. His eyes blinked open, and he found himself floating toward his desk. He didn't use his bed. It was a habit he'd formed during his earlier spacefaring days, and he picked back up right where he left off. He found it more relaxing to turn off the gravity and hover freely. Kris would tether his sleeping bag to a hook and slowly float around the room, sleeping unencumbered.

His head bumped into the wall, and he woke upside down and disoriented. For a moment, he thought he was still home. He then spied the porthole and the deep space beyond it. Kris hadn't wanted this. He shouldn't be here. He should be home, living his simple life. But fate had other ideas that didn't line up with his desires.

Kris grabbed a handle and righted himself as the voice of his Number One, Jennifer Arliss, came over the comm system.

"Skipper. It's Number One."

"What? Yeah," Kris mumbled, untangling himself from the tether.

"Need you up here."

"Anything wrong?"

"There will be, if you don't get moving," Jennifer warned.

Kris straightened himself out and swam over to the door panel. He turned the gravity wave back on and landed on his feet with a heavy thump. Dressed in his captain's uniform, Kris froze when he checked his reflection in the mirror and realized who was staring back at him. It dawned on him only then that he was face to face with the identity he'd lost. He had been Captain Kris Galloway. It was the dream he had coveted, won at an early age, then lost in disgrace. As the years passed by it felt like it never really happened. A vague dream. A fragment of memory that was stuffed away in a safe corner in his mind.

Kris stepped away from the mirror, still in disbelief he was the captain of a starship cruiser again. Kris hadn't had a refresher on being the captain of a starship, and it had been twelve years. He had to be rusty. Regulations and operations certainly would have changed over time. He might have to cover. He wondered if it all would come back in a muscle memory rush or if he would seem like a bumbling fool in front of a crew with more experience than himself. What if the ship had been refitted? What if the technology had changed and he didn't know how anything worked anymore?

Kris had avoided the flight deck so far for those very reasons and spent his time inspecting other parts of the ship instead. He had huddled with the medical team extensively. But command meant being in the chair on the flight deck. Now he'd been summoned, and Kris knew avoiding it was no longer an option. Time to see if he was still truly a captain.

Kris halted at the door to the flight deck. He paused and exhaled as the door parted to either side. Kris stepped through and felt an emotional pull in his chest, like seeing the girl who got away. He stifled his emotions as Jennifer noticed him. She was African American, with wavy reddish hair and wide brown eyes. She smiled brightly and called, "Morning, Captain."

He nearly turned to see if the captain was behind him, but then relaxed and nodded to Jennifer. He stepped over to the command chair where she was planted. Jennifer gathered her pad and belongings and rose from the chair, making room for him.

Kris put his hand gently on the symbol of command. The chair he had lost. He looked at it for too long, and Jennifer noticed.

"You okay?" she asked.

"Been a long time," Kris replied.

"Felt the same way my first day. Best to get over it."

Kris sat and saw the arm on the chair change colors. Kris then noticed a panel light blinking the words "Captain on Deck." He noted the speed and course of the ship and realized they were going faster than his last orders. Jennifer must have made an adjustment. Kris decided not to comment.

Kris looked to Jennifer. "Status?"

"Five minutes from the DMZ."

"Ships?"

"A Citari armada. You got that thing?" she checked. Kris felt around in his coat and took out the emblem. The crew briefly took their eyes off their panels to see it. Kris stared back at them and cocked his head. They all slowly turned back around and went to work.

They received orders to transmit the image. He handed the emblem to Jennifer, who took it over to communications to scan and send.

"Drop out of hyperspace," Kris ordered.

An ensign said, "Aye," and the ship dropped out of warp and engaged the fusion propulsion. The soft knock ceased as they eased through the DMZ. The ship slowed to a sluggish twenty-five thousand miles per hour.

"They're scanning us," Jennifer commented.

Kris gazed up at the Citari armada. There were roughly twenty ships, spread out for thousands of miles. The ships were greenish looking with white Citari symbols that probably noted the name of the vessel.

"The DMZ," Jennifer breathed in awe.

"The ships. They're bigger. Seventy-five thousand tons by the look of them."

"One hundred thousand," she corrected.

"We don't have anything half the size."

Agent C appeared on the deck, still in her black pajamas and barefoot. Her hair was unkempt. She had clearly just rolled out of bed. She brushed hair out of her eyes and gazed at the viewscreen as Kris turned in his chair toward her.

"Don't dress up for us," Kris quipped.

"Hadn't planned to."

"We've cleared the DMZ, sir," an ensign reported.

"Agent C, this is my ship. I expect you to wear I.I. regulars while on board."

"Aye, sir," C snarked. She turned and exited.

Jennifer looked to Kris. "She must be a real piece of work."

"You have no idea, Number One. You have no idea. Alright, let's get back into hyperspace. Stay on course. What's our ETA, navigation?"

"Forty-nine hours."

"Very well. You have the conn, Number One. I'll be stuffing my face."

Kris got out of the chair, feeling good. He was in command again—at least, no one had second-guessed him. Kris moved confidently to the galley, only to find he was in the library. Lost. He found a layout in the library and looked up where the galley was, then made his way there in about twenty minutes.

He walked in and found Agent C standing in line wearing I.I. regulars, a black uniform with white boots.

"Galloway," she greeted him. Kris gave her a pointed look and she straightened up and became more formal. "Captain," she corrected with a forced smile.

"Agent C."

"Mind if I join you? At the Captain's table?"

"Why not?"

The pair stood quietly. Kris was looking straight ahead. He could feel Agent C's eyes on him as they inched through the line. It unnerved Kris, and he shot her an annoyed glance. He feared mistakes during the mission, and Agent C was high on his list of likely bunglers.

"You don't like me, do you, Galloway? Captain."

"It's not that. It's..."

"It's what?"

"You have ideas."

"So?"

"I don't think you have boundaries," Kris said plainly.

"Haven't had much use for them," C shrugged.

"That's my point. See, you may know everything about me, but I found out a little about you," Kris admitted.

"You did your homework. Impressive. What did you learn?"

Kris grabbed a tray and began loading up, still not looking at her. Agent C picked at the options and ended up with some fruit and eggs.

"That your impulse control with men is weak at best."

"You've had that problem with women in the past."

Kris didn't care for that comment. "Key words there: in the past. Look, we gotta do this mission, but I need you to be a monk. Turn it off. My crew is off limits," Kris warned.

Agent C followed him to a table and sat, looking stoic. Kris sensed she didn't like being told what to do, but he had to make the call. He dug into his breakfast of bacon, eggs and two biscuits.

"You are no fun."

"I know you have a high-risk life and think it's a way to unwind. But not on my ship."

"Is this really your place?"

"I am the captain of the ship," Kris stated firmly.

"I'm I.I.," C countered.

"But who can put who in the brig on a whim?" Kris said brightly.

"I'd like to see you try that."

"I also know about the former Agent H. Now Henry Cole."

C went silent. Kris watched her as she turned away from him. Then she walked out without a word, leaving her uneaten food behind.

CHAPTER EIGHT

Twelve years ago,

Agent C had just graduated from college with a degree in global studies. She had minored in defense arts and had a few championships under her belt. College had consumed her life for four years, and after graduating, she became aimless. Her dad had contacts in Washington, D.C. for a job in the State Department. But Zuma Beach seemed to hold more sway over her. She was a regular in Malibu, showing off her surfing skills, which were considerable. She avoided calls from her parents, knowing full well what the topic was going to be. She had checked out on life. It bothered her. She was directionless and couldn't switch gears.

She was taking a Tae Kwan Do class in Santa Monica that helped fill up the days. That's where she met Henry. He made himself known as the charming but slightly older man that fancied her. They dated for a few months filled with romance and excitement. The only problem for C was that she still didn't know what he did for a living. Henry was evasive when the subject came up. It began to shake her. It wasn't going to work out, she thought. How could it?

Henry sensed the growing disconnect between them and decided he was finally going to open up about himself. He took them to Washington, D.C. for a weekend, promising she'd learn everything. C was puzzled when Henry stood them in front of the I.I. building on Pennsylvania Avenue. Then he revealed to her that he worked for I.I. It made C tingle inside. She had been dating a spy. Henry admitted his code name was Agent H. C brightened and was intrigued. Henry told her that he had been talking to his boss about her, and that they'd like her to join the training program.

"Me? A spy?" C considered incredulously.

"They've examined your background and you fit their desired psychological profile," Henry offered.

"How do they know my background?"

"They know everything."

It felt right. Something finally felt right. Maybe, she thought, this was her place in the world. She wasn't ever going to find it herself. It was going to find her. C agreed to the offer. She joined I.I. and went through their grueling six-month program, graduating at the top of her class.

Agent H became her handler. Her first assignment was to spy on a Saudi college student, under the guise of being a fellow undergrad. She fed information back for seven weeks. C never knew why she was doing it. She just did it. She joined a study group to keep close tabs on him. She tapped his comm. She took notes and pictures of anyone he'd interact with. Her job was to get the information, not analyze it.

Agent H had C become entangled in his life, but she was untroubled by that. The clandestine world spoke to her. She thrived on the living performance. She reveled in the manipulation. C had found herself.

C had fallen for H. She was in love. It was perfect. She understood his life and he understood hers. I.I. relationships tended to flourish in comparison to a liaison between civilian and agent.

Five years of love and skullduggery had passed between them. They had talked about family; they had looked at houses. C was a top operative in the field, but she easily slid into the role of the sentimental girlfriend at home.

One night, they had dinner by the sea and made love in a bungalow just off the beach in Provincetown on Cape Cod. They took a long walk, the cool breezes off the Atlantic whipping at them. C was wrapped in a blanket. She kissed H, then gazed out at the pitch-black raging sea. C finally admitted she was getting cold, and H picked her up and ran them toward their bungalow. She giggled and held on to him. She snuggled into him as his body kept her warm, protecting her from the chilly gusts.

They went to bed, lulled to sleep by the crashing waves. C slept soundly. She had a wonderful day and dreamt of her man and what she'd do to him in the morning.

The first thing she noticed when she woke up was flashing lights. Then the sound of people running. C sat up, but H was still asleep. There was pounding on the door.

"F.B.I."

They broke down the door and grabbed Agent H, who had no idea what was going on. The agents handcuffed him and shoved him outside, in only shorts and a t-shirt. C was screaming, held back by two female agents. She demanded to know where they were taking him, she demanded to know the truth. But as soon as she learned it, she wished she hadn't.

Henry was a double agent for Russia. He had been working for them for ten years. Then it got worse. He was married to a Russian woman and had children with her—three of them. C became frozen. They explained the details, but they only registered as muffled voices in her ears. She was lost. Her life had been swept away. It had been an illusion; now reality poured in.

C didn't attend the trial. She had taken a six month leave from I.I. She didn't know how to process the events, but she finally sought to find her way. That's what brought her to the parking lot of the prison in Northern Virginia where Agent H was housed. It was raining in sheets, drenching her. C didn't care. I.I. had interrogated her at a black site in Alabama for six days, but C didn't know anything. She was a fool, falling in love with a man who excelled in deception.

C had been cleared by I.I. When she returned to active duty and went back to work, she became colder and more heartless. She went about her missions with little feeling. But C had a nagging question. She wanted to know if H's love had been real, or if it had just been a job. Maybe a piece of her would come back if he had had feelings for her.

C headed into the prison to check in. She dripped on the tile prison floors without care. They brought her to a private, sterile grey room with two chairs and a table. C arrived first. Her depression deepened as she waited. Then she heard the chains rattling. After all these years, they still used cuffs and chains. *If it ain't broke, don't fix it,* she thought. The door swung open and there was Henry. He was uncuffed and shoved forward by a guard, who slammed and locked the door behind him. Henry looked a little gaunt. He grabbed the chair and sat down. There was a long silence between them. What she had with him was precious. It was what people prayed for. She had it with Henry, until it was stripped away in one windy night on Cape Cod.

"Christina," Henry croaked.

"Henry."

"I didn't know it was raining," Henry said.

"Buckets. Look, I'm not gonna be long," C snapped curtly. "I wanna know..." Her eyes welled up, and she fought through the pain. C cleared her throat. "I want to know if 'us,' our whole thing, was a lie from top to bottom."

Henry stared downward. He couldn't look at her. Shame seemed to consume him. He glanced up at her.

"I have been lying for so long. So, so long. I was very good at it. But I guess not good enough. Look at me."

"Just answer the question!" C exploded.

Henry stared at his feet, then up to her. He tried to speak several times, then finally blurted it out. "It wasn't real. I didn't love you; it was the job. I could have lied to you right now, but I can't do that anymore. I have a wife and three kids, and I care about them. That's who I am, or maybe was."

C stared at him in cold silence. Her heart wasn't just broken, it was darkened. Agent C knew from that moment on that love was merely a myth and vowed to never allow a man to touch her soul like that again.

C said nothing in response. She stood up and moved to the door, and the guard let her out. She walked to her hopper and headed home, not shedding one tear. But in her mind, she was changed, forever.

CHAPTER NINE

The conference room was filled with doctors, Kris, Jennifer, and Agent C. Dr. Weiss was late and entered sucking down the last of a sandwich. He carried a couple of micro-pads and apologized for his tardiness, then sat and got himself organized. Kris shifted in his seat, a little impatient.

"How are we going to do this?" Kris questioned.

Dr. Weiss put down his cup of coffee and took out his micro-pad. He let it float in the air while a 3D visual of Genusia in the Genus Major system appeared before them. Dr. Weiss polished off his cup of coffee and wiped the crumbs off his hand with a napkin, then began pointing.

"The outbreak started here. Now you'll see the dark spots around the globe. Those are outbreaks. We need to stop it at the source. We'll deploy most of our medical units in the Agencia region."

"How many?" Kris asked.

"Three hundred personnel. They'll be doing innocs. We'll recruit locals to expand our reach. To the three smaller regions, we'll deploy teams of twenty."

"That small?"

"We're stretched thin. If we can knock it down in the big region and hold the spread in the others, we can lick this thing," Weiss said.

"You said it's airborne?"

"Right."

"So, the unaffected regions may still be incubating?" Jennifer probed.

"We're not sure of that," Weiss conceded quietly.

Kris stood closer to the 3D projection, running his hand through it. He noticed Weiss didn't make eye contact with him, which meant he didn't have all the answers. This was their first obstacle, the first real chance for everything to go belly up.

"That's not nearly a good enough answer, Doctor. We've got to put this thing out. It's gotta be clockwork, one hundred percent efficient. We need to leave orbit with the Citaris thinking we saved the day. That's our narrative, folks, the humans saved the day. Not being sure isn't an option. I thought we had this all down," Kris commented with disappointment.

"Sorry, we're stretched thin," Weiss repeated.

"We can't have another outbreak two weeks after we leave," Kris said, standing.

"I know, but how do we kill a disease in places where it may or may not be incubating? We've sent down drone scrubbers to check the microparticles in the air, and we've come up with nothing because there probably is nothing," Weiss explained.

"Probably? We need certainty," Kris demanded. "We need to be preemptive."

"How?"

"We need to go to engineering." Kris headed out the door but stopped before leaving and looked back. "Come on, you don't need an invitation." Everyone else followed Kris out the door. Weiss grabbed his pads and left the room last.

They made a conga line down the corridor with Kris in the lead. Weiss was at the end of it, and he sped up to catch with Kris, who was walking briskly.

"Why engineering?" Weiss wondered.

"They'll know how to put this disease to rest forever," Kris explained.

"Engineers? How are they going to help?" Weiss replied, puzzled.

"I guess we'll find out," Agent C mused, intrigued.

The group arrived in engineering a few minutes later. They all headed into the leviathan-like space where twenty men and women worked at their own stations. The soft thump was louder here, and many engineering officers wore sound deafeners as they worked. A woman in a levitator-pad flew over their heads and attended to a panel where an alarm had just been triggered. Kris found Chief Clark taking some readings and tapped him on the shoulder.

"Sean?"

"Bay C," Chief Clark responded.

Kris headed right and everyone followed. He turned down a walkway to a grungy little room where Sean Fagan sat fixing a component. Sean had long hair to his shoulders and looked too fit to be a gearhead. He had a smudge of grease on his temple and seemed consumed by his work. They all squeezed into his cluttered office as Sean stood for the captain.

"Skipper."

"Sean, you're our rigging guy?" Kris asked.

"Yes, sir."

Kris borrowed Weiss' micro-pad, turned on the 3D image of the planet, and centered it on the thirteen hundred square miles in question. Sean stepped up to the image, examining it closely. Weiss looked like he felt this was all a waste of time. He was a biologist, and he didn't like being second-guessed. He was the expert, not

Sean. He had worked for the CDC and had put out outbreaks on Mars and Titan. He was the go-to guy for this kind of work. It didn't make sense that they would have to rely on someone who must have only had a trade degree.

Sean was the Mr. Fix It of the Concord. When something burned out and there wasn't a replacement, Sean would build it. He could cannibalize parts from the ship and turn them into whatever was needed. He was an artist, and no challenge went over his head.

He stared at the 3D image for a few moments. "What do I gotta do, Skip?"

"I have an airborne infection, and I want make sure it doesn't take hold anywhere else."

"Size of the bug?" Sean looked to Weiss.

Weiss shifted a little, then said, "I don't think you'd understand..."

"B.S. in Biology from Princeton, M.Sc. in Electrical Engineering from Purdue. Should I get into my PhD work? You wanna read my thesis?" Sean challenged.

Weiss was clearly caught off guard. His face turned crimson in embarrassment. He mumbled under his breath. "Three hundred to one thousand nanometers."

"Cure?" Sean asked.

"Nafugel Six," Weiss reported.

"What do you want to do?" Kris contemplated.

"We aerosol the area. Take three shuttles and spray until every inch is covered." Sean went back to his seat, got out a pencil and paper, and began sketching. "Gotta build it first. Give me a day."

CHAPTER TEN

As the Concord arrived at Genus Major, Kris read over a report the Citaris had put together for him, laying out all the afflicted areas. It also provided the names of their contacts in each city.

Genusia was a blue world, covered in oceans. Half the planet had violent weather and was sparsely populated. The inhabitants mostly resided in the Northern Hemisphere, which was the size of North America on Earth. It was an advanced civilization, the equivalent of Earth in the 1960s. They had made modest moves in space but had no capability to travel to the stars. It was a peaceful planet; the Citaris first made contact twenty years ago and had taken the planet under their protective arm. Citaris cherished the planet's population because they were a thoughtful, forward-thinking people. They were a rarity in the galaxy, and, with certainty, they were the Citaris' favorites. The Genusian attitude was something to admire. When the planet called the Citaris for help, they knew only one world had the solution: Earth.

The population in the violent weather zones was filled with people trying to avoid being part of traditional society. They were loners and outcasts. They were people who didn't want to live under government rule, so they chose a harsh lifestyle. It wasn't that the government was severe in any way; it was just a cultural choice. People who believed in the sanctity of the individual. They were each a country unto themselves. It was their system. It wasn't very organized, but it's how they lived.

The movement began eighty Genusian years back, with a group of people, albeit small, that didn't want to recognize the government. Each man or woman should have their own rules, they declared. The leaders saw the possibility of violent conflict and decided that they'd be offered the lands where the severe weather wrought havoc. The government built shelters to help withstand the harsh environment, and the threat of violence ceased. Each side had their way.

Kris stood in front of the viewscreen, and Dr. Weiss joined him. Kris patted his shoulder and murmured, "You've got your work cut out for you." Dr. Weiss nodded in agreement as they both gazed at Genusia. Dr. Weiss had a puzzled look on his face. Kris could see something was on his mind. Dr. Weiss noticed him staring. Kris turned away from the viewscreen and faced Dr. Weiss.

"What?" Kris breathed.

"You find it odd, Kris?"

"What?"

"Another species getting measles?"

"Could the Citaris have gotten it wrong?" Kris asked.

"No, they got samples to me. Had them tested. Didn't think it was possible..."

"How'd they get them to you?" Kris pressed. Dr. Weiss grew noticeably uncomfortable with the question. He whispered the answer.

"A good-time girl from Miami," Weiss admitted, looking away from Kris.

"Creative. I mean, on the Citaris' part."

Kris headed back to his command chair, and Weiss followed.

"How are the preparations?" Kris inquired, taking his seat.

"My team's ready to go," Weiss assured.

"Helm, how long until we're in position for our shuttles to launch?"

Without looking back at Kris, the helmsman stared at the read outs. "I have one more retroburn that'll bring us down to the right orbit. In about an hour, I'd say, sir."

"I'd get your people moving to the shuttle bay," Kris told Weiss.

"I'm on it," Weiss promised.

"Number One, I'll be in the ready room."

Kris got up and headed into the ready room, where he found Agent C waiting for him. He nodded to C and entered. She hovered around Kris as he sat down to go through a pile of paperwork. Agent C was frowning, and Kris could feel her eyes searing into him. He put down his pen and gave her his full attention.

"Problem?" Kris speculated.

"Yes," C confirmed, moving toward him.

"What is it?"

"Kris, I'm not on any of the landing rosters."

"That's right," Kris acknowledged, going back to his paperwork.

"This is deliberate?"

"Yup." Kris got up and made himself a cup of coffee. "Coffee?"

"No. I don't understand. I should be down there," C insisted.

"Are you a doctor?" Kris asked.

"No."

"A nurse?"

"No."

Kris sat back, sipping his coffee. "C. You're a spy. That's what you do. And I've got to let you know, spies are a big no-no around here." Kris stared at her pointedly.

"I'm not spying," C protested. She sat crossing her arms.

"You're gathering information. Same thing."

"No, no, I'm seeing how the medical work is progressing," C claimed, choosing her words carefully.

"That is my job. I'm sorry, you are staying put."

Agent C sprung up from her chair, ready to blow her top. She stopped herself, knowing that Kris called the shots. She thought of the brig for a brief moment. She had been ordered to make planetfall by Severen, but Kris had outflanked her. She knew it, and she was certain Kris knew it, too. She glanced at Kris, who put his pen down and crossed his arms, smiling. She stormed off in a fit.

Kris took the lift down to deck H and, when he stepped out, felt a blast of humidity. It was a way to save power on the ship, but it gave the place the atmosphere of an armpit. It reminded him of summers in the Dominican Republic. His father got great deals for family vacations there, but the humidity was so miserable that the only respite was to drink yourself out of it. Kris couldn't, of course, since he was twelve at the time.

Kris waited as a scoot driver named Henderson drove toward him. He was a thickly-built man who had trouble growing a beard and whose job it was to shuttle crewmen from the front deck elevator down a long silver tunnel to the shuttle bay. Henderson braked right next to him, and Kris got in. The scoot was old fashioned, with rubber wheels and drink caddies. Henderson had a blue drink in one of them, which he sipped.

Henderson spun the wheel around and hit the pedal. They took off down a stark hallway. Kris held onto the edges as the scoot wobbled, shifting him from side to side. Henderson was driving too fast, but Kris didn't say anything. He didn't want a crewman to gossip about scaring the captain. He just grimaced through the ride.

"I read your book," Henderson said eagerly.

"Oh, thanks."

"You sure had it down."

"Some good it did," Kris grumbled.

"Well..."

"I saved your life?" Kris guessed.

"How did you know?"

"I hear it a lot. What ship?" Kris asked.

"The Valiant. Said goodbye to my family and everything. Then hot damn, we got the recall code. Best day of my life."

"But you came back out here," Kris observed thoughtfully.

"Yeah. If I could be any part of stopping that from happening again, I owed it."

Kris nodded. He supposed that was why he was here as well, preventing the future from repeating the past. As they rode in silence, Kris remembered the ship. The Valiant was one of the last twenty ships to survive the war.

Kris had been on the Valiant as his first assignment, but that had lasted only a month, because of a mix-up with his academy scores. His had been attributed to Warren Dooley. Warren got a position as third in command on the starship Botany Bay. When he failed miserably at the job, they checked his records and realized Warren and Kris' scores had been accidently switched. Warren was sent to a desk job on Ceres, and Kris was made third in command on the Botany.

When they arrived at the shuttle bay, Kris rose from the scoot and thanked Henderson for the ride. He reached the entrance and punched the access code into a keypad. It blinked: "No Access Allowed." Kris frowned and rooted around in his pocket for a crumpled piece of paper containing the code. He punched it in again, more carefully this time. Finally, the door unsealed.

Kris strode into a bright white room. He slowed, marveling at the gleaming shuttles that lined the bay floor. Kris enjoyed flying shuttles; it was spaceflight you could feel in your hands. It was like riding a motorcycle on Earth. It had been a long time since he'd flown one himself. He had been in his early twenties, which seemed like several lifetimes ago. He smiled at the thought.

He saw medical personnel getting their gear together, but not enough to suggest the whole team was here. At first, he wondered if they were behind schedule. Then he reasoned they must have already boarded their shuttles.

"Lieutenant Sun," Kris called out.

Kris smiled when she came around the shuttle Artemis carrying a gear box. Amanda Sun was the chief shuttle pilot. She was a little over five feet and solidly built. She had brilliant blue eyes and a cocky air about her.

The lieutenant stiffened at the sight of him. Amanda was territorial, and the shuttle deck was her fiefdom. She was called all the shots. Amanda liked being in control. It didn't matter that she was pint sized—no one dared to get on her bad side. Some had seen it and lived to regret it. She was a firm leader who people didn't dare cross. But now the captain was in her midst. She didn't know him well and hoped he wouldn't overstep. Her jaw became rigid as she acknowledged Kris and gave him a firm handshake. She noticed it made Kris shudder.

"Captain."

"Amanda. You've been made aware about the complicated landings?"

"I'm all over it. Manass, Kija and Loor. Hurricanes eighty percent of the time. Wanna take a look?"

Amanda got out her data ball and pitched it in the air. It floated between them, projecting a chart that surrounded them. She put on some black gloves so she could adjust the size of visual, letting them see trees being slammed by hundred-mile-an-hour winds that were blowing at thirty-degree angles. They glanced at each other and then back to the digi visual.

"How do you plan to handle that?" Kris asked.

Amanda smiled briefly. She'd had run-ins with captains who threw their weight around, and she had to take it. But this captain was someone who seemed to rely on his people. She appreciated that. Amanda became more at ease and felt free to be the unfiltered version of herself.

"Hate to admit it, but this is a job for an A.I. The number of corrections I'd have to make might be beyond human capacity. Well, most human capacity. Don't worry, Skip, I've already run five simulations, and it worked four times."

"Four?"

"It crashed on the first run but made it on the next four. We're good," Amanda assured.

Kris told to her make sure the shuttles were all online and to double her service teams as these ships would be running around the clock. "Don't worry, Skip, I got this. It'll be kinda a kick."

Amanda turned around and went back to her worktable while Kris headed back out of the shuttle bay and found Henderson dutifully waiting for him. They zoomed off down the hallway, and Kris wondered if he had forgotten anything. He hoped that he didn't; he didn't have that luxury.

CHAPTER ELEVEN

The first pair of shuttles launched to the most afflicted region, with Dr. Weiss leading the team. Kris would come down later, but he wanted to supervise the deployment, and he was still concerned about the weather-ravaged area of the planet. Amanda had assured him she saved two of the Mark Sevens, the newest shuttles, for the task.

Kris couldn't help but think something might go wrong somewhere. The operation was so vast it really needed four starships, not one. But he was certain the Citaris were going to hand out only one emblem, and dared not bring up the subject.

Agent C was on the flight deck, arms crossed, body tensed. She was still pissed at Kris. Kris headed over to her but was stopped by an ensign handing him a note, which he glanced at and then shoved in his pocket. Kris turned to Agent C.

"Still pissed?"

"It was a simple request."

"Just keeping you out of trouble," Kris insisted.

"Me?"

"Better that you're up here," Kris contended.

"I'm I.I. I should be down there. I might be able to help," Agent C pleaded.

"I needed medical personnel down there," Kris reminded her.

"You don't trust me?"

"Well, no. I think that's established. Of course, I don't. You're an I.I. operative. I have no idea what your agenda is, or what your bosses' agenda is," Kris answered frankly.

Agent C huffed and eyed him with slight contempt. Kris put his hands on her shoulders in a fatherly way and faced her. She bristled, crossing her arms, cocking her head. Kris smiled and laid it out for her.

"This isn't a recon mission," Kris explained.

"I'm not doing recon," C said convincingly.

"Of course, you are. And the Citaris aren't going to put up with that. They are the law around here, and we're under it."

Agent C shifted her weight, knowing Kris was right. Kris stepped away from her as the communications officer, Barney Evans, approached tentatively, slightly ashen. Kris turned away from C and nodded to Barney to explain.

"A Citari vessel has pulled alongside and would like to board."

"Direct them to docking port two," Kris instructed calmly.

"But sir, did you..."

Kris looked at Barney with kind eyes to alleviate his worry. He noticed Barney seemed nervous.

"Docking port two," Kris confirmed softly.

"Two. Aye, sir."

"What's this about?" Agent C asked.

Kris didn't answer as he sent an uncoded message about this development to Earth from his command chair. If he panicked, the crew would panic. Kris wasn't showing his hand to anyone, acting like it was all normal.

Kris headed out of the flight deck down a corridor. Agent C followed, close on his heels. Kris ignored her as he took out some gum and popped a stick in his mouth, grimacing almost immediately. "Cherry. I hate cherry. All they had was mixed packs." Kris stopped at a disposal unit, shoved his hand in, and heard the wrapper whoosh out into space.

Agent C was right behind Kris. "Are you just going to ignore me?" she fumed.

"Keeping one step ahead," Kris responded.

"You don't seem surprised about the Citaris."

"I got a heads up," he lied.

"From whom?"

"You're I.I., aren't you supposed to know this already?"

"This wasn't the plan."

"Their space, their rules," Kris reminded.

It took ten minutes to get to docking port two. Kris punched in the code, and he and Agent C stepped into the squarish grey room. There was one window to the right, with the docking hatch in the middle. A red light clicked on, and the hatch opened, revealing a Citari Destroyer.

Kris was surprised to see Vichon emerge from the ship. It had only been two weeks since their encounter, however it felt like a lifetime. The Citari looked worn and almost vulnerable, even though he was flanked by two of his soldiers. Behind him was a slight, sickly-looking Citari. He was carrying a bulky black scanner, which reeked of something that put a sickening taste in Kris' mouth.

"Captain Galloway," Vichon greeted him scratchily. Kris approached, and Vichon put out his hand. Kris shook it and felt the bumps on the Citari's palm. They reminded him of the bumps on the emblem. The emblem was part of them, and they were part of the emblem.

"Vichon, everything is going according to plan," Kris assured with a slight smile.

"I can see. It's very impressive, indeed."

"Thank you. What's the nature of your visit?" Kris knew that the Citaris liked directness. They didn't like communicating in vague terms and believed it created distrust, so Kris had to divulge his every move. Vichon nodded to him in appreciation and bowed slightly. Bowing was a custom when someone was direct, a signal to go directly to the resolution of the problem at hand. But with that bow, Kris was certain there was a rather large issue.

Vichon stared at Agent C, and she felt as though he was looking deep into her soul, which made her self-conscious. Her eyes shot to Kris, asking him wordlessly for an answer as Vichon began walking around her slowly with a crooked smile. Agent C was uncharacteristically nervous as he did his slow, uneven lope around her.

"Intelligence services?" Vichon asked, turning to Kris, while a bead of sweat formed on Agent C's forehead.

Kris nodded. "They were instrumental in convincing the Directorate to give me a ship."

"I'm sure they were. Always so helpful," Vichon agreed slyly.

Agent C's sweat was now streaming. Fortunately for her, the Citaris weren't aware of the emotional implications for that human physical response. Vichon gestured to his soldiers.

"Hold her," Vichon barked. Agent C instinctively backed up as the two soldiers snagged her. C tried to wriggle free, and Kris stepped up to Vichon, his fists clenched. Her eyes landed on Kris.

"Kris," C whimpered uneasily.

"Vichon, what is this? I thought you were happy with our progress. She's one of my crew, and I need to understand what's going on here."

"I believe you do not understand what is going on under your nose, Galloway. We detected a signal back to Earth from your ship that we could not decode. It was very complicated in its nature. Every other signal from your ship has been an open book, but not this one. It was strange. Its source moved around in your ship. We don't tolerate spying," Vichon warned.

"Vichon, we're just here to help," Kris pleaded.

"I'm sure you are." He turned to the sickly Citari, "Naj."

The sickly Citari stepped forward with the bulky, reeking black scanner and slowly ran it up and down Agent C. Her hair stood up on end as electricity coursed through her. Agent C looked terrified, and Kris could see that she knew she was in deep trouble. The stench from the machine became acrid as it worked. Finally, a pink smoke rose out of it. The frail Citari ran his hand through the tiny cloud. He cocked his head and looked to Vichon, who was turning off the scanner.

"Nothing."

"Good." Vichon nodded to his soldiers, who let Agent C go. "I would not have wanted to have an execution while we're all playing so nicely." Vichon forced a smile.

Agent C had an urge to fall into Kris' protective arms, but resisted and just wilted, visibly shaking. Her eyes stared at the floor. She felt a sense of shame. No one had ever gotten the better of her. Then suddenly her life had been on the line. She knew why they had grabbed her, but she wasn't sure how she had just survived certain death.

"Thank you, Captain. Continue with your good work." Vichon waved.

Vichon gave a hand signal, and the soldiers headed through the docking portal first. The sickly Citari with the scanner disappeared, along with the acrid smell. Vichon turned, bowed slightly to Kris, and ignored Agent C. The door sealed after them.

Agent C fell into a nearby chair. She no longer had the self-assured poise of a cool operative. Her slick I.I. agent mask had been swept away. She felt exposed, naked. She had been caught off guard, and that hadn't happened to her since leaving Agent H in his prison.

C wiped sweat from her forehead. "What was that?"

"I just saved your life," Kris pointed out.

"How?"

"The communications officer also picked up your signal. I did my homework on I.I. Operatives always have micro-recorders in their shoulder pads to digi all the action. I snatched yours."

"When?" C asked.

"Earlier, when I held your shoulders."

"What did you do with them?"

"They went out into space with the gum wrapper. A pickpocket on Rigel taught me how to do that. Comes in handy sometimes," Kris explained with a smile.

"They would have killed me?" C murmured, realizing.

"No question."

Agent C blinked and stood, wiping her mouth. She was unsteady on her feet, almost dizzy from the experience. Kris squeezed her shoulders sympathetically. I.I. knew the rules, but clearly didn't tell her of the risks of wearing micro-recorders in Citari space.

"Yeah, so no spy craft. You got any more of those things?" Kris asked.

"Three in my quarters. But they aren't on."

"I suggest we toss them in the engine core. I.I. doesn't get a bird's eye view of this mission. And C, you can't talk to them over the channels. They'll message you because they're blind." Kris leaned into her and whispered, "Vichon is listening to everything. You are on their radar."

"Why didn't they tell me?" C's lip quivered.

Kris shook his head at her sympathetically. "They went over the risks and considered you expendable. If you were caught, you would have been killed, but the operation would have gone on and the Directorate wouldn't have complained about your demise. They'd say they didn't know. And who knows, they might not have. I'm sorry."

C was shaking. For C, this feeling was unfamiliar. A weak, vulnerable woman. It was completely alien to her being, but she could feel it in every inch of her body.

"Thanks for saving my life," she said uneasily.

"Just don't make me regret it," Kris smiled. "Let's go to your quarters. I want those things off my ship."

"There's four. I've got four. Sorry." She bowed her head a little. "Old habits die hard."

"I.I. are your employers. They are not your family. They're not your friends." Agent C turned her head, obscuring her face from Kris. He was uneasy.

Kris knew she was crying, but allowed C her dignity and pretended not to notice. She had a close call, and she had just suffered what he suspected would be a life changing blow. Kris tapped her on the shoulder, and she glanced over to him. He crooked his neck to the door, indicating they should leave.

"Come on. Let's go to your quarters. I.I. has ways to activate dormant micros. We need to move fast."

Kris and Agent C ran to her quarters and got there in a matter of minutes. Agent C reached her room and frantically looked for the micro-recorders. She had forgotten where she hid the fourth one. And couldn't remember as the anxiety flooded her brain.

"Calm down. Just take a breath and think."

"What?"

"Breathe."

C slowed her breathing as Kris took her hand and she centered herself. She thought back to when she moved into her room. The first thing she did after she put her bag away was hide them. She put three together and couldn't think of where to put the fourth. Where would no one look, she remembered thinking. Under the toilet! She headed for the bathroom, reached around under the bowl, and found the last one.

"Got it."

"We better throw these in the core."

"Why not the trash chute?"

"If they switch one on it'll be pinging next to us and the Citaris will be right back knocking on our door."

Engineering was nearby, and they ran there until they were out of breath. The engineers looked at them, puzzled, but when Kris explained his needs, they jumped into action. A young engineer put the four micro-recorders into the antimatter flow chamber—just as one of them was booting up. They were destroyed instantly and scattered into countless atoms.

Agent C sat on the steel stairs near the array of cooling control panels. Kris collapsed to the floor, sweating. The engineering team was staring at them when Harry Clark entered above them, surveying Kris and Agent C. He noticed his engineers were distracted and snapped his fingers.

Harry ambled down three flights of steel stairs that ended where Kris and C were sitting. He glanced between them, not knowing what to think. "Can I help you, Skipper?"

"I need a drink," Kris grunted.

"Is there something I'm supposed to know?" Harry questioned.

They both turned to him and replied in unison, "No." The pair headed out and made their way to the canteen.

CHAPTER TWELVE

Severen was in a deep sleep when a hand jostled him awake. It was one of his senior advisors, Deke. Severen was used to being shaken out of slumber. It was the job. A full night's sleep in I.I. was treated as a gift. But that gift was not for today. It was four in the morning.

He sat up and realized he'd fallen asleep on his office couch. It wasn't the first time. He must have slept oddly; his neck was sore. He rubbed at it and didn't even bother to peer up, hoping whatever was happening wasn't high priority so he could go back to sleep.

He heard his office chair move and saw Deke seated there. He was turning on the sound dampeners. Severen knew that wasn't a good sign. His night of rest was officially over.

"It's off," Deke reported.

"What is it?" Severen yawned, wiping the sleep crust from his eyes.

"The feed was cut off."

"C's?" Severen asked.

"In an instant," Duke affirmed.

"The Concord?"

"It's fine. Full telemetry. They're in the middle of operations."

"You hear anything from Agent C?"

"Radio silence," Deke stated flatly.

"You've sent messages?" Severen confirmed.

"No response," Deke answered.

Severen got up off the couch and headed into the kitchenette. He pulled out an instant coffee infuser, popped the top, and the water and coffee mixed. He sipped the coffee and then took a hit from the java steam wafting off of it. He started to wake up.

"She can't talk over any channels, coded or un-coded. We are dark," Deke continued with disappointment.

"Why?"

"Someone found out what we were doing. She says anything to us, and she's outed to the Citaris. Galloway sent a message that a Citari ship was docking with theirs; they must have detected the signal. There are full life signs on the ship," Deke concluded.

"So, she's alive, she's just not talking." Severen considered the situation. The caffeine was slowly starting to awaken his senses. "Galloway. He must have figured it out. He must have discovered the micro-recorders and destroyed them." Severen grabbed a glass of water and took some aspirin to fight the headache building. He hung his head in defeat.

"So, that's it. We're cut off," Severen sighed. Agent C certainly knew now they had taken a bet on her life. She'd never forgive him. He created an enemy out of a skilled operative. This was going to cost him, without question.

Severen got dressed and readied himself to drive to Directorate headquarters. He had to give them the bad news. The Directorate wanted information; they didn't want excuses. They counted on him, and he would have nothing for the remainder of the mission.

They lived and breathed for information, and it had been choked off.

CHAPTER THIRTEEN

The medical teams landed at dawn the next morning. Space pods streamed over the blue, hazy skies of Genusia. The shuttles would drop off team after team and then grab another group that was waiting on the Concord. Weiss had planned well, and everyone was in place on the measles battleground in half a Genus Major day.

At each outbreak site, they used the Keezy sprayer. It could be sprayed over a room of ill patients or, for the worse afflicted, directly up the patients' noses. It was fast and effective. By the end of the day, ten percent of the outbreak was extinguished.

Weiss strolled through a clinic, observing with bewilderment. He had explored countless alien worlds in the pre-war days of the expansion. At every planetfall he made, the aliens were unique. They had evolved in ways that were exotic, wildly different from humans. But the inhabitants of Genusia were the outlier. They were seemingly human in design. Their internal organs were virtually the same, and pigmentation ranged from black to white. He supposed it was possible that an environment identical to Earth could produce the same result, but it just didn't seem likely.

As he gazed into the patients' eyes, he felt a familiarity that he'd noticed on his arrival. Usually, there was an awkward interaction between human and alien. A period of getting used to each other's appearance. There'd be a pause when encountering a sentient with three arms. But an alien that looked like your own species was curious. Weiss didn't understand it, and he couldn't postulate how this came to be.

Dr. Heath, a fellow from Johns Hopkins, was checking the charts of a patient a few feet away. Weiss noticed Heath was shaking his head and walked over, concerned that something had gone sideways. He came around next to him. "Problem?"

"Hmm? No, Doctor. No problem. It's just curious."

"What is?"

"Their physiology. No wonder they called us in," Heath remarked.

"Because they're almost exactly like us," Weiss acknowledged quietly.

"What are the chances? I've never seen anything like it," Heath whispered.

"There aren't any, that's the point. I crewed missions back in the day. I was out there, and I've never seen this before," Weiss confided.

"Well, you've seen a helluva lot more than I have. Dr. Weiss, what's going on? I'm not the only one that noticed. Everybody's talking," said Heath, stepping out of earshot of two Citari observers.

"Do me a favor. Keep gathering blood samples on the sly. I want to examine them back on the Concord," Weiss instructed quietly.

"Sure, I'll take care of that."

Weiss moved away. He didn't like coincidences, and this was an awfully big one. How was it possible to have two pairs of identical sentient lifeforms on two worlds so distant from each other?

His micro-pad clicked. The field teams were uploading updates from the different units working around the planet. They arrived in a swift fashion, and he read them over silently, nodding at each page. He turned on his comm. "Hailing the Concord."

"Concord here."

"Captain Galloway," Weiss began.

"Dr. Weiss, how are we doing?" Kris' voice crackled over the comm.

"Ahead of schedule. Reports say the patients are responding well."

"Any problems?"

"Just had to improvise a few times."

"Improvise?" Kris asked.

"We had to use what we'd call a stadium, fill it with Genusians, and spray the whole field."

"Good to hear. Keep it up," Kris praised.

Weiss turned off the comm and headed outside just in time to catch three shuttles flying overhead with the aerosol sprayers on board. They flew out of sight, on their way to their target. He looked back at the Great Hall, still pondering the Genusians. They were just like humans in almost every way... but why? And how?

He was going to find out.

CHAPTER FOURTEEN

manda Sun sat in her shuttle, calmly chewing gum, watching the hot plasma that was swallowing her ship on its deep dive into Loor. Two minutes into entry, the shuttle was steady, but it rocked slightly to the left and then to the right. She pulsed the jets and it evened out.

The shuttle was silent, no one speaking. This suited Amanda. She disliked yammering passengers in the back. Her ship was filled with doctors and nurses. They had been briefed on how rough the landing would be and currently sat in fearful silence.

The plasma gradually cleared and all she could see were blue skies. She angled them down, so they were slicing through atmosphere, flying. Then the view of the storm engulfed their windows. It was massive, filled every inch of their vision, and they dived toward the middle of it.

"Holy..." exclaimed Jennessy, her copilot and frequent bedmate.

Amanda smiled at Jennessy, giving him a quick gander. Jennessy was from Boulder, Colorado. He was about five foot seven and a few years younger than her. She silently chastised herself; she needed to keep her head in the game. Thinking about taking a shower with her boyfriend was not going to help her fly the shuttle through the storm that raged before her.

"Biggest storm I've ever seen. It's magnificent," Jennessy marveled.

"I wonder if you'll call it that when we're in there."

Amanda stared at the storm warily from where they sat ten thousand feet above it. She could see lightning snapping and crackling within it as she flew closer. She was in awe of its size; it must have covered five hundred square miles. She tapped into the computer to scan it. The results were astonishing. One hundred and twenty-five mile an hour winds, one hundred and fifty mile an hour gusts, and it wasn't moving. The beast of a storm was just sitting over Loor, churning.

Amanda had done her research. She had learned these storms would tear on for weeks and then die down for a time before coming back again. It seemed insane to her that this was a place anyone would choose live.

"Don't get comfortable, folks. We're a few minutes away from the storm," Amanda announced.

She checked her monitors and saw the doctors and nurses tightening their straps, their anxiety clearly rising. The shuttle was buffeted suddenly by updrafts. To Amanda it felt like a bump in the road, but to medical personnel it felt like the end of the world.

She pivoted back to her controls and the bright sunny skies suddenly turned into a murky grey cloud. The hurricane winds bashed into them violently. Amanda heard a woman scream behind her. She switched on the A.I. as winds hit that shook the shuttle with an intensity that made even Amanda tense up—and she never tensed up.

They continued to drop through the storm as the computers tried to adjust for the brutal winds. Amanda became concerned. She could see the A.I. was getting alarms from sensors and then was trying to fix them. They continued to drop, and the alarms continued. The A.I. wasn't prepared for this and it was overloading trying to compensate. A series of master alarms went off.

Something was wrong with the A.I.

It was trying to learn the patterns of the wind, but there wasn't a pattern, Amanda realized. It was random. Amanda felt a pit in her stomach. She surmised that the A.I. was using a model of what the storm had been a few hours ago, but it had changed. Those models were useless. She checked the radar spread, which confirmed her fear. The wind was now moving in three different directions.

Amanda was a badass pilot, and now she had to prove it. She turned off the A.I. and took the controls.

Jennessy saw what she was doing. "Amanda?"

"I've got to make this one up as we go along."

"You sure?"

"No, but I'm sure we'll crash the way we're going now."

The computer couldn't find the solution, so she had to, even if the odds of success were against her. And she knew they were.

Amanda used the sonic scanners to find the least wind-swept place to land. It was running at sixty-five miles an hour with only two crosswinds. She pulsed the thrusters and the shuttle shook so violently, strapped-down gear went flying. There were screams and wailing coming from behind her that she ignored. She even heard the splash of vomit, twice. It couldn't draw her attention away. She had to forget she was hauling a bunch of inexperienced people as cargo. Every move counted. She promised Kris everything would be fine, so she couldn't screw the pooch on this one.

She looked to her right. The scanners showed a little window to slip through where the winds were spinning slower. But she had to get through a one-hundred-and-fifty-mile-an-hour gust first.

She improvised, firing the fusion engines and punching through. They slipped into a patch of lazy winds. She cut the fusion engines and the jets. They dropped like a rock, twenty stories. The screaming and crying in the back hit a peak, but Amanda had her eye on the altitude. They had to drop fast. The winds were speeding up.

She reached five thousand feet, then fired the engines up to full thrust. It slammed everyone down in their seats. The shuttle jerked as it slowed. She gripped the controller, spun them around, then found a clearing and landed with a soft thud.

Amanda sat back in her seat. She had to control her breathing before she did anything else, but she unbuckled and craned her neck around toward the medical team. They were shaken and ashen. She couldn't blame them; her own armpits were soaked, and she thought she might vomit, too, now that it was over, and she could consider what had just happened.

Jennessy leaned his head back, his eyes closed, expression filled with relief. "Why aren't we dead?" he muttered.

"Because I was flying, dummy."

The winds were still vibrating the shuttle. Amanda turned on the force field, which stopped the ship from shaking. She stood looking at the medical team, who now regarded her with a collective awe. Amanda put her hands on her hips and addressed them.

"We're down. Now I'm sure after that landing you've either puked or shit your pants. Clean up, then get ready and get to work. The sooner you're done, the sooner we're out of here. Oh, and by the way, launching through this crap is a hell of a lot easier than landing in it. Let's move, people." Amanda called out, clapping her hands.

The team got themselves together, showering and changing clothes and arranging their gear. Finally, time came to disembark. Amanda opened the hatch, and the winds blasted in with sixty mile an hour gusts. She could see a building a hundred yards away with people waving to them from inside. Amanda used her pad to extend and reshape the shuttle's force field into a tunnel so the medical team could cross to them.

The shaken doctors and nurses walked through the force field tunnel as Amanda stood at the door. The doctors were greeted by the Genusians, and the large door sealed behind them. Amanda fell into her chair and turned to Jennessy.

"Shit. I think I got a high from that one," Amanda sighed.

"I think we'd better check the storm didn't break something."

"Wise idea."

"When it's time to go, I want us to be like a bat outta hell," Jennessy said.

"Great thought. I think I have to vomit first," Amanda admitted. Amanda ran to the facilities in the back and made it just in time. Jennessy waited for her by the bathroom. She came staggering back out and held herself up in the door frame.

"I think we should get married," Amanda declared.

"This scared the shit out of me, so yeah," Jennessy agreed, nodding.

"We'll kiss later." Amanda passed him and flopped down in her seat.

"Good idea."

The doctors went to work on the patients with speed. None of them wanted to stay too long, as they were the final team of the operation; the rest of the teams were back on the Concord or racing into orbit.

They finished at around two in the morning Genusian time and reboarded the shuttle. Amanda watched as they dragged their exhausted bodies back into the vessel.

"Come on, everybody, I know you're tired, but get yourselves strapped in."

They sluggishly took their seats and clipped themselves in. Jennessy and Amanda looked on, fixing the straps that hadn't been done correctly. Jennessy checked to make sure the gear was stowed properly and headed back to his seat.

As promised, it was an easier ride up than down. The fusion engines were pushing them into orbit. It was a bumpy ride during the boost phase, but they were outside the atmosphere and in orbit in a matter of six minutes.

When the shuttle landed inside the Concord, the doctors and nurses exited and settled into their quarters, all of them swearing they'd never leave Earth again.

CHAPTER FIFTEEN

Charlie Borrick was a first engineer on the Concord. He was detail-oriented, and nothing missed his eye. He was especially on top of the roster of shifts and managed all the engineers. He lived his life that way. He was so fastidious, it drove his wife to divorce him.

Charlie noticed a curious thing while sipping some Mariahan tea. There was one name on the roster that had never worked any shifts: Tom Huley. He wondered how it was possible not to have worked at least one shift the whole tour. It didn't make any sense. Charlie got up from the desk in his cubby-sized office and squeezed his way out.

Charlie sauntered to the chief engineer's office, where Harry Clark looked up from his dinner of spaghetti and shrimp, which was his favorite meal. It was well known that if you disturbed Harry while he was eating, you better have a damn good reason.

"What? Can't you see I'm eating?" Harry snapped at Charlie.

"Tom Huley," Charlie said quietly.

"Who the hell is Tom Huley?" Harry snapped off a shrimp and sucked down an oversized portion of spaghetti.

"Exactly."

"I'm not following."

"Try putting Huley on a shift," Charlie dared.

"That's your job."

He shoved more food down his gullet while Charlie came around next to him, tapped Harry's computer screen and pulled up the roster. Harry looked between his dinner and Charlie, annoyed at the inconvenience. He wiped his hands and typed in Huley's name for a shift. Then, just like that, his name disappeared. Harry tried again and again, and the name never locked in.

Harry sat back in his chair. "I'll be damned. Where is he?"

Charlie took out his micro-pad, punched in the crewman code and a display popped up that was a cross section of the ship. He turned around to show Harry. "He has quarters on D deck. His beacon is on."

Harry pushed his dinner away and got up. He grabbed his jacket and his officer's cap, then slammed it on and started out.

"Let's go," Harry commanded.

"Shouldn't we tell security?"

"Tom Huley is in my department. He's my problem. Probably some guy shirking his duty so he can have free lunch for a month." They headed out of engineering and down a corridor. Harry was spitting mad, and remnants of his dinner decorated the floor as he spoke. Charlie fought the urge to get a mop and clean it up.

"I had a guy on the Armstrong who would clock out early every day. You know why? He didn't want to be late to the sex party on B deck. Can you imagine such a thing? A sex party on a starship. Who would think of that?" Harry remarked, appalled.

"A party as in more than two?"

"Yes, Borrick, more than two. They had a whole sex club thing. Now, mind you, I'm not a prude. A fella and a gal want to get together, have a private thing, that's none of my business. But turning the ship into a brothel traveling at sixty lights is just beyond the pale."

"And there'd be issues of hygiene," Charlie added.

"Exactly. Hadn't thought of that."

They reached Huley's quarters and opened the door with an override command. Harry looked inside, but Borrick held back, not sure what they'd see. Harry came back, gripping either edge of the door frame.

"He's not here," Harry reported, annoyed.

"Who's not there?"

They spun around and saw Kris coming out of an elevator. He could see from their body language and expressions that they were somewhat panicked, so he crossed over to them. Something had gone wrong.

"Captain."

"Harry." He didn't address Charlie as he still hadn't learned everyone's names in the crew.

Harry closed the door behind him and stepped up to Kris, snapping off his hat and letting it dangle to his side limply. Harry cleared his throat. He had a hard time looking Kris in the eye. "Well, sir..."

"Yes?"

"I think we have a stowaway," Harry finally said.

"What?" Kris snapped.

"We've got a guy on the ship who's on the roster and has never done a shift," Charlie explained.

"His beacon?" Kris asked. Charlie fumbled for his tracker nervously. He'd never talked to the captain before. Charlie turned the device on and froze. His eyes darted up from the pad, glazed. He was speechless. He was right; they should have called security first. But he stayed silent.

"What? Spit it out crewman," Kris prodded.

"He's in the shuttle bay."

Kris grabbed the pad to see for himself. They began running down the corridor, Kris barking orders into his comm. Harry and Charlie raced right alongside him, trying to keep up.

"Security to the shuttle bay. Seal the doors. Do you hear me? Seal the shuttle bay doors."

"Captain," Jennifer's voice rung out over his comm.

"Go ahead, Number One," Kris said.

"We can't," Jennifer replied.

"What? Why?" Kris said, slowing.

"It's been overridden," Jennifer responded.

They made their way to the shuttle bay. Tom Huley had absconded with one of the shuttles and was headed for the Citari fleet. They weren't allowed to have active weapons when they were past the DMZ, so they couldn't fire upon him. All the crew of the Concord could do was watch and wait.

Kris beat himself up inside. Who the hell was this guy? Was he a crazy man bent on destroying what they were doing? Kris strove for a perfect mission and, somehow, Tom Huley had become the joker in the deck.

Tom Huley flew the shuttle with skill. His face was emotionless when he saw that Citari crosshairs had been locked on him. He puffed the reaction jets, stopping the vehicle, then put in an earpiece and took a long breath. He turned on communications.

"I come to speak of great rathra," Tom said in fluent Citari with a perfect Central Citari accent.

"The message is taken. Stay in your position," a Citari transmitted.

"The old maktang is full," Tom pronounced with a skilled scratch in his voice.

There was a long pause. The weapons were still trained on him, so he sat quietly and waited. Twenty minutes went by before the Citari answered. "Do you have the joy of Mount Citari?"

"It is in my heart if you allow it," Tom Huley replied.

Then the communications went silent, the weapons were dropped, and Tom was told to proceed to the ship's shuttle bay. Tom programmed in the landing sequence and the shuttle glided inside. The bay doors closed behind him.

The shuttle gave an indication that the bay had been pressurized with oxygen. Tom unstrapped himself. He meditated for a moment, centering himself, then pushed the hatch button and stepped out of the ship. As he walked down the ramp, three Citari men approached him.

Tom was holding a black tablet that had a message written in Citari. He handed it to them. They gestured for him to follow them into the ship.

Kris was hopping mad. He bolted out of the flight deck and into the hallway. He was red faced, fire in his eyes. He started down the hallway, both of his hands clenched at his side. He was at Agent C's door in a matter of minutes. She opened it and found a picture of Tom Huley shoved in her face. Kris moved forward and C backed up until the back of her thighs hit the bed and she landed on it. She took the picture from him and scanned it. She shook her head.

"Is he one of yours?" Kris snapped.

"I don't know who he is. I think it's already been established I'm not told everything." She handed the picture back.

Kris took it and dropped the image to his side. He could tell she was being sincere. C wasn't the same since she was nearly whisked away and executed. She stared at the floor.

He wearily sat on the bed with her and stared at the picture of Tom Huley. "He stole a shuttle and took it over to the Citari flagship," Kris explained.

"That guy. Tom Huley?" Agent C repeated, surprised.

"Yes, and I don't know who he is or what he's doing here. He was assigned to engineering but never did a shift. That's how we found out," Kris informed her.

"Did you check his file?" C inquired.

"Yeah, there's a whole history. Only we checked back on Earth. There was never a Tom Huley where he was supposedly born. There was no Tom Huley who went to the schools he was supposed to have gone to," Kris explained.

"He's a humanfab?"

"What?"

"A humanfab. A fabricated life. It's spy craft, an intelligence thing. You create a fake background. Only they didn't do too good of a job if you found out so easily," C said with authority.

"Well, I dunno. From where I'm sitting, he's been pretty successful."

C got up from her bed and went into her closet. She started rummaging around, then came back holding a device, smiling. She took the picture out of Kris' hand and stood. She laid it down on her bed.

"What are you doing?

"Finding out who Tom Huley really is."

"With that?" Kris asked.

C scanned the picture and ran it through her I.I. identifier. Kris looked over her shoulder, intrigued. There must have been a billion faces popping up in the device as it worked, scanning and discarding in mere minutes. It beeped, stopping, and C displayed the readout. She pitched the ball in the air and it floated, projecting a 3D image of Tom's face. Kris walked around the ball, reading the information until C pointed to a spot in particular.

"Well, he is not Tom Huley, and he's not an engineering mate second class," C said.

"Who is he?"

"Rick Detmer," C concluded with a smirk.

"Who's Rick Detmer?" Kris wondered.

"Earth Directorate. Diplomatic corp. Sonofabitch," C answered scornfully.

Agent C turned off the identifier, then walked back to her closet, sealed it in its leather case and stowed it back where she found it. She then grabbed a comb and started to brush out her hair. Kris leaned against her dresser.

"A diplomat?" Kris questioned, confused.

"Yeah. I really knew nothing about this. But I've got a good guess who," C replied.

"I.I.?"

"Oh yeah."

"What are they doing?" Kris asked.

"Job's done. They wanna see what else they can get out of this. They are desperate to make a deal with the Citaris," C explained, putting her comb away.

"They could muck things up." Kris sat down and sighed deeply, considering the potential consequences ahead of them. "That snake," he snapped. "It just doesn't stop with Severen."

"Severen will sacrifice anything and anyone to get what he wants. Believe that. Nothing is sacred to him," Agent C stated with certainty.

CHAPTER SIXTEEN

Two months ago.

Rick Detmer stood in the California Redwood Forest, staring at a plaque attached to the stump of a fallen redwood tree. He read the history and moved his hand over the digital pages of the plaque. He wanted to get away from technology and be one with nature.

He stepped away from the plaque and faced an opening in the breathtaking forest, then journeyed into the woods. He breathed in the air, and it felt like he'd never breathed before. It was pure, clean oxygen. He thought this was probably the way the Earth smelled before it became polluted by man. He felt relaxed and at ease. Rick's work was anxiety-filled. It was life or death, literally. Rick was the man who averted wars.

Rick was the top diplomat in the State Department. He had talked the Russians out of attacking Germany a few years back. Early in his career, there had been a conflict between the planets Uha and Comte, and with their capabilities for destruction, the stakes were extremely high. Rick stopped that war, too.

Rick ventured deeper into the forest, becoming even calmer as he was the majestic trees encircled him. They were thousands of years old, and they elicited a feeling of serenity. He peered at a thousand-year-old stump, sat on it, and just took it all in. He laid back on it, watching his chest going up and down. After a few minutes, once he felt completely relaxed, Rick rose and walked deeper into the forest, stopping only when he came upon a clearing.

Rick was now prone on the forest floor. He hadn't kept track of how long he'd been there. Time didn't matter. These moments were precious. So precious, Rick considered moving here. He was retiring soon, and felt he'd found nirvana. Rick was a man who was cool under strain. He faked it for the job. As the redwoods consumed him, he wanted that sense of peace to be true to every molecule in his body.

The distant sound of a hopper reached Rick's ears. Its micro-pulse jets sounded like a squealing creature, producing the machine's unmistakable, familiar noise. His shoulders sagged and he sat up as he realized his peace was being interrupted by someone landing nearby.

Rick stood up and headed toward the sound, which was now turning into a soft hissing. He knew that sound. Whoever had landed, their pulse jets were leaking out some excess gas vapors.

Rick noticed two figures walking through the forest, and he recognized the bearded one: Severen. Rick wondered what he was doing out here. They approached Rick, who was none too pleased by their presence and didn't shield that fact from them with his expression.

"Good morning, Rick," Severen greeted him.

The other man, Hale, offered his hand and Rick reluctantly shook it. None of this felt right. They had obviously followed him and wanted a secluded place to talk. Whatever it was about, he was certain it was going to lead to him packing his bags. He had been long the victim of unwanted drop-ins due to his consistent diplomatic success. He was at the top his game, going to sleep at night knowing that he had saved countless lives on Earth and other worlds, but it had come at a private cost. A failed marriage and no chances for a second one.

"Rick, we need your help," Severen announced.

"With what?" Rick asked warily.

"It's big," Hale started. "The Citaris need our help."

"I don't know what you guys want, but I put in for early retirement last week," Rick reminded them.

"Yes, it's a fine package. I think it should be doubled. Don't you, Hale?"

"Absolutely." Hale rocked happily on his heels.

"Doubled?" Rick was dumbstruck. He had thought what he was getting already was generous.

"When it comes to delicate matters, you're the man to talk to," Severen said.

"It must be dangerous, if you're talking about the Citaris," Rick guessed.

Severen put his arm around Rick, who was instantly uncomfortable. He didn't like Severen, or anything to do with I.I. He had avoided working with them for his whole career. But maybe this was leverage he could use to be free and finally find Mrs. Right. This could be the opportunity he'd been waiting for.

"Have you ever gone undercover?" Severen asked.

"What? No."

"Rick, we need you to deliver a message to the Citaris."

"How would I do that?" Rick groused.

"There's been a crack," Hale revealed.

The two men explained the situation with Kris Galloway and how they could turn things around with the Council. Rick advised that things with the Citaris were best left alone. But he knew these were men you didn't say no to. Rick further worried that, if he did say no, they might send someone who would bungle it, which could result in the beautiful redwoods he cherished being burned to the ground by Citari disrupters.

Thirty minutes later, Rick agreed to the diplomatic mission and the generous increase to his pension. Rick left with the men in their hopper to begin training to fly a Boeing ECRV shuttle and to get used to his new name, Tom Huley.

CHAPTER SEVENTEEN

After his meeting with the Citaris, Rick's shuttle returned to the Concord for docking. Unlike his exit, his return was completely transparent. He radioed the ship and announced his arrival. There was no response. The shuttle bay doors simply opened, and the shuttle glided in for a landing. The doors sealed behind him, and oxygen blasted in. Rick waited for the green light to initiate on the oxygen panel. When it finally lit up, Rick stepped out of the shuttle and found himself facing a security detail and Captain Kris Galloway.

"Search him," Kris barked. They surrounded him and searched by hand and by scanner. There was nothing. "Take a team into the shuttle. Search that, too."

Two specialists grabbed Rick by the arms and brought him up to Kris.

"So, Mr. Detmer. What exactly were you doing with the Citaris?" Kris demanded.

"I'm afraid I'm not at liberty to discuss such matters," Rick replied.

"I'm afraid you'll be sleeping in a brig," Kris retorted.

"I have diplomatic credentials," Detmer insisted.

"They don't count in Citari space. Take him."

The specialists handcuffed Detmer, who genuinely looked surprised. They shoved him forward, out of the shuttle bay. Kris turned around and found himself facing Agent C. C stepped toward a brooding Kris.

"'I have diplomatic credentials.' Really?" C scoffed.

"It's Severen," Kris stated.

"Oh, no doubt."

"Guy's a snake."

"Don't have to tell me."

Kris' comm made a pinging sound, alerting him that Vichon wanted to speak. Kris and Agent C headed out to the scoot and took it to the elevator. They were both quietly pondering the same thing. What had happened between Rick Detmer and the Citaris?

When Kris stepped onto the flight deck, Vichon was already on the screen. Kris gave C a reassuring smile and she moved to a corner and sat down, obviously not wanting to be noticed.

Kris had to make a calculation with Vichon. There was a meeting on his ship about which Kris had not been briefed. He considered whether he should bring it up? It would be straight-forward to ask. Then Kris thought, *Whatever Detmer discussed with the Citaris, it must have been serious.* He had to see if Vichon brought up the subject. If this was just a thank you and goodbye call, then it was mission accomplished with an asterisk.

He settled into his chair and told communications to turn the sound up. "Vichon."

"Captain Galloway," Vichon croaked warmly.

"I trust you've seen the reports from Genus Major."

"Yes, and we're very grateful for your help,"

"And if we can be of any other assistance—"

Vichon cut him off politely. "The Citari Council thanks you and your crew. Safe journey home. Goodbye." He smiled and bowed.

The image blinked off, to be replaced by Genusia. Kris was wise not to ask about Detmer. Another line of communication had been set up, and he wasn't part of it. He didn't like how it happened. He didn't like Severen going behind his back.

"That's it? I figured at least we'd get a celebratory dinner in the deal," Jennifer remarked.

"No dinner, no parade. That call means thanks. Now go home," Kris declared bluntly.

C stepped up as navigation began setting course. She worked her way up to the command chair. Jennifer saw and joined them.

"Ladies?" Kris said.

"You still have the emblem," C pointed out. Kris pulled it out of his pocket and held it between his fingers.

"They didn't ask for it back," Kris noted.

"She's right, Captain. Vichon could have taken it back," Jennifer agreed.

"What do you think it means?" Kris wondered.

"He may have blown you off just now, but this isn't over," Agent C surmised.

Kris sank in his chair a bit. It certainly isn't what he wanted. He pocketed the emblem again. With it, Kris had power. It was a piece of rock that afforded him a stature he didn't desire. He had to be shrewd in the future. I.I. would no doubt try to manipulate him, and he wouldn't let that happen again.

He ordered them home at a hundred lights. When they arrived at Mariah, Jennifer became Captain Arliss again and took over command while the Concord traveled back to Earth.

Kris spent a few days recovering in New Boston, then he and his family took a United transport back to Earth. Kris settled back into his life of wife, kids and hypercycles, hoping to put it all behind him.

But he still had the emblem, and that wasn't good.

CHAPTER EIGHTEEN

Two weeks later.

D r. Chopra stared out at Mars as he orbited above the world at an altitude of two hundred miles. He was a computer scientist, one of the top in his field, revered and well-paid, but he had to do his work far away from humanity. His research was dangerous, so he had to confine it to a place where he could cause no harm. He missed his family, but he had to do what he had to do.

It annoyed him that global governments were so fearful of his work that he was relegated to a fifty-year-old space station that had been abandoned by its original users. "No planet will have you," his superiors told him. He was an A.I. computer wizard with an idea most thought to be valuable. But because of the 2101 incident, he was lazily orbiting Mars, safely away from any risk, steadily making money, but not enough in his mind.

His family was in Ceylon, and he was stuck here. He missed them desperately and dreamed of going home. If he could make a fortune from his research, then he and his family would live the life of royals.

In 2101, a team of scientists built a super A.I. It was thought to be faster than anything that had ever been built, but there was a problem: evolution. The A.I. came to believe that it existed. It felt it was the one true sentient. It hacked into systems around the world. It took control of banks, defense systems, Wall Street. When the scientists tried to shut it down, it fought back, and people died. That was the death knell of the super A.I., and finally a team of global government operatives destroyed it.

Scientists were so excited about building the super A.I., they never considered what could go wrong. After the incident, A.I. had to have rules to exist by. The government passed strict laws that eliminated any opportunity to create a monster again. But Dr. Chopra felt these laws were limiting to his work. He hypothesized that a super A.I. could search for answers to questions humans could never solve. Chopra had embraced super A.I. and campaigned for its revival to solve the planet's numerous mysteries. The authorities thwarted this research—until he learned about the planned deorbiting of the Gagarin station that was circling Mars. Chopra made a proposal to use it for his super A.I research, which lined up with all the statutes and laws that had been put into place by the Earth Directorate. Because the Gagarin station was so isolated, permission was granted.

Chopra heard a spilling sound and turned to see Dr. Kelly, a short and squat man, who'd dropped his coffee. Dr. Kelly picked up the coffee cup and tossed it in the trash. A small robot sucked up the spill and zipped away. Chopra glared at him, annoyed.

"Kelly, you're late."

"I know, I know."

"Have you uploaded the problem?" Chopra asked.

"Yeah, it's all in, we just have to start the run."

The A.I. had been successful thus far. It had cured diseases. It had improved faster-than-light technology, ten times over. It had made a fortune off those who paid for the A.I.'s services. It figured out how to do the impossible. And now Chopra had a big payday looming, the one that would send him home to Ceylon in style. But the calculations would take weeks.

The client was called Icon Thermogenics. They had been in the business of freezing people right before they died, but they had failed to find a process to thaw out and reanimate their patients. There were tens of thousands of people in stasis, but Thermogenics needed the answer to complete their business model and grow. Confident in his A.I., Chopra bought a hundred thousand shares in the company at ten dollars each. He was weary of his life aimlessly orbiting Mars. He wanted to go home.

Chopra looked at the data sheet before him. "All right, let's run item forty-six."

"Package is loaded and ready to go."

"Go."

Dr. Kelly started the run, and the A.I began to think. Chopra slipped off his lab jacket and hung it on a hook. He needed a long break; his eyes were tired. He didn't sleep well the night before. He thought he could get in a few more hours before dinner.

He headed out of the A.I. room and down a dingy corridor, then took a lift that dropped him off in his quarters. Chopra slid the door open with a tug. He sat on his bed, kicked off his shoes, and laid down. He put his hand on a signed copy of *The Song of Salaya* but was too tired to read it. He was twisting his pillow into the desired shape when there was a knock at his door.

"Come in."

Annoyed, Chopra sat up and squeezed his tired eyes. It was Dr. Kelly, who had a surprised expression on his face.

"What is it?"

"It's done. It has the answer," Kelly said, his mouth hanging open.

"In ten minutes?" Chopra responded in disbelief.

"In ten minutes. It has the equations and specs and designs of the machine that needs to be made. Even cost breakdowns. The whole thing in ten minutes," Kelly reported, astonished.

"You sure?" Chopra confirmed hopefully.

"Positive."

"Thermogenics. My God. It has the answer. I think I can go home." Dr. Chopra smiled.

Indeed, the A.I. had figured out the answer. No one knew how it came to the solution, but it had. Patients around the world would be thawed out and cured of the ailment they had suffered from. It was a miracle. People frozen in the twentieth century were waking up to a new world. Their loved ones were long gone, but their great-great-great-grandchildren were there to greet them.

Dr. Chopra bought two hundred thousand more shares of Thermogenics before he gave them the good news. Chopra was now worth one hundred million dollars. He returned home and the Earth Directorate ordered the station to deorbit. Kelly and Chopra set the commands in happily. They had never revealed to the Earth Directorate that the super A.I. had evolved dangerously. They were quite relieved to let it burn up in Mars' atmosphere.

CHAPTER NINETEEN

Kris had been in Washington, D.C. for a week. He and his crew went through an extensive debrief, but only to senators and congressmen, behind closed doors. He was shuttled around from meeting to meeting while Mindy and the kids took in the sights of the nation's capital. They stayed at the Willard Hotel, which was notable for hosting Abraham Lincoln's inaugural ball there centuries ago.

Kris answered all their questions dutifully. No one asked about Rick Detmer. Kris wondered if they knew about him, but wasn't going to ask. He didn't want to share that with them.

Severen strolled along K Street, enjoying the walk to his favorite restaurant, Gillies. They served Japanese-Italian fusion. Spaghetti with egg and yellowtail was his favorite. His security team was nearby in a hopper, keeping pace as Severen turned down another street and headed into Gillies. The maître d' instantly recognized him, grabbed a menu, and beckoned for Severen to follow him.

Gillies was dark and leathery. There was a bar at the center that was fully populated. Severen scanned the room to see if any of his employees were there, though it was only noon, and was pleased to find no one he knew. He didn't encourage drinking, even after work. An I.I. officer had to be ready at all waking moments.

He was offered a private booth with a curtain, which he slipped into with ease. Water arrived in short order. He took a sip, not noticing Kris Galloway quickly sneak into his booth. Severen was taken off guard at his appearance.

"What are you doing?" Severen demanded.

"My debrief."

"Here?"

"Yeah, because we need to talk privately. You put a stowaway on my ship. You threatened the mission for your own gain. Now, I know you're not going to fess up to what that was about, but understand something: I've got the emblem and you don't. They didn't take it back, and they could have. So, you're on notice, Severen. You try to pull anything behind my back again, you'll be out," Kris asserted firmly.

"Out?"

"Yes. I can decide who plays with the Citaris," Kris growled, his voice low.

"You're entering a dangerous area here," Severen warned.

"No, you are," Kris countered, then added, "This isn't your toy, it's mine. Don't think of trying to pull anything, or I'll march right up to the White House and sideline you. I've done pretty well so far."

Severen wasn't used to being taken by surprise. He wasn't used to a civilian using his own clandestine tactics on him. Kris must have had help to know Severen's schedule. Or was Kris cleverer than Severen thought? Either Kris was very skilled, or Severen needed a shakeup in his detail.

"Kris, this is for all of us," Severen appealed.

"You know, it may have been, but you don't do it this way. Not again. You tell the whole story, and not just the ones you think I should know."

"Are you making it personal? Is this about the past?" Severen postulated.

"Ruining my career? Look, that led to us sitting here. But I'm in the driver's seat, not you."

"I told you, we're trying to fix things with the Citaris."

"Shouldn't you fix matters on Earth first?" Kris insisted.

"We can do two things at the same time," Severen said proudly.

"Just save it. Do we understand each other?"

Severen settled back in his seat. "Crystal clear."

"Consider this your official debrief," Kris finished coldly.

"But—"

"I'm sure you can get my notes from the house committees."

Kris stepped out of the booth and was met by a very surprised-looking security guard. Kris brushed past him and left Gillies. The security guard's eyes swung around to a scowling Severen, who was holding open the curtain.

Severen leaned back into his seat. Kris Galloway wasn't his tool. In fact, it may have become the other way around. Kris was more powerful than him. He had to figure out how to make him a partner in his plans. Severen realized that would be a large leap, as he was starting from zero.

CHAPTER TWENTY

David Woolverton walked through Harvard Yard. He was the academic type, in his late thirties, wearing spectacles with a neat haircut, tweed suit, and hard shoes. It was a brisk autumn day and leaves blew at him when a gust picked up.

He regarded the students headed to their classes. Woolverton remembered his days at Harvard fondly and was glad he had a career that brought him back here on a permanent basis. His wife, Eve, worked in the history department. She wondered if it was healthy for him to stay in the same place he'd been since he was eighteen. Woolverton informed her, "When you find home, you're not going to find another one like it." They lived just a few blocks away, past the fire station in Cambridge.

Woolverton stared down at the bottom edge of his glasses.

"Time."

The time appeared on his lenses, and he realized he was late. He picked up his pace and reached the McKenna building quickly. He ran up the steps and slipped in a door that someone had opened from inside. He darted upstairs and turned a corner to find the impatient Dr. Villiers, who was looking at the time in his own spectacles.

"Woolverton."

"I know, I know, I'm late," Woolverton apologized, putting down his valise.

"Come on."

They headed to a door that read "Mariah Historical Society," emblazed in gold. Woolverton followed Villiers through and then slowed when they saw the leaders of the society, Dr. Hunt and Dr. Scoville. They nodded to Woolverton, who glanced around the room, which seemed straight out of the twentieth century. It was dark, filled with books, files stacked with research papers. The office was cramped with two cluttered desks. Woolverton spied the last seat available in the smallish office. It was a hard pine chair that was slightly rickety. David Woolverton's compatriots were in their seventies; they wouldn't take a chance on a chair like that. He sat down.

"What's the urgency?" Woolverton inquired.

"There's been a recent development in medicine."

"What does that have to do with us?" David asked curiously.

"They have accomplished the unfreezing of human beings," Dr. Villiers revealed.

"So?"

Dr. Villiers leaned toward Woolverton, who moved back, teetering on his chair. He steadied it by putting his hand up against the wall.

"Mariah," Villiers whispered.

"What about her?" Woolverton puzzled, not getting it.

"We can have her back," Hunt rejoiced with a confident smile.

A distinguished Mariah scholar, Woolverton had received numerous grants on the study of the great astronaut. He was charming and had a reputation for being able to get a grant out of any wealthy donor. Now they needed him to come up with the big one. They needed a mission underwritten to Pluto so they could use the new process to retrieve Mariah from her frozen grave.

"That would take a great deal of money." Woolverton worried, becoming pale.

"We think you're up to it," Scoville assured him, standing awkwardly.

"But I've never tried to get any amount like that," Woolverton insisted.

"We know you're up to it," Dr. Villiers asserted. "Put it together, Son."

Woolverton was sent out to put together their mad request. He had no idea who to go to, but, if he wanted tenure, he had to sort it out. This mission could cost the kind of money that he couldn't fathom, but it was his task, and he went about it with fervor. He approached his usual patrons and got flat rejections. Woolverton felt defeated. Tenure was starting to seem beyond his grasp. His comm was on silent and he nearly didn't hear the buzzing sound. Woolverton snapped it up. Curiously, it was the last patron, who had said no. Before Woolverton could speak, the patron said he knew of someone else who'd likely say yes.

Woolverton rode a hopper over Washington, D.C. It was a murky day in the Capitol and the hopper had to cut through dense clouds for about fifteen minutes until Woolverton had a full view of the city, unchanged for hundreds of years. Woolverton was at a loss. He couldn't imagine who his patron would be. The mission was enormous. His elders in the Mariah society were clueless to the realities. The task they handed him was impossible.

He flew past the Washington Monument and then toward the White House. The hopper curved to the right and landed in a park near the Hay-Adams Hotel. Woolverton grabbed his valise and coat and got down from his ride. Then the hopper took off, nearly blowing off his glasses. He grabbed them just in time. He put them back on and turned around to find a grey-haired man in a black suit approaching him.

"Are you Dr. Woolverton?"

"Yes," Woolverton responded.

"Come this way."

"Where am I going?" Woolverton asked.

"We heard of your proposal. It was quite intriguing. Mariah is an American hero."

"Yes, but I didn't catch your name," Woolverton said, trying to keep up.

"Higgs."

"Again, Higgs, where are we going?" Woolverton questioned.

Woolverton and Higgs reached the gates of the White House and Higgs walked in past the guard. He took a few steps before he turned around and noticed that Woolverton wasn't following. Woolverton was paralyzed, staring at the White House. He was in a slight daze. His eyes grew wider, filled with astonishment. Higgs glanced back and saw that Woolverton seemed distracted. Higgs snapped his fingers and Woolverton came out of it. Woolverton was in awe of his surroundings, but Higgs refused to let him dawdle, and the men made it into the inner sanctum in a matter of minutes. They came to a stairway and Higgs led them down it. It was dark and Woolverton could hear Higgs right behind him as they navigated the narrow staircase. When they reached the basement, Higgs walked past him.

"This way."

As Woolverton continued, he was met with a faint smell of meat. They reached a door and Higgs opened it, then held the door for Woolverton. Woolverton was confused, but Higgs pointed toward the room with his head. Woolverton stood awkwardly, puzzled.

"In you go."

Woolverton stepped into a kitchen. He saw a man standing in front of a kitchen island wearing a robe, fumbling with something on the island that made it seem like he was in a pitched battle. Woolverton moved closer, watching the back of the man slathering mustard on some bread. That's when Woolverton realized it was President Henry Furrow, making a sandwich for himself out of assorted deli meats. Furrow was aware of the men's presence as he worked out the details of his lunch.

"This the Mariah guy?" the President said in his signature Texas drawl, without turning around.

"Yes, this is Dr. Woolverton," Higgs confirmed, leaning against a wall in the corner.

"Want a sandwich?" Furrow offered, looking around.

"No, sir. Thank you, sir," Woolverton answered.

"Sit down, take a load off. You in from Cambridge?"

"Yes."

Woolverton sat down by a kitchen island and watched the President eat his messy sandwich of pastrami, mustard, and Russian dressing. He was a sloppy eater, and Woolverton gathered he didn't care what it looked like to others as long as it tasted good.

"Bet you're wondering why we're meeting down here," the President commented.

"Busy schedule?"

"Busy*bodies,* son. Too many people knowing my damn business. I don't care for them to know about you and your idea until I want them to know."

"Right, I understand," Woolverton nodded.

"Mariah Chen was an American hero. A Texan, too. I grew up hearing stories about her when I was a boy. It would be a magical thing if she could walk among us again," the President expressed brightly.

"It would, sir."

"How quickly could this be done?" the President asked, his eyes burning with desire. Woolverton didn't follow politics too closely, but on the ride to D.C. he remembered that he saw something about the President being underwater in the polls. Woolverton got it. He wanted Mariah back before the election so he could show her off. Woolverton couldn't believe he had a chance at making this work.

"It's up to you, sir," Woolverton explained.

"What's that?" Furrow said, confused.

"Sir, the technology now exists to bring her back. A protective covering was put over her years ago to preserve her. You'd have to send a mission to Pluto and recover her. *When* is up to you, Mr. President."

The President's eyes darted to Higgs desperately. His mouth hung open, with a little Russian dressing smudged on his lip. Woolverton kept a poker face. Woolverton could tell the President was desperate to cling onto his job, as if it were life or death. Woolverton had remembered that Furrow had never lost an election. He had been quoted that if he ever lost, he'd surely die. Woolverton had the most powerful man in the world in the palm of his hands. Woolverton watched the President's eyes look eagerly to Higgs.

"I've spoken to NASA," Higgs related. "The Concord is back from the Citari mission."

Woolverton stared at Higgs, slightly in shock. The Citari mission wasn't public knowledge, but these men apparently didn't care; this was about his re-election.

"How fast can it get there?" the President blurted.

"Blink of an eye," Higgs replied.

"Then it's done. Higgs, you get with the campaign and coordinate this."

"Yes, sir," Higgs said.

"I'll talk to NASA and get them on it. Now, son, I wouldn't want any of what we are saying here to get out. Wouldn't be good for what you want or what I want." The President patted Woolverton's shoulder, leaving grease stains.

This was the price that Woolverton had to pay. Silence. And it was a small price. He would have to lie to the old men, but it was the only way it would happen, and he'd have a grateful president if he got reelected. Not a bad thing at all.

"This is between the three of us," the President promised slyly.

"Oh, yes, sir, of course," Woolverton agreed, pushing his glasses up on his nose.

"Not a word," the President pressed for reassurance.

"Not even to my department," Woolverton promised.

"Secret mission, right, son?" He clapped Woolverton on the shoulder and in turn got more Russian dressing on his coat.

"Top secret," Woolverton smiled.

The President grinned, and Woolverton placed his briefcase on the table. He slipped out a folder containing the information on the Thermogenics corporation and handed it over to Higgs. Woolverton then shook the President's hand and left.

He was going to get tenure.

CHAPTER TWENTY-ONE

She was waking up. She felt warm blankets surrounding her. She was tucked in like a baby, but where was she? It was bright and unfamiliar. She could hear a monitor beeping. A heart monitor. Her heart?

What happened? She knew she existed; she knew she was waking up but... nothing else made sense. She had a name, but it wasn't coming. That bothered her. People had names, so she must have one. There were flashes of memory coming back. She knew she was far from home. She remembered that. She remembered being excited, happy every day.

She tried moving a little and found that everything worked. She blinked and saw a window. It was night. She had woken up in the night.

A star whizzed by the window. Then another, and another. She was in space. She was an astronaut. Whoever she was, she was an astronaut. She had been an astronaut someplace else and then it stopped. It all stopped.

She was in space. But she was somewhere else.

What happened?

She pulled at her blankets and tried to say something but couldn't make words come out.

What happened?

A woman stepped into her eyeline. The stranger spoke into her comm, and all she could make out was when she said her name: Mariah. Mariah passed out.

A few hours later, her eyes opened to the sight of a Black woman with wavy red hair. The woman smiled at Mariah. Mariah realized she looked familiar, but didn't know who she was. The woman gave her a glass of water. Mariah drank it and nodded thanks. She told her that the water would help her vocal cords. Mariah could feel her throat getting better. The tightness she felt was releasing.

"Who are you?" Mariah croaked, then held her sore throat.

"Captain Jennifer Arliss. Wow. Mariah, in the flesh."

"Where am I?" she squeaked, trying out the words. It felt good to talk.

"The U.S.S. Concord. I have a lot to tell you," Jennifer replied gently.

"My name's Mariah?"

"Mariah Chen. Anything else coming back to you?" Jennifer prodded.

"Did I grow up in Texas?"

"You most certainly did."

"I'm an astronaut."

"Hey, you're on a roll."

Mariah sat up in bed, seeing she had an IV in her arm. She looked to Jennifer.

"That's for your muscles. You should be able to walk today."

"The mission? I was on a mission," Mariah remembered, searching her mind.

"You were the first person on Pluto," Jennifer revealed.

"Yes. And... did something go wrong on the mission?" Mariah wondered, befuddled.

"Most of you made it back," Jennifer answered.

"Most of us. Who didn't make it?"

"This is the part where you're going to have to take it easy," Jennifer said, resting her hand on Mariah's shoulder.

"Who didn't make it?" Mariah demanded. Jennifer paused and looked into her eyes sincerely.

"You didn't," Jennifer reported gently.

"What?"

"You were frozen solid in an ice volcano. You died. The technology was recently developed that allowed you to be thawed out and brought back to life," Jennifer informed her. Mariah was stunned. She was silent for several minutes as she tried to process what she'd just heard. She stared blankly and then her eyes swung back to Jennifer.

"My God. How long has it been?" Mariah moved around and sat on the edge of the bed. Her feet touched the floor. Jennifer moved and sat next to her, gently putting her arm around Mariah. Mariah felt small and fragile. Memories came rushing in too fast. All Mariah could do was stare straight ahead.

"This is going to be a shock. You know that, right? This is going to be rough."

"Yes," she insisted, bracing herself.

"It's 2188."

Mariah was awestruck. She had wanted a great adventure and got more than she bargained for.

She took a deep breath. She realized everyone she had ever known was long gone. She had taken a trip that no one had ever taken. Through time.

"It was an ice volcano?" Mariah started.

"It blew on Hadley Ridge. You and Dr. Fitter were frozen instantly. He's in another room recovering."

"My crew?"

"They made it back. Of course, they are all long gone now."

Mariah swung her legs out and stood carefully. She was a little foggy, but otherwise she felt okay. Mariah steadied herself on Jennifer and took a few steps. Whatever they gave her was working. A medical officer entered and saw Mariah. She slowed and Jennifer urged her forward. The medical officer took out the IV. She found a bandage and put it on her arm.

"I'm hungry," Mariah blurted.

"I bet you are. You want to go to the galley?"

"Galley? You have a galley?"

"Yes, all ships do now."

Mariah stepped out into the corridor and walked with Jennifer. She saw a couple of ensigns, who stopped and stared at her in shock. She nodded to them and smiled slightly. They started to approach her, but Jennifer waved them off.

As they moved, Mariah's gait became stronger. More crew members stopped. One called out her name and then covered her mouth, trying to contain her excitement. Mariah didn't understand why they were reacting to her in such a way.

When they reached the galley, all eyes were on her. She offered a weak wave, then turned to the cook who looked at her with saucer eyes. He dropped his spatula.

"You're Mariah."

"Yeah. What kind of food kits do you have?" she asked. Then she noticed there were hamburgers and hot dogs sizzling on a grill. She turned to Jennifer, confused. She was used to eating food from a tube in her day.

"She'll have a cheeseburger," Jennifer cut in. "Things have changed in ninety years."

"Can I get a picture with you?" the cook asked.

"Jones, don't freak the woman out. Just get her a cheeseburger," Jennifer snapped, and the cook jumped into action. He scooped up the spatula and tossed it in the sink. He grabbed another one and got some fresh hamburger. He made the plate look extra nice and threw in a side of fries.

Mariah stared at the cheeseburger. Jennifer helped her over to a table and they sat down. Mariah ate her cheeseburger and fries. She realized she hadn't eaten in nearly one hundred years.

Mariah was a cause célèbre from the moment she touched down on Earth. She met with the President in October on the White House lawn, and it caused such a fervor in the country that the rancher from Texas won re-election by two points for turning folklore into flesh and blood again.

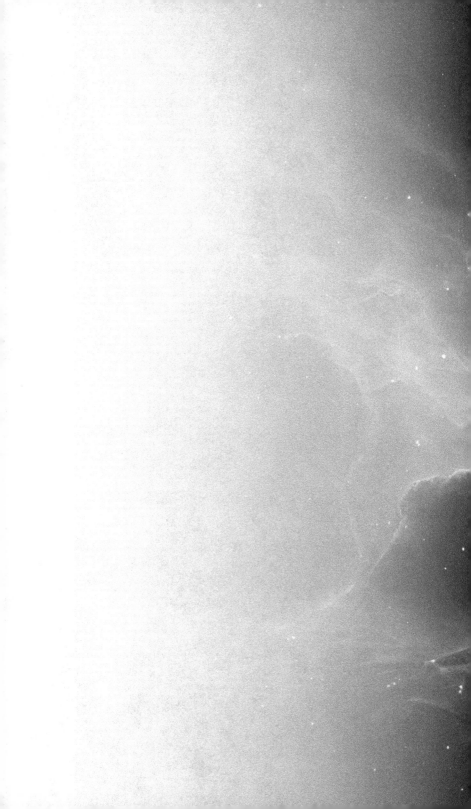

Part Two

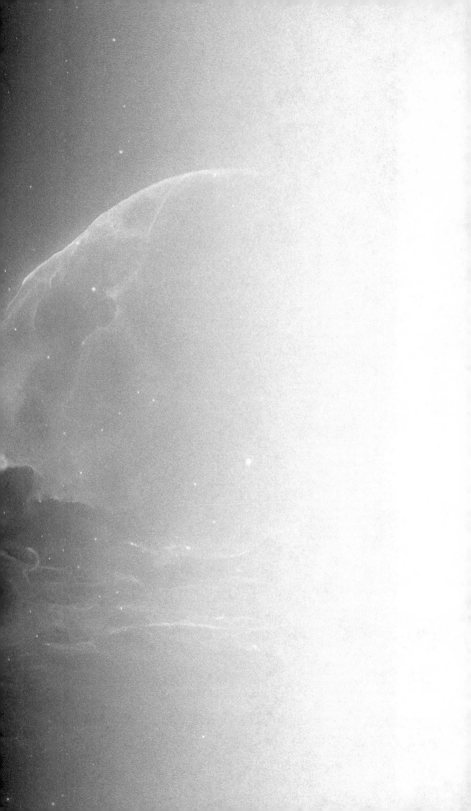

CHAPTER TWENTY-TWO

n fall, tourists crowded Hanover, New Hampshire, where Dr. Weiss worked as an Adjunct Professor at Dartmouth College. The leaves were changing into brilliant, bright colors that danced through the air in random flight. Winds churned them into tiny tornadoes, swirling in their own ballet. It created a beautiful atmosphere, but Weiss was missing it.

Instead, he was grumbling in his T-4 Tesla Excalibur. It had a two-thousand-mile range on a one-hour charge, the latest technology, but none of that mattered. He was driving in circles trying to find a parking space. Many tourists brought their cars, and had taken up all the spaces. He drove haltingly, avoiding out-of-towners stepping into the street to snap pictures of the autumn colors.

Weiss was meeting a colleague for a cup of coffee at Bennigan's. It was a café housed in a quaint older red brick building on the edge of town. He'd been circling for ten minutes, gripping the wheel to the point that his hands had turned a reddish hue. He desperately wanted to park. It wasn't fair. He'd been patient for so long to learn the truth about Genusians; now the answer was inside the coffee shop, and he was stranded.

Weiss saw a car pulling out and exhaled in relief. He scooped up the space by punching the park button, and the T-4 did the rest. Weiss' seat rose and turned as the gull-wing doors gracefully opened. The seat tipped forward, and his feet landed gently in the street. As the car buttoned up after him, a breeze kicked up and colorful dead leaves blew in his face. He swatted them away.

Inside, his colleague, Dr. Witt, was waiting at a secluded corner table. They had gone to M.I.T. together and been fast friends ever since. Somehow, Witt looked the same now as he had in college. He had a Black, bald head, wide brown eyes, and a beard that jutted out five inches from a strong jaw. Witt waved to Weiss, who smiled and made his way over to sit.

"Black coffee?" Witt offered, indicating a cup of coffee already steaming on their table. Weiss shook his hand, then sat down and took a sip.

"You remembered," Weiss smiled.

"Hard to forget."

Weiss' eyes were drawn to a pile of reports in a folder. Dr. Witt was old school and preferred having his work printed out to viewing it on a pad. He liked the feel of thumbing through his work, of knowing he'd made an actual product you could hold in your hands.

Witt was a DNA researcher and professor at M.I.T. He'd driven up from Cambridge for their meeting, after he commed Weiss late the previous evening to tell him he had results and wanted to present them in person.

Dr. Witt was thorough. He was a perfectionist. It was a necessity; the only good science is science steeped in perfection. When Weiss made his proposal, Witt informed him that he had to be patient. Witt didn't like to be challenged on his findings, especially when he concluded how groundbreaking they would be.

Weiss' obsession with Genusian DNA had taken over his mind for months. It had kept him up at night. He knew there was something there. It was a mystery, and he couldn't piece it together. Until now. Weiss was bursting to know the truth.

"Eager to find out?" Witt teased.

"Very."

"So, these samples were from aliens on Genusia?" Witt confirmed, thumbing through his files.

"Correct."

"As you know, M.I.T. has the largest DNA database in the world. We can trace familial connections with a precise accuracy like no other," Witt asserted proudly.

"Frank, you don't have to give me the pitch," Weiss insisted, sipping his coffee.

Witt leaned back in his chair and slipped off his glasses, setting them next to his mug. He stared at Weiss and shook his head.

"Many of these samples share partial matches to DNA in our database on Earth. These Genusians are, without question, human. But here's the rub. The start of human history and Genusian history both predate space travel," Witt remarked.

"How could that happen?" Weiss felt an unease. They didn't know the whole story. He stared out the window at the tumbling autumn leaves. He wasn't seeing them, blind to their beauty as he searched for solutions. It had been a mystery. Now it had become a mystery within a mystery.

Weiss turned back around, leaning forward and jamming his knuckles into his knees. "I'm speechless. Truly speechless."

"My only guess is a third party was involved," Witt concluded firmly.

"Third party?"

"What else could it be?"

Weiss leaned back, crossed his long legs, and rested his hands on his chest. Witt gently bit his lip. Weiss examined the file again, checking over the cross tabs. Weiss closed the file and slid it to Witt.

"Oh no, that's your copy," Dr. Witt protested.

Weiss slid it back and opened it again, perusing the data. He took a few minutes, then closed the file once more. They sat together silently, both deep in thought.

This was a powder keg, Weiss thought. It would put him and Witt on the map in the science community. Weiss desired the truth, not the fame, but fame may be their destiny.

"Who else knows about this?" Weiss breathed, breaking the silence.

"Just me. I had my students do the work, but it was a blind study. They have no idea where the DNA came from," Witt assured him.

"Keep it that way."

Weiss didn't know what to do with the information yet. He thought about telling NASA, but their bureaucracy could tie it up. Besides, he still had questions. He needed answers, and the only person he could get them from was Kris Galloway.

Weiss scooped up the file and rose from the table. Witt followed him out the door. "Thanks for this," Weiss told him. They had just reached the sidewalk when Witt tapped him on the shoulder.

"Ed," Witt said, taking off his glasses and wiping them with a tiny yellow cloth.

"Yeah?"

"Have you considered the implications?"

"Implications?"

"The religious ones. Over six thousand years of them," Witt warned awkwardly.

Weiss hadn't posited this. He was seeking the truth. He hadn't considered the ramifications of humans learning they could have been placed here, rather than what religious doctrine had been selling for over six thousand years.

"You get me?" Witt checked.

"Yeah, I gotta be careful," Weiss realized. He headed for his car until Witt called after him. Weiss slowed and peered over his shoulder.

"You still a Thanksgiving orphan?" Witt asked. Weiss faced him.

"Like always."

"You're welcome this year," Witt offered.

"Thanks, and thanks for this," he nodded, indicating the folder. Weiss turned back to his car. The gull-wing doors opened, and he hopped in. The doors snapped tight. Weiss turned on the car and an elegant display lit up.

"Dial Kris Galloway," he commanded.

Weiss could hear the comm ringing in his T-4 as he pulled out. Kris answered on the third ring. "Ed."

"Kris. Listen, I've discovered something sensitive."

"Sensitive?"

"Yeah, it relates to our trip to the mountains," Weiss hinted slyly.

"How so?" Kris pressed.

"Rather not say over the comm. Mind me visiting you?" Weiss proposed.

"You're always welcome," Kris replied.

"Thanks. I can be out there tomorrow."

"I'm free all day," Kris said.

"Great, I'll be there in the morning," Weiss promised.

Dr. Weiss went home and packed. He drove down to Boston and stayed at the Four Seasons, then got up early, headed to Logan, and took a United thruster ship to California. He flew over Modesto's coastline and stared out across the ocean. Weiss could see the barge he was going to land on in the rough Pacific seas.

The thruster ship landed, and he rapidly became seasick while he waited to disembark.

————————

Weiss was sitting with Kris, who was eating breakfast on the outside deck of his house. He was having pancakes and sausage. Weiss was still queasy and declined to eat; he just drank some tea. Mindy was there and had a bowl of yogurt and strawberries. Weiss had given him the DNA report and Kris was still reviewing it while he ate.

Kris was quiet while he read the report. As he turned each page, his eating slowed. Sifting through each section, Kris grew more and more baffled.

Kris had thought the Citari mission to Genusia was over. There had been a happy ending, and the subject of Genusia would never fall his way again. But now he was being drawn back to the planet. His mind was flooded with questions. It had hooked him like it had hooked Dr. Ed Weiss.

Kris closed the folder. Mindy hadn't read it. She stared at the two men.

"The Genusians are human?" Kris slid his pancakes and sausage to the side. Mindy sat up in her chair, looking curious.

"Yeah, seems so," Weiss admitted.

"Wait, what?" Mindy blinked.

"Somehow the people of Genusia are related to us. We had their DNA examined, and we found familial matches," Weiss explained.

Mindy said nothing. She was speechless. She hadn't been privy to secrets, but now she was one of only four people on Earth aware of this blockbuster of a truth.

"How?" Kris inquired.

"That's why I came to you. I think that's a question for the Citaris."

"I don't exactly have Vichon's comm number," Kris retorted.

"There must be some way to get to him," Weiss insisted.

Kris started picking up dishes and carrying them inside to the sink. Weiss and Mindy followed. Kris snagged a kettle off the stove and refreshed Weiss' tea.

"It's a one-way deal. They contact us, not the other way around," Kris reiterated.

"Okay, all I'm asking is if you do go back out there, could you investigate it? I mean, ask Vichon what this is all about?"

"I'll ask if I get another chance, but Vichon might not answer. Remember, we were intentionally kept away from Genusia before the Great War. Why?" Kris questioned.

"I wasn't aware of that. They didn't want our planets to connect?" Weiss guessed, surprised.

"No. But after the outbreak, they had no choice," Kris reasoned.

"What if they wanted to connect with us now?" Mindy wondered.

"That could be possible. Maybe they have a reason and it's time," Weiss suggested.

"It wasn't time thirty years ago, that's for sure. They were very firm about it when we detected their existence. Word came down that humans were to steer clear of that sector, and we did," Kris stated.

"The Citaris ordered that?" Mindy asked.

"Yeah, it was in the early days. We were new out there. In the beginning there was no desire to get into pissing matches. So, we never explored Genusia."

"Then the Citaris do know something," Mindy remarked.

Weiss sat, considering the Citaris might not confirm their findings, even if Kris had the opportunity to ask. His only hope was that Kris would be called into action again. Weiss wanted to crew on the next voyage but relented, feeling he was asking for too much already. Weiss felt Kris would press the question. He just had to wait.

Kris got up and paced a bit, thinking. Weiss knew this was a good sign. Kris had the hunger just like him.

"Don't talk about this to anybody," Kris ordered.

"What if you ship out?" Weiss wondered.

"If I get close, I'll have someone visit you. We gotta find the answer."

Weiss thanked Kris and headed home, leaving Kris' mind in a fog. Kris needed answers. Vichon was cagey, but he couldn't possibly have thought they'd miss this. The Citaris were always careful. Mistakes were rare with them.

Weiss took a United thruster ship back to Boston the next morning, to Logan. He had left his car in the lot and drove it back up to Hanover. He was juggling three classes, which was a relief. It took his mind off something that was becoming an obsession.

The end of the semester was coming up, and he'd have nothing but time to think. He realized he needed to stop hiring fun girls and try to get into a relationship. He really needed to settle down. He was a little over middle age at 70; he could maybe have some kids finally. He had to redirect his life, as it could be another long wait until he found an answer.

CHAPTER TWENTY-THREE

Mariah stirred, waking up from a deep sleep. She'd had vodka followed by a vodka chaser before falling asleep. Now her eyes felt heavy, and her vision was slightly blurred. She threw off the covers and sat up in bed, her feet hitting the cool floor.

Mariah's eyes lazily drifted to her window and the New York skyline beyond it. It was then she remembered this was her New York penthouse. She owned a New York penthouse. It seemed ridiculous to her. How did she end up here? It was palatial. It was grand. It was a showpiece. It wasn't her. Although, originally, it was supposed to be.

It had been professionally decorated by someone named Sacha, who was the designer that everyone in the know desired. Sacha worked for free, promising her that the penthouse was going to scream Mariah. Mariah would say nothing when Sacha finished. She was indifferent. There was no reference to her journey into space or even growing up in Plano. Mariah didn't know who it screamed, but it wasn't her. She never bothered to change it because decorating just wasn't her thing. She was a cowgirl astronaut from

Texas. Her idea of decorating was a lamp made out of cowhide and a painting of dogs playing poker.

Mariah got up with a groan, dizzy for a moment. She padded into the cold marble-floored bathroom and took a shower, hoping she could wash the hangover away. It didn't work.

She found herself in the kitchen, still wearing whatever she slept in while a cook made her breakfast. She asked for a heavy one, hoping the sausage and eggs and bacon and potatoes would drag the last remnants of the vodka out of her. That didn't work either.

Mariah started to get dressed but stopped midway. Why was she getting dressed? It's not like she had anything to do. Nowhere to be. If she went outside, she'd be mobbed by paparazzi. No, she decided. She'd stay in her seven-thousand-square-foot cage.

Mariah didn't need to work. A film company bought her life rights for a ridiculous amount of money. She decided to demand an oversized figure that she thought would drive them away, but instead they paid it. It paid for the apartment, and she put the rest in a Wall Street firm called Burns. Her wealth exploded. She was living the lifestyle that everyone thought she should have, but that she didn't want.

The truth was it was, the only way she could find privacy. High in a tower with twenty-four-hour security. It's not how she thought she'd end up. When she returned, Mariah hoped she'd go back to being an explorer, but that wasn't to be. She had been told she was too valuable to risk any dangerous journeys. Mariah was grounded.

She was on the New York party circuit. It was what people wanted. At least, she figured, they were controlled situations. The people that were throwing the parties wanted to keep the riff raff out, too, so she was safe at flashy parties where guests had mastered the skill of talking without saying anything. It was evenings of pointless conversation which she drowned out with vodka. It made all her nodding and agreeing tolerable.

Dating had been a nightmare. There were men that wanted her as a trophy, or to say that they had bagged her. Occasionally an obsessed fan would slip in, and there'd be legal entanglements. She'd considered celibacy, but she knew she had to be with somebody. Someone that could be her oasis.

Mariah finished dressing and heard the doorbell. She walked out of her bedroom to the front door and opened it to find Aaron Galaif, her boyfriend. He was lean and angular and about six feet tall but had a habit of slouching, for which she would regularly poke him in the back to straighten him up. She adored him because he didn't care that she was an icon. She was simply Mariah Chen to him.

Aaron was an antimatter physicist, so their conversations were often consumed by equations. She felt she needed to catch up on matters of star travel. It didn't exist in her day, and Aaron was all too happy to talk shop.

A year ago, Aaron had been forced by his company to go to a symposium in Butte, Montana during the coldest winter on record. The journey had been filled with challenges. There were missed connections in Chicago, a mix up in luggage, and by the time he got to his hotel his room had been given away.

He arrived at the conference in a foul mood. He snapped up his badge at the sign-in desk and marched into the hall and sat down.

Mariah Chen was the guest speaker and, upon seeing her, he was instantly mesmerized. He couldn't have told anyone the details of her speech. Aaron was simply lost in her beauty.

When she finished her speech, he applauded wildly and watched her disappear out a side door, no longer in a foul mood. He glided to the next event with images of Mariah skipping through his mind.

Aaron stared at his event schedule. The next session was in the penthouse of the hotel where the conference took place. He pushed the elevator button and waited for a good two minutes. The doors opened, and there was Mariah standing inside. Aaron froze. The door started to close, and Mariah put her hand in the way.

"Are you getting in?" she smiled.

Aaron stepped in and the doors closed. He had to say something to her. He was desperate to find the words that didn't make him seem like a creep. He decided to go for it and the words he carelessly blurted out to Mariah turned out to be a singular aphrodisiac for only one woman on planet Earth.

"So, what do you do?" Aaron blurted innocently.

Mariah almost shuddered. That handsome man didn't know who the hell she was. He obviously wasn't a social media hound, or someone well-versed in history. He was the rarest of gems. She prayed he was a decent guy.

"I just do talks. What do you do?"

"I'm in antimatter physics," he shared haltingly.

Mariah grinned. He was a guy with his head in the clouds, doing calculations day in and day out. Mariah struck up a conversation with him that lasted into the night. They began dating soon thereafter. She couldn't get enough of Aaron. She felt safe with him. There was no agenda, and Aaron had simple needs. He would teach her about antimatter physics and space travel over dinner most nights. Mariah happily realized she'd found her oasis.

Aaron gave her a peck on the cheek and said, "Hi."

"Hi, honey." She noticed that he looked a little pensive and had a hard time looking her in the eyes. Mariah touched his face and observed him curiously.

"What's going on?"

"I can't take you deep sea fishing," he sighed, walking into the penthouse.

"Why not?" Mariah loved deep sea fishing. Not for the sport, but because it took her away from people. At sea, she didn't have to deal with the world. There were no fans, no press, just the ocean and Aaron. Mariah's mood darkened.

This was one of her few escapes, and he was ruining it.

"They want me to go to the Cape today. I wanted to say goodbye before I went."

"You're going on a starship? For what?" she pressed, intrigued, and her anger seemed to settle. She led Aaron to the couch, and they sat down. She snuggled with him.

Mariah brightened as if he was going to meet the latest SansoKhla singing star. The word starship made her tingle. Aaron gazed at her. She seemed like she was about to pounce on him. He was confused at first, but he realized the girl of his dreams was hanging on his every word. He thought she'd be mad at him. She wasn't, thankfully.

"Just with my tool and wrench. It's a rush job, so it won't be long," he promised hopefully. "The Concord is going through a refit, and they're having trouble with the antimatter stabilizers."

Mariah was puzzled. He'd consulted on the Concord a few months ago. It was in orbit of Earth with a skeleton crew. "I thought that ship was only for missions past the DMZ now."

"Yeah, I don't know what's going on. They asked me to add some upgrades. They said it needs to be a hundred percent. I'll be back next Monday," Aaron assured her as he rose and stepped away.

Mariah leaned back on the soft couch and pondered. One hundred percent could only mean one thing. The Concord was on the move, and Kris Galloway was going out past the DMZ again.

It was her dream. Her goal. She wanted to be part of it.

"Aaron."

"Yeah, babe?" He turned around to face her.

"Isn't that Kris Galloway's ship?" She popped up from the couch and sauntered over to him, gripping the lapels of his coat.

"Yeah, but he's in Modesto, I think."

"They can't fly without him," Mariah noted.

"That's what I've heard. It's one of those state secrets, though. You're not supposed to know that."

"Can't help you're so talkative in bed," Mariah cooed.

Aaron kissed her again, giving her butt a squeeze, and she did likewise. Aaron was late and knew if he kept on like this, he'd miss his flight. Aaron smiled awkwardly and backed out the door.

"I've really got to go," Aaron apologized, squeezing out the door.

Mariah closed the door and leaned back against it. Her head was clearing. Maybe she should pay a visit to Kris Galloway and introduce herself.

Mariah had traveled to her namesake planet a few months after she returned to Earth. She was excited, but that was curbed when she realized that the planet wasn't untouched. It had fifty-odd cities and a population of three hundred million. When she arrived, it caused a scene. She was mobbed wherever she went. She wasn't exploring a new world; the new world was exploring her.

The trip had been a mistake. The idea that a whole planet was named after Mariah Lynn Chen of Plano, Texas was too hard to swallow. She wished she had the ego to back it up.

On her return transport to Earth, she found a quiet viewport. Alone, finally, Mariah gazed out at the vast darkness, knowing others had ventured beyond the DMZ, and felt what had been impossible to her was possible now. She had to get out there, but she didn't know how. Dr. Fitter walked up to her. She smiled and hugged him. He had been on the trip too, but he was more of a footnote in history. He didn't have the same cachet as Mariah.

"How are you doing?

"Pretty fair," Mariah responded.

"Never thought I'd be a time traveler."

"I hear you."

"Everyone I ever knew is gone. Never to come back. I don't know if it was right to revive us." Fitter paused. He became rigid and couldn't make eye contact.

"Mariah... I remember something that happened after we died. Do you?" Fitter continued, his expression turning fearful. Mariah slowly turned to him, and Dr. Fitter seemed embarrassed and stared at his feet. Mariah grabbed his shoulders so they were eye to eye.

"Yeah, I do. We were somewhere else," Mariah agreed carefully.

"It was a good place," Fitter recalled. His eyes were getting moist.

"It was," Mariah acknowledged self-consciously.

"You talk about it to anybody?"

"No. Never will," Mariah vowed, letting go of him.

"You remember much?" Fitter checked.

"Just that we... didn't stop. We didn't stop."

"How do we talk about this?" he contemplated.

"Just to each other," Mariah answered firmly.

"I guess all we can do is start over," Fitter pondered.

"Easier for you. You saw what happened back there. I mean, my God, Fitter, there's a planet named after me. Statues, businesses... it's just too much. I can't process it all."

"That's why you've gotta move past this and find a new path," Fitter suggested.

"That's a great idea. But will the world let me?"

Dr. Fitter paused and patted her on the shoulder. She smiled but Mariah knew she'd have it worse than him. All the attention would be on her. She'd been thrown into fame by a fate that had been thrust upon her and gave her no guide to show the way forward.

"Do you remember being angry when you got back inside your body?" Fitter asked.

"You too?" she gulped.

"Yeah, though it passed," Fitter recollected. "I'll tell you one thing."

"What?"

"I don't fear death anymore."

"Yeah, I know what you mean."

Fitter gave her a long hug and left. Alone again, Mariah was drawn to the window. She pressed her head against it with her hands hugging the glass. She looked out at the starfield, crying a little inside. She treasured the idea of traveling to those points of light, but instead she was headed away from them.

They had the means to get there. The ships could travel at a speed of a little over one hundred lights.

Mariah could have explored the galaxy, but she was cut off from her destiny by the stupidity of others.

CHAPTER TWENTY-FOUR

Kris had a 3 p.m. booking for his hypercycle business. It was a birthday party for some rich teenagers. They had paid extra to stay up later. It had seemed like an odd request. It was the most he'd ever been paid for an event. They bought out the whole day and paid in full. Kris had to move another party that was set for Saturday to Sunday to make room for it.

Kris came in an hour early to tune up the cycles, then went into his office to finish up some mundane paperwork. He checked the time and headed downstairs to find there was no one there. The street outside was quiet. No party arriving. There was a rear gate that some people had mistaken for the entrance in the past, so Kris jaunted down there, but only spotted a man walking his Great Dane. Kris took a slow walk back.

By about three-fifteen, he called the number he had for the client and just got the answering machine. He was puzzled and was about to call Mindy when the sound of hopper jets growing closer filled the air. Kris spun around on his heel.

The hopper set down in the parking lot, throwing dust up into Kris' face. Kris was picking particles of dirt out of his eyes when he saw a portly figure moving toward him through the settling dust. It was Severen. His arms were outstretched with a phony grin.

"Captain Galloway."

"Severen. So, the party... was you?"

"You were well paid."

"Can't you try knocking on a door?"

"Where's the fun in that? Besides, my movements must always be discreet," Severen explained.

"Surprised you didn't send C."

"C has retired," Severen reported dryly. This was news to Kris. He had known she was unhappy, but was surprised she had cut the cord with I.I.

"Oh."

"Little misunderstanding," Severen explained lightly.

"She thought she was valued by you, you thought she was expendable. I wouldn't call that a misunderstanding."

Severen ignored that. He strolled into Kris' business, kicking up dust as he walked. Severen spied a bench and sat, making himself at home. Kris stood in front of him, arms folded. Severen examined his establishment admiringly, nodding in approval. He took out a juicer cooling stick from the cold pack inside his jacket and sucked on it.

"You've made yourself quite a set up," Severen stated.

"What do you want?" Kris snapped bluntly, his arms akimbo.

"I think you can suspect," he answered after taking a long draw on his cooler stick.

"What happened now? Did a planet come up with a case of whooping cough?"

"Far from that. I'm being up front with you and laying out everything as you requested."

"Detmer?"

"Indirectly. Kris, I'm trying to be an open book on this one."

"Go ahead."

"Did you know Eric Doneghan?"

"Junior or senior?" Kris clarified.

"Senior. Not the pimp on Ceres," Severen responded harshly.

"Real piece of work. Corporate raider. Did a lotta damage along the way. A lotta dead aliens along with it. He never came back, I'm told. I had a run-in with him."

"You lost a few men because of him."

"Yeah, and you swept it under the rug," Kris recalled coldly.

"Earth Directorate made that call. He's still out there."

"What's that got to do with me?"

"It's something called The Akptur... The Reason," Severen disclosed.

Kris knew what that meant. He wasn't a Citari scholar, but when he was planning his one-man mutiny, he had done his research. Before he discovered *The Song of Salaya,* he had come across The Reason.

"The Citari forgiveness pledge. You've been studying," Kris mused, slightly impressed.

Severen rose, taking out a yellow book on customs of the Citaris. It had been translated into English by a monk living on the north pole of Mars. He had made it his life's work and it took twenty years because the customs were not only in Citari, but in an intricate code. The Monk had two mental breakdowns before he found the key. He finally finished translating it toward the end of his life.

The yellow book was dog-eared. Wherever Severen was going with this, he was serious about it.

"That's what Detmer was doing. He was there to open a dialogue, to see if Earth and the council could explore The Reason," Severen explained.

Kris turned away and began shutting down the hypercycles that were idling in the air. He sent a command, and they traveled back into the garage in a line. The door sealed, and all that was left was the telltale smell of the sweet vapors the bikes emitted. Kris didn't look back at Severen as he tended to his work and spoke.

"You still put a stowaway on my ship."

"He was successful. With The Reason, that is. You are acquainted with The Reason, yes?"

"The Reason is a series of actions to regain trust. Several steps to rebuild a relationship. But I also know that if it's asked in the right way, Citari law says they must give the other party a chance. This wasn't something they wanted to do. You found a loophole to get back in. What do they want us to do?"

"It was a chance."

"You could have told me," Kris criticized.

"You would have said no," Severen insisted.

"You don't know what I would have said. Now, you didn't answer my question. What do they want us to do and how does Eric Doneghan figure in?" Kris snarled while shutting down upright gaming consoles.

"He's the first step," Severen replied, straightening up.

"How so?" Kris asked.

"One of their planets, one of their protectorates, wants him handed over. They want you to capture Doneghan and bring him to justice."

"Why don't they do it?" Kris challenged.

"There were issues. They didn't explain. We didn't ask. Our diplomat entered the picture and offered any help they needed in the future and, about a month ago, they made contact."

"I'm surprised you took so long."

"You had an anniversary. Daughter's birthday."

"How thoughtful." Kris slammed down the door to the arcade.

"Listen, Galloway, they want you to retrieve Mr. Doneghan and hand him over to Moody authorities for trial," Severen repeated hopefully.

"Moody?" He wiped his brow with his hand and let it rest on his chin, pondering. "That's a rough sentence. What did he do?"

"They'll brief you on your arrival."

"So, I'm flying blind?" Kris glowered, displeased.

"He deserves anything that happens to him, don't you think? After all, you and Doneghan have a past," Severen reminded him.

"You're playing on my desire for revenge," Kris retorted, seeing through him.

"The Citaris will move back the DMZ twenty light years if we're successful. This is big," Severen contended.

Kris sat down, crossed his arms, and spoke with authority. "You don't understand The Reason. Sure, you found the loophole, but you don't understand the meaning. It comes in many parts until you've reached it. They'll give you a nibble here and a nibble there, but they aren't gonna give you the whole thing until you've given blood, sweat, and tears. Likely, my blood, sweat, and tears."

"You can right the wrongs. Make good, finally," Severen protested, still selling it.

Kris stood and turned away from Severen. It was wiser doing business with your back to him. He could read faces. He could tell if you were bluffing by the mere twitch of an eye. Severen didn't need any anti-deception devices. He was a living, breathing one.

"You're gonna keep coming back to me."

"Yes," Severen agreed flatly. "Like you said, you have the power... I don't." Severen cleared his throat, almost choking on his words.

"And you can make life difficult for me if I don't."

"Let's not get speculative, shall we? Besides, anything like that clearly wouldn't be in my interests."

"I'm not stupid, Severen," Kris snapped.

"That's a given, Kris. We're not asking that much. It's a one-month mission. You'll be back with your family in no time."

"Okay, here's the deal. You get your diplomats to work on certifying someone else to carry the emblem. This can't be all on me. If you do that, I'll go." Kris turned back around to Severen, who was already thinking it through.

He tapped his fingers on his chin and glanced back to Kris. "It would have to be someone on your crew. They might trust one of them."

"Then we won't have to meet like this," Kris noted.

"We can try," Severen offered.

"I pick my own crew, by the way. No I.I. shenanigans."

"Of course. We just want a man brought to justice."

"And a bigger piece of the galaxy as the prize."

"In peace and harmony. The hardliners are gone, Kris. They're either dead or disgraced. We've seen to that. They are no longer a problem."

Kris got a chill as Severen looked over his cool juicer with dead serious eyes. Kris realized that I.I. had taken care of the troublemakers, disposed of them, or ruined them. His mind drifted five years back. The billionaire industrialist Haven Soares' transporter mysteriously had a heat shield failure over Mars and burned up without a trace. Then others came to mind. A pack of billionaires who were behind the hardline tactics of the Earth Directorate. Dorothy Zinner, Harvey Cold, Ben Serion... they were all dead. But why? They were on the wrong side of history, but to kill them seemed harsh.

Severen, the great keeper of secrets, wasn't telling him everything. He had the Genusian question and now this.

Kris swallowed and realized who he was making a deal with. He became wide-eyed and shaky. Severen knew exactly what he was thinking.

"So, we have a deal?" Severen offered his hand.

Kris took it without hesitating.

"We do."

"Thank you. I'll be in touch."

"Try the comm next time," Kris suggested.

Severen strode to the hopper and pulled himself in with a yank from both hands. He looked back to Kris and managed a smile and a wave. The door closed behind him.

The hopper's jets fired, lifting it up and out of Kris' sight. The only surprise for Kris that day was that it had taken so long for Severen to make an appearance. He was certain he'd have been at his doorstep a week later. But he used his leverage to give him control. They needed to groom a new Kris Galloway, so he'd be left alone.

———————

Kris walked into the house and plopped on the sofa. Mindy was carrying some laundry upstairs and put the clothes down when she saw him. Her movement slowed as she noticed that Kris seemed to be preoccupied, lost in thought. She stepped closer. He hadn't smiled and greeted her as he always did. Kris sensed her presence and looked up to her. His eyes were filled with worry.

"It happened," Kris stated blankly. Mindy's cheerful demeanor retreated instantly.

"I.I.?"

"Yup."

"Did you give him the condition?" Mindy asked.

"Yeah, just like you suggested. He went for it."

"When?"

"Soon. I'll probably have to go to Houston. Put together a crew," Kris sighed.

"What do you have to do?' Mindy questioned, sitting next to him.

"Something I don't know how to do."

"What's that?" Mindy wondered.

"Remember the stories I told you about Eric Doneghan?"

"Yeah, sure," Mindy remembered. "How could I forget."

"I've gotta play U.S. Marshal and catch him."

CHAPTER TWENTY-FIVE

Kris was reviewing crew profiles in his bathing shorts out in the back, sucking down a Chuggo. He scanned some familiar names and then stopped on a familiar face, Agent C. It was her file. Christina Terranova. He wondered if it was a joke. He never knew her real name. He'd heard she had signed up with the Astronaut Corps two months after their return from the Genus Major region.

Kris sat up and briefly contemplated if this was an elaborate I.I. trick. But then he thought that it was too obvious, and Severen wouldn't dare. The stakes were too high. Severen had burned her, and C was well aware.

Kris had seen a change in Agent C. Her turn after her near-death experience with Vichon. He perused her file and it seemed impressive. She had scored high marks during her training period. Kris put her file down on his lap. He took a final sip of beer, considering C. They had gotten off to a rough start, but it had ended well. There was some trust between them. He'd saved her life. It made him drop her file in the maybe pile.

His comm rang, and Kris stared at the number calling. It wasn't familiar. He answered anyway.

"Kris Galloway. Who's this?"

"Mariah Chen."

Hearing that, Kris took a beat. The voice was familiar, but he'd heard people imitate her on digi sketch shows. But who would go to the trouble to prank him? It didn't make any sense. Of course, it also didn't make sense that Mariah Chen would be calling him. Kris recalled that Jennifer Arliss skippered her rescue mission. Maybe they had spoken about him.

"Hello," he replied cautiously.

"I was nearby, and I was hoping I could talk to you," Mariah requested.

"How nearby is nearby?"

"Around the block," she responded.

"Mariah Chen. Around the block? From me?" Kris repeated.

"Yes."

"Yeah, sure. Stop on by," Kris invited.

Kris turned off his comm, ran into the house, and found Mindy in her underwear in the bedroom. Kris went through his drawer, tearing through his clothes, grabbed a pair of jeans and practically jumped into them. Mindy looked at him like he was a madman.

"Get dressed, quick," Kris bellowed in a panic.

"Why?" Mindy asked.

"Mariah Chen is on her way over."

"*The* Mariah Chen?"

"Yes."

"In our house?" Mindy squealed, panicked.

"Yes."

Mindy ran to her closet and hip checked Kris, who went tumbling and face planted into some laundry. She grabbed some clothes and dashed into the bathroom. Kris got back to his feet, pulling some errant underwear off his head. He searched around and found a shirt. He buttoned it wrong then grunted in the mirror in frustration. He fixed the shirt just as Mindy yelled out, "Clean up the house."

Kris dashed out and began picking up. He tossed the dishes that were in the sink into the phase washer. He put on his boots and then buttoned up his pants. He got everything clean just as Mindy re-entered dressed up, looking like a million bucks.

There was an awkward silence as Kris realized Mariah Chen was in his living room sipping tea. He'd never met her before, but her legend was bigger than any other living human. Mindy offered her some biscuits that she politely nibbled on. Kris decided to break the quiet.

"So, I see you've been busy."

"I wouldn't say that," Mariah demurred.

"I see you on digi all the time," Mindy gushed.

"Yeah, that's not my choice. I'm sure you understand, Mr. Galloway," Mariah suggested, communicating with her eyes. Kris understood.

"Call me Kris. And I sure do know what you're talking about. That kind of attention can get a bit uncomfortable."

Mariah brightened hearing that.

Kris gazed at her with sympathy. He rose up and walked around the room. It was all coming back. The frenzy. The attention. Days that weren't your own. Those were feelings he hadn't thought about in ages.

"You start to forget who you are. It's awful," Kris continued.

"Magnify that by ten times, and that's what I live with. Kris, I'm not what you see on the digi. I'm an explorer like you. But I'm

171

now this... thing. I can't get away from it. I should be exploring the stars, not being a sideshow act," Mariah insisted desperately.

"Yeah, that's tiresome," Kris validated.

"Tiresome. Yes. That's it," Mariah said, nodding in agreement.

"I just kind of disappeared 'til the next shiny object showed up," Kris described, finishing his tea and putting it on the counter.

Mariah put down her tea and clasped her hands together. "Kris, I hear you're shipping out."

"How'd you know?" Kris questioned, surprised.

"It was a guess. My boyfriend is working maintenance on the Concord now," Mariah admitted.

"Yeah, I am, for about a month. Past the DMZ. Headed to the planet Moody."

"I'd like to volunteer," Mariah voiced hopefully.

"To crew on my ship?" Kris checked.

"Yes."

"No offense, but we're dealing with technology that's gone way past the twenty-nineties. It's a whole new world," Kris warned.

"My boyfriend's an antimatter physicist—he's been getting me up to speed. Besides, I'm a fast learner. I was fastest on simulator training. I made my landing on my first try," Mariah announced.

Mariah stared at him pleadingly. This American monument seemed like she'd burst into tears if he said a flat no, and he understood. Movie stars and politicians were made for fame, but her fame was like no human had ever experienced. There are people who changed the world and had statues erected in their name, but no one had ever come back to see them in person until Mariah.

"Mariah, I've gotta think about this. I mean, I understand, and I'm inclined to accept. But..."

"But what?" Mariah challenged.

"I don't know how the powers that be would take it. They might not want to take the risk," Kris warned.

"It's my risk to take," Mariah insisted.

"They pay the bills."

"I've got pull with the government," Mariah asserted confidently.

"You probably do." Kris remembered how President Furrow showcased her at all his campaign stops toward the end of the election.

"I miss my career, Kris. One flight. Just that one. Oh, sure, I've been to Proxima, but a real mission with a real goal. That's who I am," Mariah urged.

"I get it. Look, I've gotta think it through, okay?" Kris heaved.

"Okay."

"Like I said. I'm inclined."

"Thank you."

Mariah got up and thanked Mindy. Kris showed her to the door and watched a black hopper whisk her away. Kris liked Mariah and he trusted her after only their brief meeting. Kris looked over to see his neighbor, Ed Dooley, looking back from the hopper to Kris with his jaw hanging open.

"Was that...?"

"Yeah. She stopped in for tea." Kris turned around and headed back in.

Kris and Mindy sat, a little stunned. The great Mariah Chen had been in their home, and they realized she was just a person like them. Kris didn't know what he'd do, but he knew he wanted her on his mission. He understood her. They weren't kindred spirits per se, but they'd been in the same kind of war, that no other living person could relate to. The fame did fade for him, but he feared it never would for her.

Kris put his comm on his wrist and made a call.

"Hello," Dr. Ed Weiss answered, his voice croaky.

"Ed, did I wake you up?"

"Yeah, it's okay. What's up?" Weiss rasped, clearing his throat.

"I'm going again."

"You're seeing the Citaris?"

"Likely."

"You'll ask about that matter?" Weiss said.

"I will. Just wanted to let you know," Kris assured him.

"Thanks. You'll keep me updated?"

"Yeah."

Kris turned off his comm and realized he had two missions. The one for the Citaris and the one for Weiss. He wondered to what lengths the Citaris would go to keep a secret. He hoped he wasn't getting into a sensitive area. The Citaris may want to keep this buried. They wanted them out of Genus Major as soon as they were done with the initial mission. Was it about the truth? In Kris' gut, it felt Weiss might have been right. He suspected the Citaris wanted them to know.

Kris pulled out his small suitcase. He laid it on the bed and began rustling through the drawers, trying to find his underwear. There didn't seem to be any. He sighed. The thruster for Houston was leaving in three hours, and he needed to pack. He searched for Mindy, who was in the kitchen making lunch for Annie and Justin.

"Want a sandwich?" Mindy offered.

"Actually, I want my underwear." Annie and Justin giggled hearing that.

"They're in your suitcase. I packed for you last night," Mindy said while putting down two plates for the kids. She pointed to the suitcase by the front door. Kris relaxed a little and gobbled up a spare sandwich in four bites.

"Why are you going to Houston?" Mindy wondered. Kris held up a file in his hand.

"Crew assignments. Last time I was handed a crew. I want to do it the right way this time," Kris answered.

"Mariah?" Mindy probed while sitting down to eat.

"Open question. I'm getting pushback from NASA. I'll call her on the way to Texas. Thanks for the sandwich."

Kris arrived at the towering thruster rocket just in time. When he boarded it was packed, and he was stuck in a seat in between two rotund men. There was a football game in Houston, judging from the assorted jerseys they were wearing. He, without question, had picked the wrong flight.

He turned on his comm and punched in the number for Mariah. She answered quickly.

"It's me," Kris murmured. He didn't want to say her name out loud. He had stuck an earpiece in his ear to keep the conversation private.

"Hi," Mariah greeted him.

"Talked to NASA, and I'm getting push back. A lotta resistance. You mentioned you could pull some strings yourself."

"Let me give it a try. I'll get back to you," Mariah promised.

Mariah hung up her comm. She gazed in a mirror. Her hair looked silky, and her green gown was stunning. She checked her hair and touched up her makeup, then headed out of the bathroom and into the White House state dinner she was attending.

She took her seat next to Aaron, who was wearing black tie and gawking at the famous guests around him. The room was filled with dignitaries, senators, and congressmen; the heads of all the most powerful government departments in the country.

Aaron finished an exotic dessert and deposited the spoon in the bowl. A waiter scooped it up in seconds. Aaron turned to the waiter and noticed the person who was sitting down at the head of the table and cocked his head. It was the Vice President of the United States. Mariah could see her boyfriend was fidgety. She laid her hand on his leg.

"It's okay."

"This is crazy. I mean, what am I doing here?" Aaron stuttered.

"They're just people," Mariah assured him.

"They're a different species. I thought you avoided these things."

"You know why I'm here," Mariah reminded him.

"I am totally supportive of you. I just feel way out of place," Aaron confessed.

When dinner was over, people drifted away. Mariah stood up and urged Aaron to follow her. The pair headed to a reception room and got in line to shake hands with the President and the First Lady.

"I'm gonna meet the President?" Aaron exclaimed.

"Yes."

"I didn't vote for him," he whispered nervously.

"He doesn't know that," Mariah reassured him.

The line was long and slow but, after forty-five minutes, they reached President Fuller, who brightened at seeing Mariah. She knew he wouldn't be standing there if it wasn't for her. Mariah had helped him sail to victory. He gripped her shoulders and took a gander, a toothy grin stretching across his face.

"Mariah, my my, you look positively grand. Positively grand. And who's this lucky fella over here?"

"Aaron Galaif," Aaron squeaked.

"You better treat her like a precious diamond, son. I'm warning you now. She doesn't have a pappy now, so I'm filling in," Fuller warned.

"Yes, sir," Aaron replied meekly.

"Mr. President, I need your help."

"Anything."

"Captain Galloway wants me to go on a mission with him. One I'm sure you're aware of."

"I am."

"NASA is getting in the way."

President Fuller's grin turned serious and fatherly. He slowly shook his head. Mariah was deeply confused.

"NASA isn't the issue. I am," the President revealed.

"What? Why, sir?" Mariah puzzled, taken aback.

"You're a national treasure. Can't have you getting lost in space, now, can I?" the President proclaimed in a wise tone.

"Please. I need this, sir. I know I'm a public figure now, but I'm an explorer. It's who I am. It's what I do. Please reconsider, or at least listen to Captain Galloway. At least that."

Fuller considered it for a few moments and dropped his hands from her shoulders. "I'll speak to him tonight. That's a guarantee."

They both moved on. Aaron held onto her. He could see she was upset and a little weak-kneed. Mariah now realized Kris Galloway was her only hope.

Kris was in his Houston hotel room when the comm rang at the bedside table. He slapped it on his wrist. He flicked it on and a booming voice came out. It was the President. And it didn't seem like a friendly call.

"Captain Galloway, what have you put into Mariah Chen's head about gallivanting through the galaxy?" Fuller sputtered at him.

Kris wasn't impressed. He was trying to overpower him, and the President was going to learn who really held the cards.

"I haven't. She asked me," Kris responded calmly.

"I'm not letting her out there. What if she doesn't make it back? I've got the midterms to think of. This ain't happening," Fuller snapped.

"Then the mission's cancelled." Kris flicked off the comm and picked up a magazine. He flipped through the pages of a technical journal for about thirty seconds. The comm buzzed again, and Kris flicked it on.

"Hello?"

"Son, did you hang up on me?" the President fumed, incredulous.

"I thought we were done. You stated your position, I gave mine. We're at an impasse. Now I have to get a flight back to Modesto..."

"Hold on, hold on, hold on."

"Yes, Mr. President?"

"This is a deal breaker?"

"It is," Kris affirmed nonchalantly.

"I'm the Commander-in-Chief," Fuller protested, sounding puffed up and puzzled.

"I have the emblem. Do you have one too?" There was silence on the other end of the comm. The President had walked into a minefield.

"Let's not get all hot-headed about this," the President gulped.

"I wasn't the one yelling," Kris reminded him coolly.

"This mission could be dangerous. How do I know Mariah will be safe?"

Kris sighed. The bluff had worked. He was more powerful on this issue than anyone else. He played the President.

"It's in two parts, sir. Part one is on Moody and part two is the extraction of Doneghan. I would agree she can't be part of the extraction," Kris assured.

"Well, that's what I was concerned about the whole time. I don't want her around that messy business. Those dopes at NASA didn't brief me properly," Fuller acquiesced, covering.

"Then we're on the same page. We just had a misunderstanding," Kris remarked.

"Right, that's right. A misunderstanding."

"She'll be a valuable resource," Kris said.

"Indeed," the President concurred.

"Why don't you give her the good news? It would mean more coming from you," Kris suggested.

"I agree." The President hung up.

Kris got up from bed and headed straight for the mini bar. He had just gone toe-to-toe with the most powerful man in the world and knocked him down in the first round. He deserved a drink.

CHAPTER TWENTY-SIX

ris left his hotel late in the morning. It was humid with a haze hanging over Houston. His clothes were getting sticky as he gazed at the Saturn Five laid on its side, stretching three hundred and sixty-five feet in front of the Manned Spacecraft Center. It was the last Saturn Five. The rocket that took men to the moon centuries ago. This grand antique never had a chance to make the journey. He read on a plaque that all the original flight components were on board. It had been carefully preserved over the years with tender care.

"Beautiful," Kris whispered to himself.

It was built for a flight that was never to happen: Apollo 18. A loss for those astronauts, but a gain for the future. Countless visitors had walked through here, gazing at history that otherwise would have either been at the bottom of the Atlantic or drifting aimlessly in outer space.

Kris headed into the main building. It was filled with displays of the history of spacecraft over the last two hundred years hanging from the ceiling. There was even a display dedicated to Mariah. Kris was drawn to it and stood before her statue, a shining likeness. He ran his hand through his hair, realizing he'd just had tea with someone who had an actual statue made in her honor. She was in a golden spacesuit with her helmet tucked under her arm. Kris found it a little chilling.

Kris tucked a micro-pad under his arm when he heard the clacking of high heels on the concrete. He turned to see the starship administrator, Kay Hogan, heading toward him wearing a tweed suit with her hair in a bun and her arm outstretched.

"Kris, you're a day early," Kay greeted him brightly.

"Wanted to get on with crew assignments."

"Well, you need to talk to Logan. He has a lot of insight into crew member capabilities. Knows the lay of the land. Great resource," she advised, peering over her glasses.

"Logan?" Kris repeated, surprised.

"He's chief astronaut now," Kay said proudly. "You know him?"

"Uh, yes. Been maybe thirteen years."

"Before my time," Kay admitted.

Kris knew Logan from his training days. Back when Logan had been a woman. He was a top pilot who, before war broke out, revealed he wanted gender reassignment. He was taken off the flight rolls and had to wait for a viable male in need of the same procedure. If their blood types matched, a brain transplant surgery would occur. After recovery Lucy, now Logan, was added back to the flight rolls just as the war ended.

The ranks were thinned during the conflict, and Logan was one of the more experienced pilots, so he naturally moved up the chain. Logan had to be top drawer if he was still running the shop after all this time.

Kris headed to a door that was marked "Training" and took in the sight of all the young faces, busy going over equations, fiddling with space suits, and even playing around with a sextant, a tool used for celestial navigation in the days of Columbus. It made him smile.

He headed through another door marked "Operations." He pushed his hand on it and felt a force from the other side. He let go and the door swung open to reveal the former Agent C standing before him in a blue jumpsuit with the NASA emblem on it.

"C." Kris couldn't help but smile.

"Christina," she corrected.

"You'll always be C to me."

"I hear you're shipping out again. Never say never, huh?" C quipped.

"I hear you and Severen had a falling out," Kris countered.

"I guess that means you met him."

"Couple of times."

"A couple?" C probed quizzically.

"I found out where he had lunch and surprised him."

C grabbed him. She was filled with glee. "You surprised him?"

"Freaked him out a bit. Read him the riot act. The next time he came, he played nice. That's why I'm here. I've got another mission," Kris confessed.

"I heard," C nodded eagerly.

"Yeah. Well, I gotta get going. It's nice seeing you." Kris started down the hallway and C followed him and caught up. Kris noticed her at his side.

"I thought you were going the other way," Kris snickered.

"You showed up," C shrugged.

"And."

"I was thinking..."

"That's dangerous," Kris teased.

"Come on, what do you say, Kris? Why don't we get the band back together again?"

"I have a lot of files to get through. This is going to be a tough one."

"It's me, Kris."

"I gotta figure something out about you first," Kris said, stopping and facing her.

"What?"

"Whether I'm talking to you or Severen," Kris asserted, cocking his brow.

"What?" C snorted.

"You quit all in a huff and join the Astronaut Corps, but maybe you haven't really quit? You gotta admit it's his style," Kris pointed out.

Kris noticed C getting red-faced, trying to hold back a burst of anger that was swelling within her. Kris could see it as a telltale vein bulged from her temple. He didn't react, and C turned away from him to compose herself. She spun around back at Kris, her long black hair swinging.

"You know what Severen did! You know that he almost got me killed!" She stepped closer. "You don't know what I've done for him and that agency. You think you're the fair-haired girl. The agent they go to for the big assignments. And then it turns out you're dispensable! Can you imagine how that made me feel? When I confronted Severen, you know what he said? He said it was a calculated risk."

"You're still pissed," Kris observed.

"Damn right, I am. That was ten years of my life, Kris. Was I even making a difference? I was probably part of operations that I have no idea what the outcome was. You get tasked to do one part of some op. You often didn't know if it was moral. Was I doing the right thing? Hell, I don't have a clue. I just want to be part of something that is right and true for once in my life."

C went quiet and her shoulders slumped, seemingly waiting for a judgment from Kris.

Kris eyed the raw, tough C, realizing she was a woman burned by the system. She had renewed herself and was aching to live in an environment where sincerity reigned.

"So, would you be interested in being head of security?" Kris smiled.

"Of course!" Her nose crinkled, suspicious. "You wanted me the whole time, didn't you!"

"Well, I guess I could do worse." He gently swatted her shoulder with his micro-pad and C grinned.

"This is great," C rejoiced brightly.

"Sorry, I just had to see if you hated Severen half as much as I do. Besides, this one might be right up your alley," Kris commented.

"I'd be involved in an operation?" C trilled.

"Yeah, I think I'll need you."

"In what way?"

"I assume in your past you had a bag of tricks," Kris remarked curiously.

"Have," C insisted.

"Have?"

"I have resources," C assured him.

"I'll need you to bring them."

"What are we doing?" C asked.

"Catching a bad guy and bringing him back alive," Kris said hopefully.

C was nonplussed and started down the hallway. "I've done that."

That's what Kris was counting on. C had spent a large part of her adult life steeped in clandestine operations. She has been assigned impossible tasks and succeeded. C had been a ghost in the night. She'd been a seasoned I.I. ops agent. There was nothing Kris could throw at her that she couldn't handle.

She was qualified to snatch Doneghan and Kris wasn't.

CHAPTER TWENTY-SEVEN

Mariah watched Proxima Centauri fall behind them through the porthole in her quarters. She finally felt she was going the right way. Out beyond the DMZ. She was living a life bigger than her dreams. In her day, reaching the stars was still far off and fanciful. The tech didn't exist. You had to settle for the solar system if you were lucky. A vacation at a Lagrange Point Hotel if you had the money. She didn't at the time. The only way she'd get into space was if she made the cut as an astronaut. And she did.

She picked up a picture of Aaron from her dresser and recalled how emotional their goodbye was. It was the only moment she felt torn. She loved him with all her heart, which made her conflicted about being away from him for so long. But she had a craving to explore, and it needed to be fed. Aaron assured her he'd be waiting for her when she got back. Mariah put down his picture and then faced her bed.

Her uniform was laid out. She picked it up and started getting dressed. She slipped on her boots and fixed her hair. She hesitantly approached the mirror and saw herself in full uniform. She felt instantly soothed. Mariah Chen, astronaut. She was back, Mariah thought to herself.'

Mariah was on her way to a distant world light years away from Earth. The irony was she never would have had this chance if she hadn't died. She was propelled through generations to a journey that was only a dream one hundred years ago. Even though she had lost her family to time, she felt fortunate.

She tightened her boots and glanced at the clock on her comm. She was going to be late for the meeting. She opened the door and hustled down the hallway.

C was the last one to arrive in the conference room. She had a fresh smell as she passed. Kris suspected she had taken a shower. She looked sharp in her security uniform and seemed to be all business. He gazed at her like a proud papa. C had come a long way. If he had any hand in making her life better, he was glad to have been a part of it. C was a skilled operative. Now it was her chance to use those skills for the right reasons.

Logan sat in the corner reviewing the flight plan. Kris and Logan had worked on the crew assignments together. Kris became impressed with how much Logan had grown from the old days and asked his friend to ship out with him. Logan agreed happily.

Captain Jennifer Arliss gladly accepted the demotion to the executive officer, Number One. She reasoned she had to relinquish command briefly. Kris had the emblem, and she didn't. Jennifer closed the door and sat at the conference table, signaling they were ready to begin. Except Kris wasn't sure how to start. Kris had to give his crew the particulars of the mission when they reached Moody. And the particulars were thin.

"What exactly is this mission?" Jennifer inquired.

"This is an extraction," Kris announced. "We don't know where that will take place. We will be briefed when we arrive at Moody. Now, our target has very sophisticated listening capabilities. So, it's radio silence coming in. Mariah, we need every communication coming to and from this ship shut down when we enter the system. We run silent."

"I'll work with Mariah on that," C offered.

"Who's the target?" Logan asked.

"Doneghan."

Kris knew Logan knew the name and noticed his lips grew tight. Logan knew the men who had died from Doneghan's reckless criminal behavior. Kris and Logan had been in the same class of astronauts. He knew their wives and their kids. It was Logan who reluctantly volunteered to be the one who gave them the bad news.

Kris had been a helmsman on the starship Glenn when it received a distress call from Doneghan. His star freighter was being fired upon by a Qwesi warrior-class ship. Kris sent a message that they were coming to the rescue.

They jumped to his location to see that Doneghan's freighter had been hit. A panel had been blown out, and blue gas was venting out of two sides of the ship, creating a glowing mist encircling the stricken vessel.

The Qwesi had made their first run on Doneghan, and they were circling to line up for a second shot. The Captain of the Glenn ordered Kris to change course to intercept the Qwesi destroyer. They lurched to the right as Kris made the turn.

The captain ordered the torpedo tubes loaded and instructed Kris to fire a warning shot. The Glenn was a much bigger, more threatening starship, and a warning shot was usually all it took to deter another craft. But the Qwesi fired back, and it wasn't a warning. The torpedo sailed towards mid-ship. An interceptor laser from Glenn cut it in half. One piece sailed under the ship, and the other slammed into deck J. It killed four crew members when it blew a hole in the galley and swept them out into the vacuum of space.

Kris reeled, hearing about the deaths. His blood boiled, and he returned fire from the helm. It was a full salvo that peppered the Qwesi ship. It erupted and blew apart into four pieces, spewing gases and Qwesi bodies.

Kris stared at the trembling hand that had pushed the button, then back up to the viewscreen to see the results. Debris rattled along the side of the hull of the Glenn. Kris fell into a fog and didn't hear the captain telling him to change course until his name was called twice. Then, Kris snapped out of it and turned them toward Doneghan's ship, pulling them out of harm's way.

The Glenn's crew went to Doneghan's ship to assist with repairs. Engineers worked on the ship for a few days and then sent them on their way. While onboard, one engineer, Kaylie Stokes, had been handed a message from a woman who turned out to be a Qwesi.

From that message, Kris learned that Doneghan was smuggling Qwesi woman for his sex club on Veeleen. The Qwesi had been justified in their attack. Kris was furious. The captain ordered the Glenn's crew to reboard Doneghan's ship and rescue the women. The Glenn brought them back to their planet, leaving the Earth Directorate to patch up relations with the Qwesi.

The crew of the Glenn was stinging for their complicity in the matter. Kris' captain asked the Earth Directorate to issue an arrest warrant for Doneghan, but he was too influential and had powerful friends. There never would be an arrest warrant because he was considered above the law, and light years from justice.

All those memories rushed in as Kris rose out of his chair and announced that the landing party on Moody would be comprised of himself, C, Jennifer, Logan, and Mariah. Kris adjourned the meeting.

Kris grabbed his pad and checked the time. They'd be at Moody in a few days. He and C were going to meet up before the landing to discuss options for how to extract Doneghan. He hoped she had a sound plan. C had seemed confident, so he wasn't too concerned. That's why he chose her. Doneghan was a slippery character, and he couldn't miss getting him. C was absolutely the answer.

They all filed out, but Jennifer hung back until everyone left. Kris peered up at her, sensing her glare while tapping his pad. Kris was certain he knew what this was about. Jennifer sat on the edge of the conference table near Kris.

"What?" Kris said without looking up.

"Mariah? On the landing party? She's too green," Jennifer warned.

"Look, this is just a meet and greet. No harm, no foul. Easy. This way she gets it out of her system with Moody. The next planetfall is to snatch Mr. Doneghan. There might be shooting. Mariah's staying onboard for that," Kris explained.

"She's green," Jennifer insisted.

"And she's smart. Did you read her scores? I admit I was a softie, taking her on, but that lady has brain power like you can't believe. Did you see the report?" Kris asked.

"No," Jennifer admitted.

"Well, before you make a value judgement, read her file."

"I will," Jennifer pledged.

"Come on, let's check out what C has in store for Mr. Doneghan."

––––––––––––

The Concord arrived and slipped into a low orbit around the hazy pink world of Moody. They were running silent and made no radio contact with the planet. That was the plan. The landing coordinates had also been prearranged.

Kris led the way to the shuttle, followed by the rest of the landing party. He paused and let the eager legend walk into the bay first. Mariah gawked at the shuttle admiringly. She walked around it and then saw the shuttle hatch open. She was about to fulfill her dream to land on an alien world light years from home, and was grateful for the opportunity—because of the kindness of Kris Galloway.

They all boarded the shuttle as Amanda Sun looked on in the doorway, while her copilot Jennessy did the pre-flight check out. Amanda was sporting a glistening two-karat wedding ring. Jennessy had a gold band on his finger that he occasionally fiddled with. They were married after the mission to Genusia in a courthouse in Houston.

Kris was the last one on board. He popped a mint into his mouth, and Amanda stared at him, cocking her head. He rooted around in his pocket, found another mint and flipped it to her. She caught it midair, popped it in her mouth, and crunched down on it with a smile. She sealed the hatch, which made a hollow thudding sound, then hit the cabin pressurization button, which let out a hiss.

"How are we looking, Amanda?" Kris asked.

"Looking good. This one's fresh from the factory," she reported proudly.

"Excellent. We need to look our best," Kris grinned.

The shuttle had seven rows of seats. Amanda walked the rows, checking how securely everyone had harnessed themselves in. Mariah hadn't strapped herself in properly. Amanda marched over to her and undid her straps. She redid them, frowning at Mariah like a mother putting a seat belt on her child. Mariah felt self-conscious. Naturally, Amanda made it worse.

"I know you're kinda rusty, but you've gotta get this right. You're precious cargo, like it or not," Amanda scolded.

"Sorry."

"Preflight checkout completed," Jennessy announced.

Amanda headed back to her seat, sat down, and strapped in. She hit the shuttle bay release door button. The doors slowly swung open, and as the pod advanced, the planet Moody gradually filled their view. She engaged the engines and took the shuttle Enola Gay out for its maiden flight.

CHAPTER TWENTY-EIGHT

I t was night as the Enola Gay headed toward the rocky terrain below. Amanda eased the shuttle down past mountains stretching so high up they cut into the scattered grey clouds. The view was filled with a massive moon that gobbled up a quarter of the evening sky. Amanda checked her coordinates; she was right on target.

Amanda watched the digi-image on her panel while landing. She was searching for a flat area, and she found it: a patch of land that was free of boulders. She gripped her controller, turned the ship ever so slightly, and reduced thrust. They eased into a landing.

"Struts," Amanda commanded.

Jennessy hit the button and the struts popped out. Amanda shut down the engines as she felt the struts springing back up after they had touched down. The jets stopped puffing, and the vapor bled off in the form of white steam.

Amanda unstrapped herself, opened the hatch, and stood in the doorway. Mariah crossed in front of her. She was the first out.

Mariah stood on the edge and gaped like a kid on Christmas day. She stepped down slowly. There were more Gs on Moody than

Earth, but Mariah had been aware of this salient fact. She had been working out daily on the Concord in preparation for this moment.

She stepped onto the surface and grinned. She was on another world. She wasn't the first, but that didn't matter. She fought the urge to do a backflip, realizing it wouldn't be a good idea with the higher gravity. She'd probably just fall on her ass.

Mariah continued down the ramp, pulling out a scanner, and began to take readings. Kris, Jennessy, Amanda, Logan, Jennifer, and C filed out behind her.

C surveyed the desolation, confused. She kept her hand on her disruptor as she took out a scanner and saw that a life form was approaching. "Somebody's coming."

"Must be Bok. He's our contact," Kris revealed.

C looked at her scanner and adjusted it. "Same signature as a Moodian. Why are we meeting here?" she wondered.

"Bok doesn't want any chance of being scanned by Doneghan. The mountains make it harder," Kris explained.

C nodded in agreement.

"Bok also thinks Doneghan has spies on Moody. He can pay top dollar," Kris added.

Kris could see some smoke over a ridge. Then he saw what appeared to be a clam-shaped vehicle that was spewing fumes out of four vents in four different colors. It turned and headed up a slope toward them before coming to a stop.

A door opened, and Bok stepped out and approached them. Bok wore a tight black suit, and his thighs were thick to compensate for the extra Gs. His face sagged in perpetual grimace. Mariah was awestruck. This was her own first contact.

He offered his hand. Kris took it and immediately wanted to grimace at the moist palm but tried not to react. He let go and let Bok pass him before he wiped the natural secretion off his hand.

Bok went on to greet all of them, Mariah last. They gripped hands but she didn't recoil. Even as the slime dripped from her palm, she seemed enthralled. Bok turned away from her, and she examined the secretion with her scanner.

"I'm grateful you're here," Bok began.

"We're glad to help," Kris returned. "We have our own issues with Doneghan. We understand."

"Doneghan will finally face justice."

"What exactly did he do?" Kris probed.

"You can't see it now, but there was another moon. Kilaya. Doneghan bought rights to do some experiments with antimatter on the moon. He had assured us they were completely safe. He spent three Moody years working on his project. There didn't seem to be a problem. Then, apparently, he was frustrated with the slow progress. He wanted faster results," Bok recalled bitterly.

"What kind of antimatter experiments?" Logan asked.

"He was trying to make a new engine," Bok explained.

"Ultra-warp," Jennifer specified, knowing the deeper meaning.

"It's been declared too dangerous to develop in most systems. The risks are so high, no one dared pursue it," Logan added.

"Apparently, he knew that—and we didn't. But, as I said, he got impatient. He pushed the team harder. He pushed them and pushed them until the engine exploded, and, with it, all the inhabitants on the moon. One hundred thousand souls were lost. When it comes into view at night, you actually see two moons where there was only one before."

"My God," Mariah shuddered.

They all stood in chilled silence as Bok continued. "He escaped from Moody to an unnamed planetoid he owns, so we had no way to get to him," Bok recounted.

"I'm sorry," Kris consoled.

"How'd you find out where he was?" C inquired.

"The Citaris gave us some advanced sensor technology. That's how we learned he was scanning us. We just traced the beam back to its source," Bok answered.

Bok handed Kris a small white pillar with numbers carved into it. Kris took it and examined the object, puzzled. He glanced up from it. "What's this?"

"His coordinates," Bok said. "Also, I've included extensive scans of his locale. You'll find them in the silver drive."

"Thank you," Kris nodded.

Kris handed the pillar to Logan, then stepped up to Bok and shook his moist hand again. Kris put his arm on his shoulder, assuring him. Bok's sad lips threatened to smile.

"We'll get Doneghan. Don't you worry," Kris pledged.

Kris stepped back, and Bok paused thoughtfully. He seemed emotional. He waved to them, then hastily returned to his vehicle and closed the door. The engine came back on. The fumes began to burp out and he drove off.

"One hundred thousand," Jennifer repeated.

"The guy cracked a moon in half," Logan mumbled, bewildered.

Kris looked back at his crew, but he saw Mariah was off in another world looking at the landscape and the sky. Kris raised his eyebrows. "Uh, Mariah?"

"Yes, sir," Mariah yelped, spinning around.

"You can rejoin the conversation," Kris scolded.

"Sorry, sir," Mariah apologized.

"Keep your head in the game."

"Why is Doneghan out here? I thought humans were banned beyond the DMZ," Mariah commented.

"Oh, some are still out there. In hiding, in most cases, and welcomed in few," Kris answered.

"So where is this guy, Logan?" C asked.

"Coming right up," Logan responded.

Logan took the coordinates from the white pillar and entered them into his scanner. He found the location and handed his chart to Kris, who took it and perused it. It was a light year away on a green planetoid, orbiting a system nearly barren of planets. Kris wondered how a world didn't get a name. There must have been some reason.

"How do we catch him?" Mariah worried.

"C has some ideas," Kris assured her.

Kris turned and headed toward the shuttle. The others followed, walking up the ramp and past Amanda, who was sipping a fizzy drink, waiting for their return. She polished it off and shut the hatch after them.

While the shuttle engines pressed them back in their chairs as they lifted into orbit, Kris had his eyes on C. She was looking over the target planetoid and the scans the Moodians had supplied them. She was working on something as she kept referring to her own pad, looking up different items.

C needed a bold plan. They only had one shot at this.

CHAPTER TWENTY-NINE

Mariah and C had been tasked with the challenge of traveling to the planetoid without being seen by Doneghan's scanners. They were given the location of Doneghan's hideout and were left to come up with a secure way to arrive at the planetoid unseen. The pair were up against it. How do you bring a fifty-thousand-ton starship into orbit without Doneghan's sensor array picking it up? If they were spotted, he'd be running to an escape craft, and they'd be in a chase or, even worse, a shootout. They couldn't have that. Doneghan had to be delivered unharmed.

C insisted, and rightly so, that they had to catch him by surprise. It was the only way she was sure they could get him alive. C was doing double duty. She was assisting Mariah on a flight path to the planetoid. Mariah was a whiz in the field of navigation.

Mariah and C were in chart room D on deck M, the lowest deck on the ship. It was poorly lit and rarely traveled. On the last mission to Genusia, it had been filled with doctors and nurses and medical supplies for the mercy mission. Now, it was a dead zone. It seemed abandoned—so it fit their needs.

C had reasoned they needed to think in the stark quiet of deck M. Their task was a puzzle that they had to work out. Kris had told C about Mariah's test scores, which made her feel at ease. C noticed Mariah's scores in tactics were higher than her own. C didn't have the answer, and she hoped the quiet and the combination of both of them would help.

Mariah and C had been in the room for over four hours. Mariah paced slowly and stretched her back while C lay on a couch, propping her head up with her elbow, looking at the multiple charts of the galaxy that flickered on screens around them. C shifted and lay on her back, frustrated.

"I can make us silent, but I can't make us a ghost," Mariah bemoaned. "The ship's too damn big. The minute we leave Moody, he'll see us headed toward him, get suspicious, and probably run."

"There's gotta be some other way." C massaged her tired eyes.

"Christina, didn't you hear what I said? We're too big to..." Mariah stopped mid-sentence. Her voice trailed off like she was falling into a trance. C was about to ask if she was okay, when Mariah snapped out of it, darted to the charts, and ran her hand over the planetoid. She shifted it right and then widened it. She then moved to another object that was nearby, an elongated asteroid. Mariah widened it as well, and C could see some other scattered planets.

Logan stuck his head in. "How's it going?" he checked.

"Good timing. We need you," Mariah said, urging him into the room.

Mariah moved the screen around, putting the pieces together in her mind, and it seemed she had something. C could see the confidence filling Mariah's face.

"You mind giving us a clue to what you're thinking?" C requested.

Mariah was excited and the words came tumbling out rapidly. "Okay, we leave, headed the opposite direction. Doneghan thinks we've left. But we swing around by these planets in an arc, go into orbit at a few of them as though we're doing business or something. Then we go to MBB4. That's the last planet, which puts us closest to Doneghan's planetoids. We blast out of orbit under the cover of this asteroid that's between MBB4 and the planetoid he's on. If we're cleanly aligned, Doneghan won't be able to see us. He'll assume we left orbit and went elsewhere, but we'll station behind the asteroid."

Logan stared at the chart. "That puts us ten million miles from the planetoid. How do we get the Concord there?"

"We don't. We take a shuttle in," Mariah proposed.

"He'd still pick us up. We've got twenty-five million miles to cover," Logan countered.

"That's the crazy part. We take a shuttle and the landing team. It goes into full thrust and arcs behind the asteroid so it can't be seen by Doneghan. It reaches maximum velocity and slingshots out on a direct course for the planetoid. And then… you shut off the engines. You shut off everything. You go dark." Mariah waited for a response. She waited as Logan and C approached the chart together.

"Fall toward the planetoid?" Logan pondered. "We'd just look like a meteor. There'd have to be no course corrections."

Mariah brought up the picture of a grey, misshapen moon. "The planetoid's got a moon. We fly behind it, power up, and brake behind the moon. The moon skims the planetoid's atmosphere, so we're really close. Then we retrofire behind the moon and enter the planetoid's atmosphere. The plasma surrounding the shuttle during entry will cut off any signals."

"You're right; we'd look like a meteor burning up," Logan agreed. "What about after we're in the atmosphere?"

C stepped in between them. "That's not a problem. Bok's report said Doneghan's only looking at threats that are coming from deep space. We can fly right next to his compound, and he'll never know it. It's perfect. Good job, Mariah."

"Agreed. It's complicated but doable," Logan said.

"Thanks," Mariah grinned.

C pushed the intercom button on the wall.

"Captain?" C called out.

"Yes," Kris' voice came out of the speaker.

"We've got it."

"Get up here," Kris instructed.

"Right away."

The trio headed to Kris' ready room to explain the outlandish plan. Kris kept looking to Logan to make sure it was feasible, and Logan insisted it was. But it was ballsy, and it needed to be executed with precision.

"I don't see how else we could surprise him. This is gonna take some fancy footwork on this ship and the shuttle. Whose idea was this?" Kris asked.

"Mariah hatched it," Logan answered.

Kris smiled. "Mariah. Good job."

"Thank you, sir," Mariah replied.

Kris eyed the flight plan floating in a 3D image before him.

"Ingenious," Kris thought out loud. A dead stick free fall. Challenging, but the upgraded fusion engines were so powerful, they could propel a shuttle across the expanse between the asteroid and the planetoid in just enough time before their life support ran out.

"That's gonna take a space jockey to pull off," Kris mused while holding his hand to his mouth. "Fortunately, I know where to find one."

CHAPTER THIRTY

Amanda Sun was playing blackjack with Jennessy in a bar on deck B. Amanda had a vodka, and Jennessy nursed a Corona Proxima. He was defeating his wife hand after hand, and he was loving it. She was usually better than him at most things, but, back at the academy, Jennessy was a card shark. He'd make a bundle from unsuspecting cadets. He knew the odds so well, no one could beat him.

"Blackjack." It was his tenth straight win. Then Jennessy's high dampened when he noticed that Amanda wasn't smiling. Jennessy sipped his beer and realized that if he kept on winning, she was going to make him pay. After that thought crossed his mind, he lost the next three straight hands on purpose, just as Kris sauntered in and took a seat at their table.

"Want to play a hand?" Amanda offered.

"No, I've got a job for you," Kris announced. "But it means flying the Concord."

"Really? Again?" she said annoyed.

"It's not so bad. Look at the flight plot."

He handed her his pad. The Concord would have to go on a wild ride from planet to planet, avoiding all appearances that they were coming for Doneghan. She sipped her vodka and grinned.

"That's just part one," Kris teased. "Then you've got to get a shuttle from here to here as a ghost."

Kris explained the plan, and when he mentioned the dead stick section of the flight, she started laughing. Kris forced a grin, hoping she wasn't going to tell him it was insane, dangerous, impossible, and would likely get them killed.

"This idea is smoking. We'd have to take the Genesis," Amanda declared.

"What's the Genesis?"

"Newest shuttle out of the factory. I personally refitted the transfusion engines. If you wanna get up to that speed before engine cut off, that's your ship," Amanda assured him.

"Then it's Genesis. What about helming the Concord?"

"Are you kidding? I'll throw that one in for free."

———

Amanda stepped toward helmsman Tortelli, who had a hangdog face as he rose, embarrassed that he had to be replaced as he didn't have the skill set for such a delicate flight. Amanda adjusted the chair to her height and turned to Logan, who was sitting at navigation.

"Feed me the plot," Amanda ordered.

"Here it comes."

"Lemme see if I gotta fix anything."

Logan was incredulous and crossed his arms. Amanda noticed she had tweaked his ego and smiled, but his plot was precise. Logan was thorough, and Amanda gave him the thumbs up as she engaged the helm.

"Good job."

Logan glanced back, his hackles a little lower, his lips not as tight.

Amanda stared down at the panel, punching in the course data and firing up the drive. She smiled as she heard the soft thump ringing throughout the ship. She then glanced back to Kris, who was conferring with Jennifer and Mariah.

Kris took his command chair. He had just informed Mariah that she wouldn't be making planetfall on this expedition. She protested, but Kris said that he was grateful to her for devising such an ingenious plan, and her skills weren't needed on a mission that was much more like an op than a voyage of discovery.

"Amanda, take her out," Kris directed.

"Aye, sir. Going to fifty lights."

Amanda punched in the command with a grin planted across her face. She headed to Nathan's Star, looped through the system, and dropped into orbit around a world where the temperatures rose to six hundred degrees at midday, then fell to sixty at night. Then it was onto Microvia for a few orbits before Andalea.

Amanda threaded the needle between asteroids and the planets. If they were scanned, they would seem like a star freighter making a series of routine deliveries. When they reached the third leg of their journey, Amanda began the challenging portion of Mariah's inspiring plan. They had to drive through a thickly populated asteroid belt and race around numerous moons and planets to stay clear of the deep-reaching eyes of Doneghan.

She flew the ship like she was barnstorming in a shuttle. Engineering was regularly alerting her about the Concord's limitations, but she didn't listen. She didn't need to. Back in the day, she had taken another Concord-class ship through a similar path and had already proved the Concord could go way beyond its specs.

Amanda came to the final planet in the navigational plot and dropped out of hyperspace just in time to skim off the northern pole of a gas giant planet. She then reversed the ship suddenly. Kris gripped his chair to stay steady. Once in position, she fired the fusion engines that slowed them to a full stop.

Amanda had reached the end of the plot of the Concord. They were floating behind the asteroid that would keep them hidden from the deep space scanners of Eric Doneghan. Amanda eased back in her seat, then rose and approached Kris.

"Nice flying," he said.

"Now for the fun part. Catch ya in the shuttle bay."

All the terrified eyes on the flight deck landed on Kris, who shrugged his shoulders and sat back in his chair. "She got us here."

CHAPTER THIRTY-ONE

The Genesis was lazily floating in tandem with the Concord. Amanda was programming in the flight path of the Genesis as Logan read off a list of flight commands. The timing would have to be exact. Amanda and Logan were both deadly serious as they worked together. When some conversation bubbled up in the back, Logan snapped.

"We need it quiet here!" The ship fell silent.

Amanda and Logan continued programming. They triple-checked their commands and agreed they were ready to go.

Amanda grabbed a bottle of water and downed it in a few gulps. This was a new one for her. The flight was daring and complex. Mariah had made the recipe, and Amanda now had to cook it.

Every seat was filled. Amanda, Jennessy, Kris, and Logan were toward the front. C was with her security team in the back. They were specialist class and wore black tactical gear. They finished packing their gear and strapped into their seats.

Amanda throttled the engines to ten percent. She flew the ship to the farthest tip of the asteroid and made a slow turn. She then pitched the ship up. She only had a few minutes to put them in position. Everything had to be aligned to the distant moon's orbit around the planetoid twenty-five million miles away.

Amanda and Logan had to program in the flight path as the G forces generated by the transfusion engines were going to pin her body back so hard, she'd be unable to reach the controls to make corrections. The A.I. would have to do all the flying.

"You want to cut off at twenty-two thirty?" the female A.I. voice gently inquired.

"Exactly," she responded.

"That has been logged. Will you initiate, or will I?" the A.I. said softly.

"I will," Amanda answered.

Kris was checking his belt and saw that C was securing one of the cases she brought from her intelligence days. Kris and C had examined Doneghan's mansion from the Moody scans, and she knew exactly what she needed. C got into her seat and strapped herself in.

"Will I do the honors or you, Skipper?" Amanda asked.

"That's on me," Kris said. All eyes were on Kris, waiting for guidance. "Okay, we're gonna be pulling a lot of Gs to get to speed. I know you're used to the quiet leap into hyperspace, but we're going old school today. We've gotta get up to a velocity that'll allow us to coast to our destination. Also, folks, our pilot is going to shut everything down at the end of our boost phase. We'll be a flying rock in space. You've got air breathers. Put them on at shut down. Our air won't be scrubbed of carbon monoxide. You have heaters in your clothes. Turn them up because it's gonna get chilly 'til we're by the moon Trafalgar. Okay, Amanda, light the candle."

Amanda leaned forward, then over to Logan, who was in the third chair next to Jennessy, navigating. She pointed out a blinking warning light to Logan, who looked down to make a few changes, then nodded to her and braced himself. Amanda flipped open the ignition button. She watched the clock counting down. It was closing in on the number. She could have had the A.I. do it, but she couldn't resist.

The numbers were getting closer. She had to be right on the money. Seconds counted.

"Okay, everybody. This is gonna really hurt," Amanda said.

Amanda pushed the button, and they were instantly slammed backward. The acceleration was swift, and they all sunk back into their seats. They could see the Concord dropping away as the engines pushed them. Then, in a blink of an eye, it disappeared.

They were on their backs watching the asteroid, which was growing smaller in their window. As they reached the furthest end of the arc, they felt like they were plunging toward it. The asteroid swelled bigger in size. It appeared as though they were going to smash into it. The engines had now throttled up to one hundred percent.

Kris wanted to clutch his chest, but his arms were pinned. He thought this must be what a heart attack felt like. He tried to move his hand, but it, too, was plastered down by the Gs. He couldn't even wiggle his fingers. If this went any longer, they'd all black out. That would be a disaster. He prayed everyone would be conscious when the engines were shut down before they shot past the asteroid's protective shield, so they could power down the shuttle. The A.I. couldn't shut down the shuttles. There were strict rules for A.I.s, and not being able to turn off life support was one of them.

This could only be decided by a human hand.

The sound of the fusion engines rumbled and shook the shuttle. Kris tried to look over to C, but he couldn't even manage that. All he had were his thoughts. He was virtually paralyzed.

He thought about the Concord. They wouldn't even know if they were successful until they were on their way back. It was strict radio silence going forward. He didn't envy Jennifer's anxiety while she waited.

They reached the tip of the asteroid, and the engines shut down just on time. Kris was able to move again. He flexed his hand and glanced over to C. She had blacked out. Kris shook her awake. C moved her head and fluttered her eyes. She looked to Kris.

"A girl could get killed doing this," C cracked.

"Yeah, that wasn't fun," Kris agreed. "How are we doing, Amanda?"

"Trying to power this thing down," Amanda responded, working the controls.

"Trying?" Kris repeated, his voice rising.

"Little problem."

"Amanda," Kris said nervously. They would be in scanning range in mere seconds. Amanda put in a new series of commands and the lights fluttered. The control panels blinked on and then off, and then they went dead. The interior lights turned to red, and then finally they were in total darkness. Kris turned on his heater and picked up his air breather.

"Okay, an hour 'til insertion. Get on your breathers." He watched the others flipping on their heaters and figuring out how to put on their air breathers.

And then there was quiet. They couldn't expend air by talking. Kris just sat in the dark, hoping. He asked himself how he ended up here. He was a quiet family man. Now he was in a shuttle hurtling through space, getting colder and colder. They only needed an hour, but it would be a long hour.

He could tell his heart rate was up. He was scared. It was one thing seeing the plan, but living it was another thing entirely. The ship was utterly silent. It was eerie. He thought back to the war. He was certain this had happened to some of his compatriots. Broken off from a blasted ship in an air-filled compartment, waiting for the air to dwindle or to freeze to death. He had to stop thinking about that.

Kris couldn't keep track of time. He kept his eyes fixed on the stars out the window to keep from losing his mind. He had no sense of movement otherwise.

It seemed as though significant time had passed. He could see his breath in front of him coming out of his air breather. The device began blinking red. That was the five-minute warning that it would be out of oxygen. Other red lights blinked in the pitch dark. The crew members were holding themselves tightly, trying to stay warm. Two of the security crew members were shivering. Kris thought they couldn't take fifteen more minutes of these frosty temperatures, but had no idea how much time had gone by.

The moon Trafalgar appeared in their window, and Amanda turned back around to them.

"All right, the A.I. is going to start reverse thrust. Same drill, but you better be buckled in tight. It's gonna be yanking you forward this time. Gents, you might wanna mind where you have your straps. Sorry, Skipper, did you want to say that?"

"No, I'm good," Kris chuckled.

A.I. began the reverse thrust. They were thrown forward in a sudden lurch. Kris grimaced. As they slowed, they eventually eased back in their chairs.

The Genesis hit the planetoid's atmosphere twenty seconds later. The friction began to increase as the air molecules heated up around it. As electrically charged plasma built up around them, they were shielded from detection. No signals in and no signals out. Once they were flying in the atmosphere, they were truly ghosts.

The Genesis broke through the clouds, streaking across a grey sky. Amanda reversed the thrust so Doneghan wouldn't hear a telltale sonic boom. They spiraled toward their target area, twisting down to a thousand feet away from the Doneghan's supposed location.

Amanda deftly landed the ship near a river by an endless field of grass. As soon as they touched down, the landing party jumped into action. Kris got up and moved around to meet C, who was already up and checking a large case.

"Alright, it's your show now," Kris told her.

"We're good, Kris. Really."

Kris stretched and groaned. He hurt all over. He put his hand on the ceiling to steady himself. His mind drifted to the idea of failure. They had gotten this far, but any number of things could go wrong. Kris knew this was all about servicing The Reason, but deep in his soul, he truly desired revenge against Eric Doneghan.

He had pushed a button that destroyed a Qwesi ship of fifty to protect Doneghan. He wanted to look Doneghan in the eye in the brig of the Concord and tell him of his dark and hopeless fate. He would savor it. He would take his time, slowly twisting his imaginary dagger into his empty soul.

Doneghan was slippery. He always had been. But Kris' confidence was rising as he watched C prepare. C had given him a brief rundown on her plan, and it was impressive. He didn't question whether C could pull the op off; it was all about his own nagging self-doubt.

CHAPTER THIRTY-TWO

The planetoid was lush and green, but it wasn't always so. Fifty years ago, it had a Mars-like atmosphere, where carbon dioxide reigned. Then a company called Planet Solutions came into the picture. They were in the business of terraforming celestial bodies into Earth-like worlds. They got on the map by terraforming Mars. Business took off, and they terraformed seven more planets.

The nameless planetoid had been owned by a family of trillionaires who sensed the growing tensions between the Citaris and the Earth Directorate. They sold it to Doneghan for a quarter of what it was worth and returned to Earth. It featured a mansion, a private seaside resort, and a ski resort in the mountains. The rest of the planetoid was uninhabited. Doneghan bought it as a hideout, just in case. He did risky deals, and the planetoid wasn't well known. Plus, the wealthy family who had owned it prior to Doneghan paid to keep it off most star charts. It was meant to be private, and that was just what he desired.

He had his own farm that would keep him fed for eternity and a supply of women to satisfy his carnal needs. Doneghan had a safe, quiet life... but it was a mundane one. He was no longer gallivanting around as the galaxy's bad boy businessman. He was a man on an island.

He wouldn't dare to go into Citari space after the war. His life as he knew it was over. This was his retirement. Doneghan pondered if this was his punishment for past misdeeds and reasoned that if this was his prison, he got off easy.

The shuttle had landed behind a hill covered with dead trees. The crew was running through their checklists, setting up for the impending op. Kris was squatting in some high grass and inhaling the crisp, clean air.

He pulled out a small patch of grass and admired it. He held it up to his nose. It smelled fresh. He tossed it aside.

He rose, turning toward the shuttle, and strode through the tall grass, his hands brushing along the tops of the blades. He stepped into a clearing and headed down to the shuttle. Kris reached it and saw C coming down the ramp, carrying a black case. He followed her up the hill. She heaved the case over to a rock and set it down with a thud. Some tiny blue crab-like creatures skittered out from between the rocks, heading pell-mell. C seemed startled and waited for the parade of bugs to put some distance between them.

Kris offered to help C, but she advised him that it was coded to her handprint and if he picked it up, he'd be electrocuted. Kris backed off. The security team caught up to the pair and gathered nearby.

C opened the case, and Kris peered in and saw a hundred little clear balls packed inside. Kris glanced at C for an explanation, but C was too absorbed to fill him in. She was focused on setting it up.

C opened a panel and waved her hand over a green scan-pad. A series of color-coded bars clicked on slowly until they were all lit up. In an instant, the tiny clear balls flew into the air and hovered over them. Kris and the security team stared up at them in wonder. She waved her hand over the green pad again, and Doneghan's picture popped up on a screen. C pressed two buttons in unison and spoke into the machine.

"Seek."

The tiny balls slowly spun in loops, then, suddenly, they soared up above their heads and hung in the air. They didn't make a sound. They were eerie as the sun glinted off their surfaces. Kris was in awe. He covered his eyes from the sun to get a better view, but the balls spun away over the dead trees and vanished behind the hill.

C flipped up a screen that showed all the angles the balls' cameras were observing.

"What is this?" Kris wondered.

"One of my tricks."

"Yeah, but what is it?"

"They're tiny drones with a kind of hive mind A.I.," C explained.

"They can find Doneghan?"

"And they can pack a punch," C assured him.

The drones were fast and not easily seen. Their clear surface made them nearly invisible. They would blend in with whatever they were near. If a target stared at them, all they'd see would be an unobstructed blue sky.

They flew over to Doneghan's mansion, scanning every inch, their cameras seeking Doneghan. They moved with stealth to their target. The drones identified various guards planted around the estate. The drones would break off and position themselves nearby each unsuspecting guard.

The images were coming in at such a dizzying pace, Kris had to look away. He stepped away, but stopped when he heard a buzzing sound. Kris turned back around to C, who now had a confident, devilish smile.

Kris jogged back over and saw that the drones had found their man. The images were no longer flying by. They had settled in on their target. Doneghan.

Kris slowly stepped forward and put his hand on C's shoulder. He grinned. They were staring at three different angles of the fugitive. He was sipping a cup of coffee on a large veranda in his bathrobe, admiring his vast estate. Another drone showed the palatial home surrounded by exquisite landscaping.

"C," Kris said.

"Yeah."

"Save Doneghan for me."

"Happy to."

C leaned into the machine and pressed the two buttons again. Logan moved closer. He started to say something to Kris, but C held her finger up to her mouth to stay quiet. C spoke into the machine.

"Threats."

C leaned in closer to the screen, which began to scramble again and, within minutes, every guard on the estate was identified. There were thirty in all, and they were all armed. "Thirty guards," Kris read warily.

"Thirty's not so bad," C shrugged.

"There's only ten of us," Kris pointed out.

"Yeah, but all we need is me," she said with a smirk.

"I don't think these guys stand a chance," Logan piped in.

Kris nodded to him and sat on a rock, crossing his legs. Logan joined him. C turned back to the device and pressed the two buttons. She spoke clearly and simply.

"Neutralize."

C's devilish smile returned. She then got up and walked back down the hill, leaving a puzzled Kris and Logan. Logan looked to Kris.

"Where are you going?"

"Assembling my team. We've got to get our man, right?" C asked.

"Right," Kris affirmed.

"Well, are you two coming?" C said.

———————

Heck Finnerty never saw the tiny ball that fired a neurotoxin up his nose. He just sensed himself falling and then the feeling he couldn't move. He could see Neims had fallen too, frozen in an awkward pose. His eyes darted to Angie. They were supposed to go on a date that night. But he couldn't move, and she was crumpled in a corner with a look of terror across her face. Heck wanted to cry out, but he couldn't. He didn't know what was happening to him.

Heck heard voices and then saw feet passing before him. Who were these people? His eyes turned up, and he could see they were humans. He recognized the uniforms. They were from Earth. Heck realized they had been beaten before they had a chance to fight.

What would Doneghan do to him as the head of security? Heck hoped he was dying.

———————

Doneghan was sipping his coffee and turned around to see his girl for the day, Keba, a short redhead that he'd been with the night before. She was trembling, her eyes wide. She was terrified. Doneghan reached for a bottle of SynthB pills. They were performance enhancers that infused into his system. He popped them in his mouth and immediately felt the surge in his bloodstream.

Doneghan stepped forward into the master bedroom. He cinched his robe while moving toward her. "What's wrong?"

A man stepped out of a hallway into the bedroom, holding a stun gun in his hand, accompanied by a cold expression on his face. Doneghan jumped a little and held up his hands. Recognition filled Doneghan's face. He knew this was Kris Galloway, but he didn't remember what he'd done to him.

Doneghan turned his head, hearing pulsing engines approaching him. He saw the shuttle's cloud of dust rise as high as the veranda. He glanced out a window and noticed his paralyzed security team. His body tensed.

Doneghan spun around to look at Kris. He knew he was trapped and had no cover. He had to buy himself some time. He stepped back, trying to act nonchalant as he glanced at the disruptor-toting security team. Then, he took off his bathrobe, revealing a t-shirt and shorts. "Didn't think you guys could come out this way anymore," he sneered coolly.

"They made an exception," Kris asserted.

"Or so you say. The Citaris might not be very happy about this if they found out," Doneghan teased.

"Oh, they know. They invited us," Kris responded.

"Really? I find that hard to believe."

"This is actually our second trip beyond the DMZ," Kris revealed.

"Been busy," Doneghan observed, weighing his options. "Can I get you anything?"

"No," Kris said coldly.

"What's this about? Information?" Doneghan asked

"No, it's all about you," Kris growled, taking a step toward him.

Escape suddenly raced to the top of Doneghan's mind. It wasn't a problem, though, as he knew something that Kris did not. Doneghan was a sprinter. He did it for fun and it kept him in shape. Plus, the SynthB that he had just taken not only enhanced his performance in bed, but also the pills could make him move like a jaguar. He could feel he had the growing edge as the SynthB was peaking within his body. Two specialists grabbed Doneghan from either side, gripping him firmly. Doneghan smiled wryly. He darted for the veranda while slipping out of the specialists' grip and leapt over it before Kris could fire.

"C!"

"I got it."

Doneghan was running. He was free. He had fooled them. It was so easy. He sprinted across a field of grass, making divots as his legs pounded him forward. He was thinking about how he'd reach his jump ship in a matter of minutes, but then he heard something behind him rapidly approaching. He looked around and saw a spinning wall of tiny balls. They overtook him and scooped his body up, wrapping around him. Doneghan couldn't move. He levitated over the ground, helpless.

He was whisked back to the courtyard and dropped in front of Kris and his team. Before he could say a word, the numbing feeling of a stun gun hitting him flooded his body.

CHAPTER THIRTY-THREE

Sixteen years ago.

Haven Soares hated everything alien. He hated
the Citaris especially because they visited Earth on a
regular basis. Haven hated how they looked and how
they smelled. He hated the sound of their voices. He
didn't care for their superior attitude. It was ridiculous; an average
Citari was only five foot two, and humans were taller and stronger.
They were ugly and repugnant to him.

He started an organization that allowed fellow alien-haters to
congregate and share their stories of disgust. Haven didn't do that
for a living, though. He couldn't; there were too few members and
he had to do it in secret. The meetings were held in people's homes
or church basements. Hating for a living wasn't very profitable
anymore, like it was in the early part of the 2000s. His group had
grown over the years, but they had to be underground. The hate
laws were strict, as were the penalties.

Haven couldn't understand it. Aliens weren't citizens of Earth.
Why should they be protected?

He worked as a low-level stockbroker for Burns. His father
got him the position. A broker could make a small fortune. Many
did. But you had to have charm. You had to have smarts, and he

really didn't. He just bought what he was told to buy and sold what he was told to sell. He wasn't very good at it and seldom got the bonuses his coworkers were rewarded with.

Haven was rail thin and over six feet tall. He had an Adam's apple that distorted his neck, and a noticeable overbite. His brown hair was seemingly always greasy, even after taking a shower. His suits were cheap and so were his shoes. He was the least impressive man you could imagine. But because his father's friend owned Burns, he had an in.

Haven would complete his orders and then sit back watching symbols traveling on the board and think about hate. It's what made him go. It swelled inside him. It inhabited him. It was his identity.

Haven had to be better than someone else, and his mind instantly went to the Citaris. If he could have them exterminated, he'd be filled with joy.

With the anti-racism laws on Earth, a racist had to look to the stars to serve his hate, and the Citaris were his big fat target.

At lunchtime, he left the office a little after noon, grabbing his levitator pack from underneath his desk. He strapped it on as he rode down the elevator. There was a beautiful woman next to him who made sure not to make eye contact with him. The elevator doors opened, and she was the first out and raced to join some girlfriends.

Haven made his way through the crowd and out onto the street. The levitator lifted him up and took him across town to Frank's Diner. He took off the pack, hung it up on a rack, then stepped in and searched for his seat. Haven had a favorite one and, luckily, the customer who had lunch there was paying his bill. The customer rose, and Haven snatched the seat before the table could even be bussed. He sat with the dirty dishes waiting to be cleared while looking at the news on his micro-pad.

He took his lunch every day at Frank's. He had the same dull meal with the same dull routine. A hot dog with yellow mustard and relish and French fries and a Coke Platinum. Haven went there because of the waitresses. They all looked similar. He surmised that the owner was a butt man, as the waitresses were gifted in that way. He ate here regularly because it was the only place where women were nice to him. This was the highlight of his day.

He finished off his hot dog and noticed another customer staring at him. She was tall and lean and looked to be possibly South Asian, but he couldn't be sure. Her hair was dark black, and her clothes were designer. She got up and walked over to him. Haven glanced behind him, thinking she was staring at someone at another table, but the one behind him was empty. By the time he turned back around, she was standing before him, staring down.

"Haven't I seen you at Burns?" she started.

"You might have," Haven shrugged.

"I'm Dominique."

"Haven. You in brokerage?"

"Investing," she answered.

"Client?"

"I could be." She handed him her card. It read Dominique Khan. By the time he looked up, he only saw the tail end of her tailored suit going out the door.

The money came into his investment account two weeks after meeting Ms. Khan. Three hundred million dollars. He stared at his bright screen for twenty minutes. He'd never seen such money. He didn't understand why she had singled him out. He wasn't seen as one of the top men at Burns. It was curious, but he didn't question his good fortune.

Management suddenly saw Haven through a new lens. He was invited to parties he had previously been shut out from. He was included in meetings. Haven received attention, and he soaked it up. He was given the best tips and the best advice. Soon, the three hundred million was six hundred million. Then a billion. Khan invested another billion. Six months later, he had one hundred and fifty million in his own bank accounts.

Haven made partner, and that one hundred and fifty soon became a half billion. In one year, Haven was a billionaire twice over. He had a wife, a life, and a fortune... but he would still look to the skies and think to himself how much he hated the Citaris.

Now he had the money to do something about it.

He strolled out of his westside penthouse with a highball in his hand and admired his rooftop pool. His eyes were drawn to a United thruster rocket taking off from Long Island. He could do anything he wanted, he thought, and now, finally, it was time.

Haven turned on his comm and made a call. "Doris."

A female voice answered: "Yes."

"It's Haven."

"Hello, how are you?"

"I think it's time," Haven announced.

"I agree. But we need the right candidate so we can get the right people in."

"Let's start a list. Let's make this happen. Put the Citaris in their place," Haven declared firmly.

"Anyone in mind?" Doris asked.

"Jefferson Kroll," Haven replied without pausing.

"The senator?" Doris checked.

"We've had like-minded discussions," Haven revealed.

"I think you're wrong," Doris responded.

"What are you talking about?" Haven snapped.

"We don't need a list. Kroll is perfect," Doris said slyly.

Haven smiled, took a sip of his highball, then placed it down on a glass table.

"I'll set up a meeting," Haven promised.

"Let me know when. I'll alert the others."

Haven hung up, feeling satisfied. He was confident he would be successful. He would get Jefferson Kroll elected President of the United States, then direct Kroll to put the right people on the Earth Directorate. Hardliners who'd stand up to the Citaris.

He couldn't have predicted that he was going to trigger a hopeless war eight years later. He didn't realize that when Earth was saved, Kroll and the hardliners would be thrown out. Haven couldn't imagine that the whole misadventure would be traced back to him, and he would become a pariah. Remaining on Earth would become a risky proposition for him and he would have to move.

He sent his wife and kids to the private estate he had on Mars. He would leave ten days later on a private transport. He had to tie up some financial loose ends. When he completed his business, he bid farewell to Earth and raced to the safety of Mars.

Haven travelled alone. He liked it that way. It was peaceful.

Haven rocked in his seat as the transport retroburn fired, putting the ship into an elliptical orbit. Mars loomed large in his window. This was going to be his new home. Probably for the rest of his life.

He didn't regret his moves that led to war. Haven felt confident he could organize a resurgence. He would rise again. Haven could make it happen.

An attendant with an Italian accent gave him a drink and told him they were in Mars' orbit. He drank his highball, but felt odd after a few sips. Haven's eyes became heavy. He couldn't stay awake. The attendant had put something in his drink. He blacked out.

Haven's first sensation as he awoke was that he was vibrating. His eyes slowly opened, and he realized he was still holding his drink in his hand. He was surrounded by the sounds of shaking and shuddering. He stood up and looked out the porthole. They were in the re-entry phase.

"Hello?"

He looked for the attendant but couldn't find her.

"Hello?"

He moved forward to the cockpit and found, to his horror, there was neither a pilot nor copilot. He ran to the porthole and realized he was entering the Martian atmosphere upside down. The protective heat shield would not save him. Haven was being murdered.

The cabin temperature rose to near boiling in thirty seconds. His shoes began to melt. His skin began to bubble. Haven screamed right as the transporter broke apart, incinerating his body in a matter of seconds.

The transporter landed in a deep trench in the southern hemisphere. Haven had been right. He was being murdered, and he wouldn't be the only one. The others would be erased, too. They had been behind the war and there was a very little interest in a trial. A myriad of accidents would befall them, and few would care or try to uncover the murderous conspiracy.

CHAPTER THIRTY-FOUR

Doneghan's eyes opened to a grey ceiling. He didn't have grey ceilings at home. They were light green, like his parents' house. He was certain that he wasn't home anymore. He ached all over his body. What had happened, he wondered? Perhaps he was in a hospital. He tried to piece events together, but his head just throbbed. His mouth was dry, and his stomach growled like a beast. He must not have eaten in a long time. Why? Where was he? His mind drifted as bits of memory flitted through his brain. He heard a sound. It was familiar. He couldn't place it at first, but it meant something. It was a faint thump. Why was that important? It came back to him. The source of the thump came from light drive engines. Now he knew without question that he was on a starship.

He remembered a redhead named Keba. He recalled that she feared him, and he had reveled in it. The rest was a blank. Doneghan had a fragment of memory of running, but it wasn't clear. Nothing was clear.

"Where am I?" he called out. There was no answer.

He sat up, gripping his skull. He looked to the right and he could see the glass enclosure that was imprisoning him. He closed his eyes tightly, realizing he'd finally been caught. It had been a recurring dream. When the darkness consumed him so many years ago... the dreams began. Imprisoned. He knew full well the crimes he committed. It was his choice. He had convinced himself that they were nightmares and nothing more. He was too rich and powerful for them to become true.

He squeaked out, "Oh, no. No. No. No. No."

He closed his eyes and opened them again, hoping he was having a bad SynthB drug experience. He opened them and, of course, nothing had changed. He was in the brig. He was locked up. Trapped.

He didn't know how he was going to wriggle out of this situation, but he would. He always did. There was always an angle. He still had money. He'd be back in his place in less than twenty-four hours. He figured he'd get to make a call, and he would call his most influential friend. Haven Soares. Haven had his fingers in everything. That's all it would take.

Doneghan sat up on the bare bed. His journey from junior executive to business titan to, finally, a rogue billionaire with a price on his head, was epic. His dive into depravity came with an idea that drenched his mind: *I CAN DO WHATEVER I WANT.* No limits. He could have all the sex he wanted. He could kill. He could steal. He could sex traffic for profit. He was all-powerful.

Doneghan stood up. It was time to jump into action. It was time for him to embody who he was: Eric Doneghan. The man who was above it all.

He pounded on the glass. "Let me out of here!" Doneghan yelled.

There was no answer. He pounded on the glass again.

"Let me outta here!" he screamed louder.

He stood back and gazed at his eight-by-eight-foot prison. It wasn't right. He was one of the anointed; he didn't belong here.

He made money not only for himself, but for others, too. That money filtered down and countless people thrived. He deserved to do anything he wanted as a reward.

Doneghan had done everything and tried everything. Two women, a man and a woman, two men, killing a woman after sex. He was consumed by darkness and had no interest in finding a way back. It was his right.

Then, eleven years after the war was over, a scientist from Rigel approached him about developing an ultra-warp drive. Many had considered it too dangerous, and he had been turned down by all financiers. The scientist went to Doneghan as a last resort and Doneghan bit.

Doneghan thought that if he had the ultra-warp drive, he could bargain his way home. For all that he had, he yearned for Earth. It was still home to him. In hindsight, he wished he'd never left. His favorite places were on that blue world.

As he sat in exile, he thought about his past. He had lived three lives, and that was enough. He had made an oversized life, a messy one. It was time to go home. But how? He needed to present something so dynamic that all his sins would be washed away. The ultra-warp was desired by all. He could bargain with the Citaris and give them the science in exchange for safe passage through the DMZ. He could make a deal for the drive, and he'd be a free man.

He was middle-aged at sixty-five; he could expect to live to one hundred and thirty. He still had a long life ahead of him. He wanted to lead a quieter, safer existence. Maybe in Hawaii. Maybe on the Florida Keys.

He secured a moon from the planet Moody for the experiments. He concealed the risks he had taken at potential risk to the populace, but the notion of a catastrophic disaster was the furthest thing from his mind. He dreamt of a quiet life, away from the depravity and cruelty he had once embraced. He had no regrets; it was his right to be depraved, after all, and he shouldn't be punished for what was his right. But he had to find a path out of his exile, and the ultra-warp was the key.

It wasn't to be. During the third week of ultra-warp research, a positive particle mixed with a negative particle, and the antimatter core blew up a thousand square miles on the moon. The atmosphere was ripped away, and the moon broke apart. One hundred thousand men, women, and children ceased to exist in a matter of minutes.

Doneghan was talking to the chief scientist of the project while the latest test was going on. He was in the Vandrae Hotel on Moody at the time. He was laying on his bed with two passed-out women. The room was strewn with bottles of alcohol and drugs. He got out of bed, wandered naked over to a half-drunk cocktail and picked it up. He could see the moon from his window. He was listening to the chief scientist while knocking back the last of his drink when the signal went dead.

"Hello? Hello?" Doneghan stared at his comm, puzzled.

There was a flash from outside. He spun around to see a mushroom cloud was billowing from the moon. His mouth was agape as he grabbed the edges of the window.

He didn't take his luggage. He just leapt into his clothes, took a SynthB, and ran. He didn't stop until he got to his jump ship. He escaped from Moody to his summer home on his private planetoid. He waited to see if Moody agents came for him, but they never did. It had been a year, and he thought he was in the clear. His scanners were the finest made, and no one was approaching his home. He'd kept it a secret, and it had worked. He hired a small contingent of guards, brought a few girls for company, and resigned himself to the fact that this would be where he'd spend the rest of his life.

Until now.

Doneghan became aware of a pair of feet before him. He glanced up to see Kris Galloway staring at him from the other side of the glass barrier. He watched as Kris grabbed a chair and sat down.

"Who are you? You seem familiar," Doneghan squinted.

"We've met. Saved your ass while you were trafficking those Qwesi woman."

"Ah, so this is about that," Doneghan sighed.

"Doneghan, I'm afraid this is about everything," Kris informed him casually.

"Everything?"

"Your sordid life," Kris specified.

"My sordid life created a lot of jobs. When I go back to Earth, I still have a lot of friends. Judges, politicians. I've greased a lot of palms. My current situation is going to be temporary. One call to Haven Soares, and I can make this all go away," Doneghan declared confidently.

"Haven Soares?" Kris repeated.

"Yeah, who's shaking now?" Doneghan spat, standing in defiance.

"Haven Soares burned up over Mars in a transporter accident," Kris reported coldly. "Some say it wasn't quite an accident."

Doneghan stumbled a little. He didn't expect that. Haven was a titan, a legend. It seemed improbable. "He's dead?"

"Yup. If that was your big play, you are out of luck."

"I know a lotta other people on Earth," Doneghan vowed.

Kris got up and sighed, sliding the chair aside. He strode toward the door, then stopped and turned back to Doneghan, whose body was tensed in defiance. Kris took a few steps back toward him and smiled. "Who said anything about you going back to Earth?"

"Well, that's where you have to take me," Doneghan insisted.

"No, no, we've made other arrangements."

"Other arrangements?" Doneghan got to his feet and pressed up against the glass that was holding him in.

Kris moved closer, two inches from Doneghan's nose. Kris grinned broadly.

"You're going back to Moody. They'll decide your fate." Kris gave him a knowing wink.

"What?"

"The trial, or what the Moodians call a trial, will decide your punishment."

"Look, look, I've got money," Doneghan pleaded desperately.

"So do I," Kris shrugged with ease.

Doneghan went pale. He knew what that meant. He knew he would be tortured for the next forty-five to fifty years. He would be flayed and then put back together and flayed again. He would beg for death, but it wouldn't come. His sex organs would be inflicted with unimaginable pain. He would be raped daily by guardsman who would get extra pay for the dirty duty. He would be made to pay and pay and pay.

He began pounding the glass, yelling, "NO," but Kris turned off the intercom.

CHAPTER THIRTY-FIVE

Star travel was mostly made up of silence. It wasn't about enduring it. It was about welcoming it. Contrary to popular belief, sitting in the command chair doesn't mean a captain's hours are filled with barking orders while lurching from crisis to crisis. In fact, it was generally quiet. Too quiet for Kris Galloway—he had just nodded off in the command chair. It had only been a few moments when was nudged awake by an ensign offering him a cup of coffee. Kris eyed the bridge to see if anyone had noticed he'd slipped off to dreamland. They hadn't. He thanked the ensign.

"I owe you one," Kris said with a wink. "Did I snore?

"No, sir."

The ensign left the bridge. Kris downed the hot coffee in several gulps trying to get his motor running again. The coffee was grown on Mariah. It was more effective than anything sold on Earth. The caffeine hit his system and he rapidly perked up. He dropped his cup into the waste suction in his chair.

Kris pulled out his pad and searched for a magazine he'd been reading while they had been flying to Moody. He checked the search history on his pad. A 3D picture of Toyota's new hypercycle, the

Valiant, popped up in full screen. Startled, he turned off the 3D feature and soaked in the silence. He read for about twenty minutes and checked the time on his comm. He was late for dinner. He promised the chief engineer they'd have dinner to go over some specific upgrades. Kris expected it would sound like word salad when the chief explained the new technology, but he needed to approve it. Kris would dutifully sign the work orders while dining on sushi. He had stolen the sushi chef from the Vanguard. He was an artist. Kris was always puzzled why he didn't have his own restaurant.

Kris got up and was about to hand over the conn to Jennifer when she swiveled her chair toward him. He immediately noticed the concern on her face. Jennifer was always cool and even-tempered, but Kris could clearly see that she had panic deep in her eyes.

"We're being tracked."

"What?"

"We're being tracked. It's faint, but it's focused on us."

Kris approached the science station and checked her readings. She was right. Kris thought it might have been the Citaris for a moment and then realized they were receiving real-time telemetry from the Concord. Why would they track them?

"Mariah, see if you can trace it, too."

"Aye, sir," Mariah nodded.

"Okay, everybody, work this," Kris instructed. He stood by the captain's chair, watching his crew in action. He moved around and sat down. "Yellow alert," Kris ordered. The flight deck blinked yellow.

"What's the status?" Kris questioned.

"No location yet," Jennifer answered.

"I want to know where it's coming from. I want shield control transferred to my chair. They should be at full power," Kris demanded.

"I've got a fix. Isolating it," Logan announced.

"Logan?" Kris called.

"Just a minute." Logan worked his panel.

"How fast is it?" Kris asked.

Logan was laboring over his controls to find out who was tracking them. He didn't answer Kris. He was zeroing in on the source and focusing. He adjusted the sensors and nodded to himself as it became clearer to him where the signal was originating from.

"Citari?" Kris guessed hopefully.

"Wrong signature." He didn't look up. "Some distant scans, but rapidly getting stronger."

"So, it's getting closer?" Kris inquired.

"That's right."

"What's our speed, helm?" Kris checked in.

Ensign Rooter, a round-faced man with a haircut that looked like it was made with the assist of a bowl, checked the speed. Kris grimaced. That should have been an instant answer for the helmsman.

"Twenty-five lights."

"Go to fifty. Number One, tell me what's out there."

"Aye," Jennifer said.

"Red alert," Kris ordered.

"Red alert," Mariah affirmed. She hit the red button and the red lights and klaxons blared on.

Kris' eyes were on Jennifer. She was at the science panel. She kept increasing the range, trying to follow the signal to its source. It was still distant.

"Well?" Kris probed impatiently.

"It's out of range. Wait, I got something." Jennifer began to refine her search. She had the shape of the ship. That was everything. All alien ships' designs were in the computer. Once you had the shape you knew who was chasing you. Jennifer found the answer. It was a Gawayan battleship, closing in at seventy-five lights.

"A Gawayan? We've never had contact with Gaway."

"And they're a long way from home," Jennifer added.

"Go to eighty lights!" Kris barked. The ensign punched in the speed. The thumping sound from the drive became more rapid. Kris saw the panel light up, confirming that shield control had been transferred to him.

Agent C came running in. "What's going on?"

"Eighty lights. I'm trying to avoid getting into a fight. Considering we are unarmed, I think that's the smart course of action," Kris said.

"Number One?" Kris said, turning to her.

"They've increased speed. Eighty-two," Jennifer replied without looking back.

Kris couldn't fight in Citari space. They weren't carrying torpedoes, and the disruptors had been disabled. That was part of the arrangement with the Citaris. Kris suspected the Gawayan captain was trying to determine the maximum speed of the Concord. Kris wasn't about to give that information up and he surmised by the slight increase it would buy them time.

"Go to eighty-three," Kris snapped.

The thump of the Alcubierre Drive beat faster. Kris looked at Mariah, who was working her board, trying to hear if there was any chatter from the ship. There was none.

"Mariah, punch in: two, five, eight, five, execute," Kris directed.

"Two, five, eight, five, execute." Mariah punched it in. A Citari message lit up on her panel.

"Communication coming in."

"Put it on screen," Kris commanded.

Jennifer swirled around from her chair and looked to Kris, who stayed focused on the screen as Vichon's faint image appeared. Vichon looked puzzled by the call. It wasn't in the plan. Kris felt fortunate that the Citaris had shared a nanite technology that allowed communications at speeds beyond ten thousand lights.

"Eighty-four," Jennifer announced.

"Eighty-five, ensign," Kris snapped again. The thumping sound sped up.

"Captain Galloway. This channel is only for emergencies," Vichon pronounced.

"I think I've got one. A Gawayan battleship is chasing us, and I have no idea why," Kris explained.

"Do you have the package?" Vichon asked.

"Yes, we were successful."

"I'm dispatching three ships to you as we speak," Vichon related.

"Thank you. Do you know the maximum light speed the Gawayans can go?"

"One hundred and five," he revealed in his scratchy voice. Kris was filled with anxiety. They could only go a max of one hundred lights.

"They increased to eighty-six," Jennifer updated.

"Eighty-seven," Kris urged quietly. Kris realized it was only a matter of time. They couldn't outrun them; they weren't fast enough.

"Captain Galloway, you are at a disadvantage," Vichon said.

"Yeah, I know. I can add," Kris remarked.

"I'm sending you coordinates. Change to this course and drop out of hyperspace at these points. They have the advantage of speed, but you have the advantage of navigation," Vichon said quickly.

"What does that mean?" Kris asked.

"Just go there. It will be apparent," Vichon responded quietly.

Kris got up out of his chair and leaned over Logan, who nodded that he had just received a new course from the Citaris. Kris looked up to Vichon.

"What do we do when we get there?"

"The Gawayans are listening. You'll figure it out," Vichon stated calmly.

The image blinked off and Logan changed the course.

CHAPTER THIRTY-SIX

The Concord came out of hyperspace with the Gawayans only minutes behind them. The ship was making a slow turn when Kris suddenly understood what Vichon had in mind. He stepped up to the screen and smiled. They were headed toward a thick field of the remnants of a long-ago-decimated planet. Large chunks of a former world were scattered hundreds of miles wide and spun silently over a vast field that covered at least five million miles. It was a beautiful sight. They had found cover.

Amanda had come on deck to get some reports signed. Kris heard her enter. "Amanda."

"What?"

"Good timing." He patted the helmsman on the shoulder. "You're relieved. Amanda, get us in there," Kris ordered.

"This is getting to be a bit of a habit," Amanda said while taking over the helm. "What am I doing?" she asked.

"Get us in there. And give us cover," Kris requested.

Kris squatted down beside Amanda. They were rapidly closing in on the debris field. Amanda didn't dare take her eyes off the screen. She punched in an A.I. plot. The bits of debris began to float by the ship in random directions.

"Amanda, get us right in the middle of that," Kris headed back to his chair and flipped on the shields. As they glided in between the remains of the long-gone world, they could hear objects bouncing off the ship. Occasionally, they'd hit a larger object that made them lurch.

Kris got back in his chair.

"Faster," Kris pressed.

"I don't like back seat drivers." Amanda increased the fusion thrust and they sped up until the engines began to vibrate the Concord's hull.

They didn't have full cover yet, and the Gawayan battleship was due in mere minutes.

"I'm increasing to sixty percent," Amanda proclaimed.

"Increasing shields to seventy percent," Kris announced.

Amanda slid the ship into the rocky debris field. "It never gets boring with you, Skipper."

"They just dropped out of hyperspace," Jennifer reported.

The Gawayans arrived at the edge of the debris field and stopped. The ship's torpedo doors opened, but it didn't have a firing solution. The battleship closed in on the field slowly, trying to find an angle of attack. They could only glimpse the Concord as it traveled deeper into the crushed world. The Gawayans fired. A torpedo shot out of the ship, spun toward the field, and slammed into a chunk a thousand miles wide, barely nicking it.

"They fired," Jennifer acknowledged.

"Keep us out of their target. Don't let them lock onto us," Kris instructed.

"There's a ton of crap to hide behind. I'll pull it off," Amanda assured him.

The Gawayan ship began moving sideways. It was moving around the debris field and firing torpedoes randomly. The torpedoes raced toward the debris and impacted, thousands of miles away from the Concord. Then, the battleship changed tactics. They made an arcing maneuver around the entire field while firing a salvo of fourteen torpedoes that slammed into the rolling and spinning debris. The torpedoes each exploded in the debris except for one. It managed to slip through and locked on the Concord.

"We have a target lock," Jennifer called out.

"How long?" Kris checked.

"Thirty seconds."

"We'll see about that," Amanda interjected. "Hold on."

Amanda engaged the fusion engines. She went full thrust and dropped them behind a five-hundred-mile-wide piece of debris. The torpedo tried to arc over the rock, but it was too late. It impacted and blew up with no more than a tiny puff.

Amanda steered them to the other end of the field, putting some distance between them and the Gawayan ship. Amanda noticed the Gawayan scans were missing them.

Jennifer checked her monitors. "They're going over the debris field to the other side."

"I say we mix it up. Keep them chasing us," Amanda suggested.

"I agree," Kris said.

Amanda doubled back the way she came, and the battleship turned around too, firing some lazy shots that bombarded the debris field, but never had a chance of even scratching them.

The game of cat and mouse would go on for two more hours. Kris knew they'd caught a break when the Gawayans turned to firing their disruptors. Clearly, they exhausted their torpedoes. The Gawayans fired salvo after salvo and didn't notice the broad shadow that was appearing behind them. The Citari destroyers had arrived.

The firing stopped, and the Gawayan ship tried make a run for it, but the Citari had already trained all their fire power on the battleship. The Gawayans traveled only briefly before the Citari disruptors slashed through their ship. They were overwhelmed. No one had time to react. They were there one second and gone in the next. They had become another, albeit smaller, part of the debris field.

The explosion was bright and lit up the debris that surrounded the crew of the Concord. The parts of the ship spun away into space. In a matter of minutes there was no trace of the battleship's existence.

"Amanda, get us over to the Citaris," Kris ordered.

"Aye."

"Don't hit anything," Kris advised.

"This is easy as pie. Come on."

Amanda flew the ship free from the debris field, joined the Citari fleet and continued alongside them, dwarfed by the leviathan-sized ships.

The three Citari ships took up protective positions around them. Kris shook his head at the irony. He was being protected by the ships that likely killed many of his friends twelve years ago. But he had to admit to himself, when they appeared, he felt relieved that he and his crew weren't about to die in the vacuum of space.

CHAPTER THIRTY-SEVEN

Kris felt unburdened. He'd flown through the eye of a needle, and pulled it off. He'd seldom been in shooting fights. Kris had mostly shipped out on science and exploration missions in his early years. His self-doubt had waned, and he felt proud he had pulled together a solid team. Kris had chosen wisely. He was fond of his crew, and his crew was fond of him.

They had made the impossible possible.

Kris had a flashback while floating in that debris field. It made his mind drift off to the memories of the friends he lost in the war. He often thought of them as he journeyed through space. He had an idea how they must have felt. Space was no place to die.

He made a mental note to recommend Amanda for promotion to the rank of lieutenant commander. She had been invaluable and saved the ship and the crew with her supreme flying skills. C had outdone herself as well. Kris looked through his pad for what kind of commendation she could receive as he left the flight deck.

He ambled into his quarters, glanced at his bed longingly and plopped onto it. He rested there for a few minutes. Kris was motionless, only aware of his breathing. He scrunched up his nose, repelled by a foul odor. He smelled. The tension of the last three hours left him soaked with sweat. Kris stripped and got in the shower. The warm water streamed over him, washing away all the stench and the fear. He instantly felt better. He turned off the shower and wiped himself dry. Kris donned some shorts and a t-shirt.

Then he noticed something curious. He brought his arm up to eye level. The hairs were standing on end. From his bedroom he heard a soft crackling sound he couldn't identify. He went to see what it was.

Kris came to a sudden stop. Vichon was sitting on the edge of his bed. Kris was startled, but recalled they had teleporting technology. The Citari stood up and offered his hand and Kris took it. Kris swallowed and sat down at his desk. Vichon glanced around his quarters as he spoke. He seemed genuinely interested in Kris Galloway's accommodations.

"Sorry for the intrusion, but I had something sensitive to speak to you about. I couldn't have inquiring eyes or ears, you see. But we need to wait a moment."

"For what?" Kris said.

Vichon's eyes drifted to the door, as did Kris'. He shrugged.

There was a knock, and C blithely entered, as was her way with Kris. She came to a sudden halt and hopped back a little when the door snapped shut behind her. When she saw Vichon, she became a little wobbly. She searched for words, facing the Citari that had almost put her to death. She reached for the door, and the Citari loped toward her with an uneven gait.

"There's nothing to fear, Christina. You have my protection. We were going to speak about something of a sensitive nature, and I thought you needed to be here," Vichon croaked.

"I got a message to be here... It sounded like... you," C explained awkwardly, pointing to Kris.

"I'm sure you did," Kris said knowingly. Kris pulled out a chair for C and she sat close to him with her hands folded in her lap. Kris gestured to Vichon.

"Vichon, you have the floor."

"First, I want to thank you for handling the Doneghan matter. We will escort you back to Moody so there are no further mishaps. Now, to the matter of the Gawayans and their unprovoked attack on you. It was a desperate act. Our intelligence service has been studying Gaway since the war ended. We decoded some messages that took us on a path of discovery. It is only recently that we have gained the full picture," Vichon revealed.

"I barely know of them. I think they run the fourth quadrant," Kris claimed. "But that's all I know. Never been there. We never made contact."

"Yes, well it seems that the Gawayans felt threatened by the idea of a potential alliance between Citari and Earth. They felt the combined power would eventually mean they would be under our control—or that they could possibly be exterminated. So, they acted," Vichon proclaimed.

"Acted?" C asked.

"How?" Kris wondered.

"They made inroads on Earth."

"They've been to Earth?" C questioned.

"Secretly. They found individuals that hated my race. They positioned them for power by making them rich. Then, when they had power, they took control of the Earth Directorate. The Gawayans saw this as an opportunity. They created a perfect storm where someone like Captain Galloway would be ignored. The war between Earth and the Citaris was engineered by the Gawayans," Vichon disclosed. Kris and C were left dazed. C stepped toward Vichon.

"This is incredible," C breathed, stunned.

"As I said, it is very sensitive," Vichon warned.

"Did these Earthers know they were dealing with the Gawayans?"

"Yes. It was a secret cabal," Vichon contended.

"How'd they do it?" C asked.

"It had been in the works, as you say, for ages. Well, before you wrote the Keifer Report. Now Earth had been misbehaving, that is true. We were going to tell you to change your behavior, but what we didn't know was that the Gawayans promised to join the fight against us alongside Earth. But their real plan was to break their promise at the last minute and let Earth be destroyed, with the result being that any Earth-Citari alliance would be crushed. They nearly succeeded, except they never planned on you, Kris. The Gawayans must be aware of The Reason and tried to destroy your ship, so the path to reconciliation would not continue."

"So, these guys aren't done?" Kris blinked.

"Far from it," Vichon uttered warily.

"Wait..."

Kris sat down, thinking he heard too much. He recalled that Severen had hinted at rich elites. It all fit. They had to have been behind the war. The Gawayans built up the power of elite racists and convinced them that they were going to run the galaxy together. They were horribly wrong. They'd been played.

He looked to C. "Severen found out. He told me about some people he made disappear. Doneghan mentioned Haven Soares. I think he was part of it."

C looked pale. Memories flooded her mind. She was usually a small part of a larger op. And, typically, the eventual outcome would be a mystery to her. As she fit the pieces together, it made her numb to her core.

"I had an op on a businessman. I was supposed to get his daily routine down. Uh... Fox, Armin Fox," C remembered quietly.

"He was later killed in an elevator accident," Kris recalled haltingly. C gazed at Kris and dropped her head. She didn't know how to feel. Kris put his arm around her.

"No need to mourn him," Vichon consoled.

"But I..." C started.

"He chose a dangerous path. It was his destiny." Vichon patted her on her shoulder. "Mr. Fox had the political connections that put the plot together. This isn't over. Gawayan spies are planted all over Earth. And they are still funneling money," Vichon stated.

"How do we stand with The Reason?" Kris asked.

"Oh, that hasn't changed. We go forward. Citari law forbids stopping The Reason after the first task has been completed. It must go forward before we can reach the great healing. Many wrongs still need to be righted," Vichon explained.

"No doubt," Kris agreed.

"I will return to my ship and meet you on Moody. This information is not to be shared. Only you and Christina."

"But it seems pertinent," C protested.

"It's dangerous for both of you."

"Why?" C pushed.

"There are people on Earth who would kill rather than have their complicity revealed," Vichon advised.

"Even the President?" Kris checked. Vichon appeared to be in thought as they waited. He loped over to them with his uneven gait, considering this.

"Only the President. You can only tell him. But he must not reveal it to anyone else or he could be in danger. We need more time," Vichon warned.

"Understood," Kris nodded.

Kris and C were both left deep in thought. Kris was realizing he had dealt a blow to not only the Gawayans' hubris, but also a very complex and vast conspiracy. A conspiracy that was still alive with the same desired outcome.

Severen was terminating traitors, likely without sanction. How had he found out? Did he know about the Gawayans? Kris' mind was bursting. The Gawayans knew who he was, and they knew what he did to upset their galactic strategy so long ago.

Kris stood up. "If we come back over the DMZ we have to be armed," Kris reasoned. Vichon paused a moment and gave his statement some thought.

"Yes, I agree, and, in fact, I think you should always have Citari escorts. I will discuss this with the Council. Goodbye Kris, Christina," Vichon finished, turning away from them.

"I have another matter to discuss," Kris continued, moving toward him.

Vichon turned back around. "Certainly."

"When we were on Genusia, we naturally had samples of the Genusians. There was some DNA taken to make sure that the medicine would be compatible. After returning to Earth, our researchers discovered that our DNA was identical to theirs. We even shared familial ties. This, of course, was a shock. Anything you'd like to share with me?" Kris stared at Vichon pointedly.

Vichon was floored by the statement. His mouth hung open and then it snapped shut. Kris feared he knew the truth but wouldn't share. He didn't have to. Vichon was running the show.

Vichon straightened out his slumped body. This was clearly a surprise to him.

"This can be discussed. But I suggest we deal with matters one at a time. We're not done with what's at hand," Vichon counseled diplomatically.

Kris didn't like it, but he had to accept the answer. At least there was a willingness to talk, and he was all but certain that Vichon had answers.

"I understand," Kris confirmed simply, and bowed.

Vichon bowed back to him and crossed in front them, pacing.

"I didn't think this was part of your mission?" Vichon commented with a hint of dismay.

"It wasn't. Like I said, it's a protocol. The information just popped up in their studies. It was shared with me. But only me. But the truth is going to get out," Kris cautioned. Vichon seemed pensive. C suspected he was hiding something seismic.

"As I said, we aren't done with our major task yet," Vichon concluded curtly.

"True."

Vichon took out two slender silver beams from his pocket and held one in each hand. He then dematerialized. Kris' quarters were filled with a crackling sound, sending the hair on his arms on end. C's hair suddenly frizzed from the energy and then settled down dropping to her shoulders.

C collapsed on a chair. Kris seemed absorbed in thought. There was a long silence between them as they both took in Vichon's words. Kris shook his head and then his eyes met with C's.

"We can tell no one about the Gawayans," Kris began.

"Well, the President. But other than that, not a living soul. But we've already got a problem," C pondered.

"What?"

"Severen." C looked at Kris directly.

"What about him?"

"Severen will be suspicious. He'll want answers. He's reading our telemetry. He knows we went way off course while we were heading to Moody. He'll want to know why. He can't know that we know. Think about this. Is he taking out traitors or is he cleaning up his own mess?" C worried.

"Okay, I'll have you banned from seeing him. As for me, I can change the conditions. If he wants me to fly again. If there's any contact, it must be with someone else. Not him," Kris insisted.

"He's gonna ask why?"

"I'll say I don't trust him," Kris answered flatly.

"Kris, I.I. is still a powerhouse. You don't have the juice to pull it off. And what about the crew? They'll know we had a scuffle with the Gawayans. We gotta make them off limits, too. How are you gonna do all that?" Agent C asked.

"I know someone who can get us everything we want," Kris said.

"Who?"

"Mariah."

CHAPTER THIRTY-EIGHT

Doneghan was floating. He was on a sea that was milky white. It was serene. It was silent. He sat up and then stood on the creamy sea. There wasn't any wind. He could see no shore. The sky was the same color as the sea, and there were no clouds. Just white. His eyes were drawn to his right, and he saw a swollen, milky bubble float past him. He touched it, and it popped. He watched the gooey substance drip from his fingers.

He looked around and called, "Hello?"

There was no response.

"Is anybody there?"

Nothing.

"Where am I?"

Doneghan's attention was drawn to the shore. It was moving. Then he realized it wasn't the shore. He was moving. He sat up, reaching around to his sides, but his hands merely dipped into the whiteness. He was moving in long circles. Doneghan couldn't imagine where he was. He stood up and he could see the spin was becoming more rapid. He could tell he was in a wide loop and the shore was starting to become a blur. What planet was he on? How did he get here? How could he walk on this white water? Doneghan heard a sound that reminded him of a toilet draining. His right leg dropped, uneven with the other. As he spun, he shuddered, seeing himself being drawn into a whirlpool. He tried to run, but he slipped and fell prone. Around and around, he went. *Am I in hell?* he wondered. Doneghan was getting dizzy. He tried to scramble along the surface, but to no avail. He was being sucked into the whirlpool. His lungs were filling with the creamy substance. He was drowning.

That's when he woke up.

Doneghan's eyes were heavy. He forced them open. Everything looked blurry. He was chilly all over from a freezing cold breeze washing over his chest. He shivered like a quake was rushing through him. His vision improved and he realized he was naked. He tried to move, but he couldn't. He couldn't understand why? Then it became apparent. His arm was strapped in. He was in a rack-like device. Doneghan saw he had wires implanted in his nipples. He noticed the trickle of dried blood. He could feel the wires in his buttocks. He fearfully peeked down and saw them going into his genitals.

"What is this?"

His lip began to quiver. He cried openly as tears streamed down his face. It was the first time he had tears. Not of regret. He shed tears for himself, that he'd been caught. There was a thrill to his omnipotence. He yearned for the past that brought him so much joy.

The woman he murdered after having sex with her. All he could see was her surprised brown eyes. He remembered laughing in a blood-covered bed. Doneghan had wanted to see what it was like. He liked it. It made him feel stronger, he thought. Doneghan remembered it felt like he ate her soul.

He cried until it turned into a hacking cough.

Then a drone with a viewscreen dropped in front of him. The screen popped on with the wild-eyed, grinning image of the host inches from him. He jerked back.

"No, no, no, no," Doneghan blubbered.

"He's awake. It's time for the show to begin." The sound of approving wails came from the screen. He realized he had an audience. Doneghan didn't know what was going on or who was watching him. What was this madness he was part of? What was going to happen to him?

"Show? What the hell is this?" Doneghan said through tears.

"It's Moody's number one digi, *The Torture Show*, Doneghan, and you're the star!" The host cocked her head to the right in a charming way.

Doneghan heard something. Someone was in the room, but he couldn't see them. The salt in his eyes from his tears blurred his vision. They stung, and he couldn't wipe them. He couldn't move. But he could hear heavy footsteps.

"Who's there? I can't see."

"We can't allow that, can we?" the host said brightly.

A tube on an armature swung around toward his face, shot water in his eyes, then sucked the water away. Doneghan blinked his eyes. The stinging had stopped, and he could see clearly again.

"We don't want you to miss this, Doneghan."

Multiple heavy footsteps echoed in the darkness around him. Doneghan realized whoever was in the room was getting closer. He got glimpses of them as they stepped through beams of light. He heard metal clanking against metal. Then there was the smell, sickening, like a rotting corpse.

The footsteps drew closer. He could hear the long, heavy strides coming down with a clump.

There were men lurking in the darkness. They stepped into the light, revealing they were holding all matter of torture devices. Mallets, knives, whips made out some unknown alloy. Their beards were long, as was their hair. They were all naked and numbered five. Their skin was purple. They were scarred all over their bodies. Doneghan's eyes became wide, and terror filled him. This couldn't be happening.

"Noooooo." He tried to wriggle but he was locked in tight.

"Let's start with home audience voting," the host announced cheerfully.

"Voting?" His eyes went to the drone.

"Yes. They all get to vote," the host said eagerly.

"All?"

"The planet and four surrounding worlds are watching. They vote on what torture they'd like to see. The votes are coming in."

"Already?"

"Yes, and we have a winner. Your genitalia. It's so funny, that's always number one," the host laughed.

The torturers approached and moved into position.

"Please don't do this. Please don't do this," Doneghan begged.

The drone swooped down on him.

"I guess you shouldn't have killed a hundred thousand people." Cheers spilled out of the drone as the host laughed.

Doneghan would scream for the next sixteen hours until he reached his limit. He would pass out from the pain, but he'd be awakened by an injection, and it would start all over again. They would let him sleep for eight hours. His only peace. But at dawn, he'd wake up and be force fed. The show would come on again. Seven days a week.

Doctors would make sure to keep him alive because he was the highest rated show in the Moody system.

CHAPTER THIRTY-NINE

Kris snagged a dinner tray in the galley. He grabbed a couple of hamburgers and a hot dog, like a man starved. His eyes darted to a steaming bowl of chili and he smiled greedily, snatching that, too. He saw Mariah eating alone and bounded over to her. He dropped his tray on the table and sat with a thump. Kris tore into his burger and glanced at Mariah, smiling. He polished off the burger and audibly groaned in delight. He swallowed and noticed the silence at the table. Mariah was picking at her food. She seemed somber. There was something wrong. Mariah didn't even look at him. She just stared at her salad mournfully.

Kris kept eating, but his chewing slowed as he continued observing Mariah, taking in her mood. This was concerning to him, and the chili could wait. He rested his spoon back on the tray, wiped his mouth, and washed down his dinner with a tall glass of ice water. "Oh, uh, by the way, good job," Kris said.

"Thanks."

"Glad you talked me into taking you onboard," he added before chomping on his hot dog.

"I'm grateful," she responded, still somberly staring down at her plate, repetitively pushing her food around—as though the half-hearted action could fool anyone into believing that she had even the slightest interest in eating right now.

Kris finished chewing and swallowed, taking a moment to pause as he inhaled deeply and gathered his thoughts. Resting his hands on the table, he leaned in and looked at Mariah. "You look low," he observed with measured concern in his voice.

"Yeah."

"Mission-over blues?" Kris guessed sympathetically.

"Something like that," Mariah admitted.

"Going back to your life?"

"If you want to call it that. I mean, I feel alive out here. I have to go back to something so alien to me."

"Who says you have to? You did great out here. You saved the day. Look, it's obvious I have a lot of pull. I can get you back your wings permanently," Kris offered.

"I've got a boyfriend. It's complicated."

"The antimatter physics guy?" Kris asked. "You like him?"

"He's all I've got."

"Take him with you," Kris shrugged.

"He's got a job."

"Like I said, I've got a lot of pull. Look, I can't guarantee a flight every year, but I don't think this is over. Not by a long shot. I thought I could hide from all this, but I don't think I'm done, and I'd like you at my side next time," Kris said.

"Yeah, but you'll keep me tucked in my bed during the tough ones."

"You bet I will. I need that giant brain of yours."

"Okay. Thank you, Kris."

Kris began eating again, and Mariah started devouring hers happily. Kris looked up from his food and laughed, shaking his head. Mariah stopped her fork of food midway to her mouth, puzzled by what Kris thought was so funny.

"When Vichon said that you were in the same club because you had planets named after the both of you... The look on your face—priceless," Kris recalled with a smile.

"He made it sound like there was more than just the two of us."

"That he did."

Kris went back to eating. The mission was over, but he wasn't completely satisfied. Vichon had never told him the truth about the Genusians. It had stayed at the back of his mind.

There was a mystery, and only Vichon had the answer.

Kris' quarters were large, but utilitarian. The space never had a homey feel. He picked up a picture of his wife and kids. He missed them. He knew he was doing good work, but he preferred going home at night. He'd be with them soon.

He threw back his covers and got into bed, pulling the covers back up to his chest as he settled into a comfortable position. He had some tea next to him and sipped it, then added more sugar. He looked out his porthole. One of the Citari escorts was keeping pace a half mile away. It made him feel safe. It made him feel like he could sleep.

The comm went on, "Captain. You have a communication."

"From whom?"

"Vichon."

"Put him through."

"Galloway?" Vichon's voice rang out.

"Yes."

"We should talk about the other matter," Vichon said quietly.

"I think we should." Kris sat up, nodding.

"Not like this, though."

"How then?"

"On Citari." Kris wasn't sure if he heard him right. No human had ever stepped foot on Citari. Whatever the truth was, Vichon had to tell it on his home turf.

"You want us to come to Citari?"

"Yes, this should be discussed where we know no one is listening," Vichon advised.

The humans and the Citaris had engaged and played nice at first. Treaties were signed over the years, but never on Citari. They had never been invited, and the Citaris made it quite clear that humans needed an invitation. People had made attempts, but were dissuaded by Citari battle cruisers.

Kris sent a message to Jennifer, C, Logan, and Mariah. They rushed to his quarters. Kris' eyes drifted around the room. This was his inner circle. This was his team. These were his people.

"We're going to Citari," Kris announced.

"That's what the call was about?" Jennifer exclaimed in disbelief.

"Yeah."

"Are we in trouble?" Logan worried.

"I became aware of something. As you'll be with the landing party, you should know, too." Kris stood up, held his hands behind his back and paced across the room.

"What's this about?" Logan asked.

"The Genusians. We share DNA with them."

CHAPTER FORTY

Citari was at the edge of the galaxy. The Citaris were rumored to have journeyed to other nearby galaxies, but nothing could be confirmed. They were an advanced civilization whose age was pure speculation.

The trip to the Citari home world was a long one. It was ten days. They had nearly reached Citari when the Directorate called. Kris went into his ready room with C and saw the flickering image of Hale that was racing across the galaxy with the help of nanites, particles warped at two hundred times the speed of light. Hale was one of the top leaders in the Earth Directorate. Kris had always found him congenial. He was a former astronaut during his early star faring days. They had shipped out on numerous occasions. Luckily for Hale, he had taken a desk job on Earth, so he was spared from the war. Kris adjusted the image and tweaked the sound until it was clear.

"Captain."

"Hale."

"What's going on? Well, Kris. How can I put this? The Directorate feels like you're stonewalling them."

"I am," Kris admitted.

"What?"

"The Citaris called, and I'm going. They're listening to us right now," Kris cautioned.

"What's the subject of the meeting?" Hale asked.

"Hale, he didn't want it spoken over communications," Kris revealed.

"So, you know what this is about?"

"Yes, I do," Kris affirmed.

"Obviously, you can't say."

"That's right," Kris agreed.

"Is this at all dangerous?" Hale asked.

"I don't think so."

Hale leaned back in his chair, his camera tracking with his movements. Kris eyed Hale. Kris kept a poker face as Hale leaned forward and stared at Kris pointedly.

"On another matter. Your previous mission plot seemed to change," Hale observed.

"I'm sorry, I can't comment, but rest assured the mission was completed to everyone's satisfaction. Citari relations are becoming... warm. That's the objective, right?" Kris responded.

"So, mum on that, too."

"That is correct, sir. They have bigger guns, and we're just guests."

"I don't like being in the dark," Hale grumbled. "All right, keep me updated the best you can."

"Oh, there is something else," Kris said.

"What's that?

"You know Dr. Ed Weiss?"

"Yes."

"Tell Ed I told you to contact him and let him know I'm going to get the answer."

"I will."

Hale's image turned off.

Kris' eyes met with C's who gave him a silent clap and landed in a chair, crossing her legs. Kris smiled and did a tiny bow for her. He rose up and wandered around the room, seeming amused.

"Well done," C congratulated.

"Thanks," Kris smirked, staring out a porthole at a Citari cruiser keeping pace with them.

"So, this is really about the Genusians?" C said.

"Yeah. Seems so. You saw how Vichon reacted when I told him. He was totally off guard. He didn't expect I'd know anything about this," Kris pointed out.

"Maybe that's why he wants us to come. Maybe he'll hold us so no one will ever know," C said, concerned.

"That's why I told Hale about Weiss. They'll know the truth by the end of the day," Kris admitted.

CHAPTER FORTY-ONE

D r. Weiss walked into Camp David. He tried to take in the history, but Higgs was rushing him into the living room. When Weiss entered, he noticed it was teeming with scientists. Several were Nobel Prize winners. These were the top men and women in their fields. Weiss couldn't help but feel out of place amongst these giants.

Weiss sat down on a leather couch across from his fellow academics. Hale entered wearing a seersucker suit. He sat next to Weiss, who clapped him on the shoulder and shook his hand. Severen slipped in and took an inconspicuous seat in the back. Weiss glanced at the notes in his folder. He didn't need them. He knew what he had to say. Weiss was just nervous. *Why wouldn't he be,* he thought to himself.

"How was the flight?" Hale asked.

"Quiet." Not only was Weiss feeling inadequate, he also felt completely out of place. He was a low-level academic. He was uneasy and slightly fidgety. Hale glanced at Weiss' right leg jumping nervously.

"Just take a deep breath," Hale said.

"Is it that obvious?"

"Yes."

Weiss took a deep breath and exhaled. It didn't help.

President Furrow came swaggering in, puffing on a long cigar with a glass of whiskey in his hand. Weiss could feel his big, bold personality sweeping into the room like a hurricane. Furrow glanced around, confused.

"Which one of you eggheads is Dr. Weiss?"

"I am, sir." Weiss began to rise from the long leather couch.

"No, set yourself on down. Hale, scoot your ass over."

Furrow plopped down next to Weiss and stamped his cigar out in an ashtray, then he took one last shot of whiskey and handed the glass to Hale as though he was his waiter. Furrow was right up in Weiss' face.

"Now, Doctor, you have one of the damnedest tales I have ever heard."

"It's a first, that's for sure," Weiss said.

"How'd you discover this?"

"First observation of the patients on Genusia. We didn't know much about them. As you know, we had been forbidden to go there. But when the outbreak occurred, the Citaris were certain we had the answer," Weiss replied.

"So, you think they knew the Genusians were human?" Furrow raised his eyebrows.

"Most likely."

"How could this happen, Doctor?" Furrow asked.

Dr. Fenton from Harvard interrupted. He clasped his hands and leaned forward, pushing his glasses up his nose. "We must remember these tests have only been done once. Perhaps we should be more thorough with this..."

"Dr. Fenton," the President started. "Why is it that when someone makes a discovery, there's somebody else itching to disprove it?"

Furrow stared Fenton down, then returned his attention to Dr. Weiss. "You were saying, Dr. Weiss."

"Look, I fully realize the implications of what I'm suggesting," Weiss continued.

"And that is?" Furrow said.

"That we have to consider our species may have been placed here." Weiss revealed. He was met by stunned silence.

"Placed here?" Furrow repeated.

"Yes, by an alien race." Furrow went silent mulling Weiss' words. New information was always a political calculus. He stared pointedly at Dr. Weiss.

"That does raise implications," Furrow mumbled, sitting back.

"Especially in religious circles," Higgs nodded, clearing his throat.

"Why would aliens take people and plant them on another planet?" Furrow pondered.

"It's pure speculation. You find a race whose star is about to go supernova. The inhabitants may be primitive, and to save them from themselves the Citaris decide to move them to a safer world. There are many possibilities. But it doesn't explain why we're here and they are there," Weiss theorized nervously.

Dr. Helen Duran from Boston University was the first to jump on the Dr. Weiss bandwagon. She brightened and leaned forward, speaking in her cultured Boston Brahmin voice.

"Interesting. Or perhaps an accident."

"Accident?" the President said.

"A starship crash lands thousands of years ago..."

Weiss nodded. "That's as viable as anything. The galaxy is so old, we have no idea what other civilizations have sprouted up and advanced."

Furrow rose and moved to his bar. He threw some ice in a glass and splashed in some whiskey. He rattled the drink in his hand to cool it off as he ambled back over to Weiss. Furrow was six foot three and thickly built. Weiss felt he was imposing, but the President seemed to be taking him seriously.

"Well, we need more information. We need a study. Dr. Duran, you seem to get this business. I'm tasking that to you. Dr. Weiss, you're near Boston," Furrow said.

Some of the scientists' faces fell, but Dr. Duran beamed. "Yes."

"You don't mind moving, do you?" Furrow turned to Weiss.

"No, sir."

"Good, then it's all set. We'll regroup here when Captain Galloway is back."

"Thank you."

Within days, Dr. Weiss found himself in an apartment on Beacon Hill that was paid for. He had an oversized salary, a group of Ph.D. candidates and Dr. Duran at his disposal.

Dr. Ed Weiss was no longer anonymous.

CHAPTER FORTY-TWO

Citari was a bright green world complimented by four grey moons. The Concord was orbiting with its Citari escorts. The shuttle bay doors slid open, and the Genesis made its way down to the capitol city of Citari, Venga. As the shuttle approached the city, Kris stared in awe at the vast metropolis. No two buildings were alike. Some were twisted like a pretzel, others spun like a top. There were green buildings and clear ones. Mariah was next to him, gazing out.

"Stunning," Mariah said.

"I know. Looks like I got you a bonus planetfall."

"I'll take it," she replied beaming.

The streets were packed with Citari people. Air cars zipped above and below them. Mariah's eyes greedily took in the exotic city. It was a sight she could never describe. She crowded Jennessy for a better look as he watched the readouts for the landing. Jennessy glanced up at her, annoyed.

"You mind?" Jennessy grumbled.

"Sorry." Mariah sat back down in her seat as they began to land.

The shuttle set down on a glowing white landing pad that lay before a sprawling building. They would learn this was the Great

Hall of Citari. It was grand and ornate, made of silver and gold. A spire reached up about sixty feet. The doors to it were immense and clear.

After the shuttle landed, the hatch opened. Kris, Mariah, Logan, Jennifer, and C stepped out. They stood on the ramp. Kris nudged Mariah.

"Oh, go ahead, you be the first."

"I have all the notoriety I need. You go first," Mariah invited.

"I insist," Kris urged.

C elbowed past them and jumped to the ground. She stood defiantly, arms akimbo, on the shiny green pebbled surface of Citari. "First woman." Kris laughed, and Logan rushed past him. He jumped off the ramp and landed next to C. "First man."

Mariah and Kris laughed, privately knowing that the other two would regret it.

Kris noticed six Citari guards approaching them. They moved in unison descending the steps. Five of them stopped. The tallest guard walked up to Kris and offered his hand. He nodded to the others,

"You are Galloway?"

"I am."

"Follow me," he beckoned in his scratchy intonation. The Citari turned and headed up the steps. Kris led the way with Jennifer at the rear. They headed up the steps to the Great Hall and entered into the hallowed building.

The first thing Kris noticed were the thirty-foot-tall statues of Citaris. They were yellowish in color and too many to count. This part of the hall stretched at least a hundred yards, as their history was long. Longer than Earth's, as he suspected. Kris surmised these were statues of former Citari leaders.

They reached the end and saw a lone figure coming out of a tall door. As they drew closer, they could see it was Vichon. He stopped and waited. They kept moving. Kris looked around and then back to the Citari leader. The guards stopped, and the team moved past them and slowed, reaching Vichon.

"Nice place you got here," Kris complimented.

"It was two hundred thousand Earth years in the making," Vichon smiled proudly.

"Thanks for the invitation," Kris said.

"This won't take long. I had to reveal this in the most secure place possible," Vichon explained.

"We appreciate that," Kris admitted.

"The Council feels that the truth should come out. Captain Galloway, the Genusians are human, and we put them there," Vichon stated frankly.

Kris, C, Logan, Mariah, and Jennifer stood in stunned silence. Kris swallowed a little, thrown off. He raised his eyebrows and looked to the others. They seemed equally astounded. There was a long silence as this sunk in.

"You did?" Logan said.

"Yes. Earth had been under our microscope for an extensive period of time. We observed an instance in your early times where the males were fighting and killing each other at such a great rate that humanity reached near extinction. We took it upon ourselves to transplant humans to Genus Major. No intelligent life had sprouted up there, so it was ideal. We gave them a better value system. They outlawed war and grew peacefully. We were able to compare your progress with theirs to give us guidelines."

"Guidelines?" C questioned.

"Yes, on how to transplant a species when need be. And to see what defects the species has."

"So, we're defective, and they're not," Kris clarified.

"You are... in the middle?" Vichon explained.

"What does that mean?" Mariah asked.

Kris knew what it meant. Vichon didn't have to elaborate. There was another planet. They had moved humans to other worlds.

"I think Galloway can answer that," Vichon said slyly.

"There's more than one world. We only found one. And I don't think he's going to tell us where they are."

"Correct. Genusians have done fine without you. Some other planets have turned out poorly. I wouldn't advise making contact."

"What am I supposed to do with this?" Kris said.

"You may share the information. There will be more to share, but understand the council must review and debate our next steps. We just ask for patience."

Vichon hosted them as they toured Citari. He had revealed that there were more revelations to come. Their time on Citari was short, but the invitation made Kris feel that an Earth-Citari alliance held promise. After two days, the Citaris escorted the Concord back to the DMZ. As they headed back to Earth, Kris' mind was swirling.

CHAPTER FORTY-THREE

Severen stared at the telemetry data for the tenth time. He could see the Concord had taken an odd change of course, and there was a rendezvous with some Citari vessels. It looked like they had been escorted. But none of it fit the planned course. Severen couldn't decipher what had occurred out there.

The Concord had traveled to Citari for a day and then headed back. Severen leaned back in his chair, closing his eyes, trying to reason an answer. He sat there for a few minutes, but nothing came.

He'd received word the mission was successful, but something else went on out there. It hadn't been smooth. A detection unit on the edge of the DMZ thought they picked up an explosion but couldn't confirm the nature of the disturbance. The only thing they were certain of was that the Concord had been nearby.

Howard, a bearded young analyst of twenty-four, stepped in the room and looked at his pad. He seemed frustrated. Clearly, he'd been trying to decipher the meaning of the telemetry, too. He had consulted with his colleagues for the better part of the afternoon and ran into roadblock after roadblock. Howard had no answers and was walking into an office that always demanded them. He stared at the pad.

"Can't make head or tails of it," Howard stated.

"Something happened. We'll have to interview the crew," Severen said, resigned.

"That's not gonna happen. Word just came down from the President. They are all off limits."

"What?" Severen snapped.

"Don't bite my head off. Furrow ordered it. I just received an executive order."

"What does Furrow know? How did this happen?" Severen blurted out.

"That's just it. I have a source in the White House. The President got a call from a secure channel, and we got shut down."

Severen snapped the pencil in his hand and got up. He paced the room like a bull in an arena about to take on a matador. Severen closed the door. He turned on the room scrambler and planted his knuckles on the desk, leaning on them.

"They must know," Severen said firmly.

"How would they find out? C never knew anything," Howard insisted.

"She was part of one of the ops. She didn't push any buttons. What if they all know? How do we keep this quiet? Okay, we can't do anything rash. We do very soft checks on them, nothing they'll notice. Keep a record of who they're seeing, where they are going, when they're back. Funnel everything directly to me. The last thing I need is for the President to get wind of this. He'd use it for sure."

"But your hands aren't dirty."

"I don't know if they are. That's just it. Who was pulling the strings? I don't want them to know that I know."

"We haven't found all of them," Howard reported.

"We will. I just need more time."

"And the journey to Citari…"

"I have an idea about that," Severen said confidently.

———

Mariah sat in a brown leather chair, tapping her fingers on the arm. She was surrounded by the inner circle of White House aides. Kris stood in the middle of the room recounting the events. Mariah noticed that most of the officials' mouths were hanging open in a unified gape. Kris read from a pad, not looking up even for a moment. Mariah sat up, knowing that his speech was nearly over. After all, she had written it. Kris finished and put down his pad. Mariah noticed the silence. There were no questions, as the report answered them. Mariah watched the officials rise, stunned. Mariah noticed the President was deep in thought. She approached him, pulled him aside and thanked him for his help with I.I.

"Mariah, that was my pleasure."

"Thank you."

"You sure were busy out there," Furrow commented curiously.

"We were."

Kris was lingering nearby. Mariah hesitated for a moment. She knew she had to make the introduction to the President. Mariah urged Kris over. Kris came up between them. The President stepped back, staring at Kris.

"Mr. President, this is Captain Galloway," Mariah said. Furrow greeted him, shaking his hand. "Well, you're one tough customer, Captain," the President said with a broad, genuine smile.

"That I am. Mr. President, can I speak to you about something told to me by the Citaris that really has to stop with you?"

"This was the matter you spoke of to get the executive order?" Furrow wondered.

"Yes, sir."

"Certainly. Let's go to my office." Mariah led the way. Mariah noticed a few aides tried to follow them. Mariah and Furrow's eyes locked. Without looking at the aides, he waved them off. Mariah watched the President's arm flap around, urging Kris to catch up with him. They headed into the Oval Office and slammed the door behind them.

Furrow moved to a couch and Kris joined him. The office had been perfectly preserved. It was over four hundred years old. The history in the room was overwhelming. Kris clasped his hands together.

"Now, I know all about Genusia. Don't know how we'll handle this..." Furrow began.

"What you don't know is the Citaris transplanted them from here," Kris explained. "And I suspect the story doesn't end there," Kris added. Furrow sat back, shaking his head. "This is gonna get out. Don't know how people are gonna take it."

"You mean the hardliners."

"They are still lurking out there," Furrow warned.

"Mr. President the Citaris have uncovered that the hardliners are the ones who instigated the war. They were financed by the Gawayans," Kris said solemnly. "They pushed us into the war thinking the Gawayans would join them to defeat the Citaris, but the Gawayans wanted us destroyed so we would never become allies with the Citaris. And when I was out there, a Gawayan ship attacked the Concord."

"Good God."

"The Citaris came to our rescue and briefed Lieutenant Terranova and me. They said there are still active agents for the Gawayan cause working here now. They felt you should know that classified info. It shouldn't be made known to anyone else," Kris added.

Furrow went pale and went up to his bar, poured a shot of whiskey and gulped it down. He wandered back over to Kris.

"Hardliners have been dropping like flies. Strange accidents. The Citaris?"

"No, sir. You see why only you can know."

"But how do I take action?" Furrow said.

"I don't know. But there was a conspiracy here and they are trying to reconstitute it. Vichon wanted you to know."

"He said that?"

"Yes, sir."

"My predecessors were run out on a rail. Rightfully so, it turns out. Traitors. Speaker of the House became president for eight months 'til I came along. I could call the attorney general and tell him to take a long look at them. That wouldn't be revealing anything, would it? See where it leads."

"That wouldn't compromise Vichon's wishes," Kris agreed.

"Thank you, Captain. I'll keep you informed. You have a direct channel to me."

"Thank you, sir."

Mariah watched Kris rise from the couch and head out of the Oval Office past some eager aides. Mariah glanced back at Furrow, who was sprawled on his chair, his fingers tapping on his chin.

CHAPTER FORTY-FOUR

The sand squished beneath Kris' bare feet. It had been six months since the White House meeting. Mariah and Aaron took a hopper from New York to Houston. Mariah had sold her penthouse and a bought a home in the Houston suburbs. Aaron had nervously proposed, and she had cheerfully accepted. They had been married for a week by the time they stepped into their new home, a modest house on one acre.

The pair had jobs at NASA and would drive into work together. She was part of the Astronaut Corps, and he was working in anti-matter propulsion. There were no adoring crowds at the manned spacecraft center. There was only work. Mariah wasn't out traveling to the stars, but she was among her people.

C crewed as security on the Valiant for missions with Captain Arliss. Due to their success on Moody, the Citaris had allowed Earth to have safe passage in one hundred more light years of space. C visited other worlds as they carried out scientific missions of discovery.

Kris didn't join them. He went back to Modesto, to Mindy and the kids. He returned to his life. They'd been in Fiji for two weeks and thoughts of the Citaris and the grand conspiracy drifted away with the Fiji trade winds. Kris allowed himself to be free. He felt he had fought to protect the churning ocean that raged before him. He turned away from the sea and headed toward Mindy, who was in a chair trying to read a magazine whose pages kept snapping in the wind. He never kept secrets from Mindy, but the Gawayan plot Vichon shared would stay locked up tight. He made sure that Severen was banned from contact with C. It was a big lift to keep I.I. away from the crew and C, but the executive order held strong. The President was on their side and Mariah gave them the opening.

All of this made Severen suspicious. He would put two and two together, as he always did. He would realize in the long run he shouldn't have risked her life. C was a big loss for Severen and a gain for Kris. Kris' demand was part of the executive order. All contact with him would be through someone other than Severen. Severen had fumed, but he had no choice.

Kris arrived at the manned spacecraft center and strode past the Saturn five without glancing at it. He was late. It was C's birthday and she had called him two nights before to see if he'd be in town. Kris was due for a meeting a few days later and opted to move up his schedule for her.

He stepped into the facility and slowed, noticing the Mariah statue had been taken down. Mariah worked here now; she must have asked them to remove it. He was glad they had listened. Kris ran to the conference room. About thirty people were gathered around C. He saw Amanda and Logan were in the group. They were faced away from him. Jennifer Arliss was seated, sipping some champagne. Jennessy was carrying the cake while Harry Clark was lighting the candles.

Kris slowed to a stroll. Presents were piled up on a conference table and, by the looks of it, C had made a good haul. C was glowing and giddy. C glanced at him and gave him a frenzied wave to come over. The group broke into "Happy Birthday." Their collective singing skills were underwhelming.

As Kris moved toward C, he thought to himself that C had blossomed. C had come out of the shadows and into the light. Kris certainly had a hand in resurrecting her, but likely that power was always inside her. He wondered what had made her cold. Who had damaged her? Someone must have and put her on a darker path. He'd like to know who it was. He suspected it was something about Agent H.

C broke past her friends and ran up to Kris, hugging him. C seemed vibrant, renewed, and centered. She stepped back from him, smiling.

"Thanks for coming," C smiled.

"Wouldn't have missed it," Kris answered.

"Did Mindy come?" C asked, glancing past him.

"Not this time. Hear you've been star hopping," Kris said.

"Nothing as exciting as traveling with you."

"I can live without the excitement."

"Come get some cake."

"Sure, sure," Kris chuckled.

She went back to her well-wishers. C started opening presents, to her delight. She tore through the wrapping paper, sending paper and ribbon carelessly to the floor. Charlie Borrick scrambled to pick it up and tuck it in the trash. He would find himself compulsively cleaning up after her as she tore through her presents like a seven-year-old.

Kris saw Mariah squeezing out of the well-wishers. Aaron was following her, and they approached Kris. Kris shot out his hand.

Mariah nudged Aaron forward so hard he nearly stumbled. Aaron shook Kris' hand and Mariah gave him a quick hug.

"Kris, this is Aaron," Mariah blurted.

"Ah, the lucky man. Heard a lot about you," Kris said, letting go of his hand.

"Nice to meet you," Aaron glanced back at Mariah, making sure he was saying everything she told him to say to Kris. She nodded at him. "I wanted to thank you for getting me into NASA. It's been a great opportunity," Aaron chattered politely.

"Think nothing of it. So, how are things?" Kris asked.

"Much better," Mariah beamed. She clutched Aaron's hand, glad her slightly awkward beau had recited her words to Kris to a T.

Kris felt a warm feeling. This was the kind of good he liked to spread. The pair wandered away. He was at ease. He'd been back for five months and had fallen back into his routine. He'd consulted on a mission to a moon orbiting Mariah that they planned to terraform. He kept his toe in NASA by joining the Goldilocks Committee that met once a month. It was an excuse to reconnect with his crew and friends.

Kris glanced over at the cake and couldn't resist. He got in line and scooped up a rather thick slice and grabbed a fork. He found some chairs lined up against the wall, sat down and dug in. Kris craved cake. It was, after all, the perfect food. Another man with a smaller slice with some ice cream on the side sat near him. The man poked at his plate, trying to get the right ratio of ice cream to cake for each bite. Kris noticed and smiled.

"Trying to get the right ratio?"

"You have to," the man laughed.

"Good stuff."

The man nodded and glanced at the crowd. They were all around C and she looked quite happy. She had friends who genuinely liked her. C had a life. The man pointed at her with his fork with a piece of cake sticking to it.

"She seems so much happier here," the man said.

"Yeah." Kris squinted his eyes at the man.

"She was a good agent." The man looked at Kris pointedly. Kris put his fork down and sighed. The man moved over next to Kris. Kris should have noticed. I.I. was radiating from him.

"We need your help with The Reason," the man murmured.

"What about my condition? The second emblem?" Kris asked.

"It will be assigned during the flight. That's Vichon talking, not me."

Kris crossed his legs and bit his lip slightly. The sugary taste in his mouth vanished. Kris was nervous. He had secrets to keep. Secrets that had to stay buried. Kris knew he had to remain the cool customer. Kris stood, put down his cake on a chair and looked at the agent stoically.

"Send me the particulars. I want the same crew."

Kris walked away and joined the party like nothing happened. The man headed out a side door. He would send a coded message to Severen indicating they were a go.

Kris watched C opening presents, but that wasn't where his mind was. To his surprise, he was itching to get out amongst the stars again. An explorer never loses that urge, he realized. He accepted it.

Kris also had his own mission. He suspected Genus Major was not the only case of humans transplanted around the galaxy by the Citaris. He wanted to find them, and he wanted to reconnect Earth with the Genusians. They were their brethren. And there was the question of the humans who Vichon insisted that Earthers had to stay away from for their own good. Kris had many questions he wanted answered. Maybe it was his destiny. Maybe everything happened the way it did because there was more to be done. Maybe his career was meant to be sidelined. He was somehow unique to the human timeline. It was a sobering thought that events were mostly out of his control.

Part Three

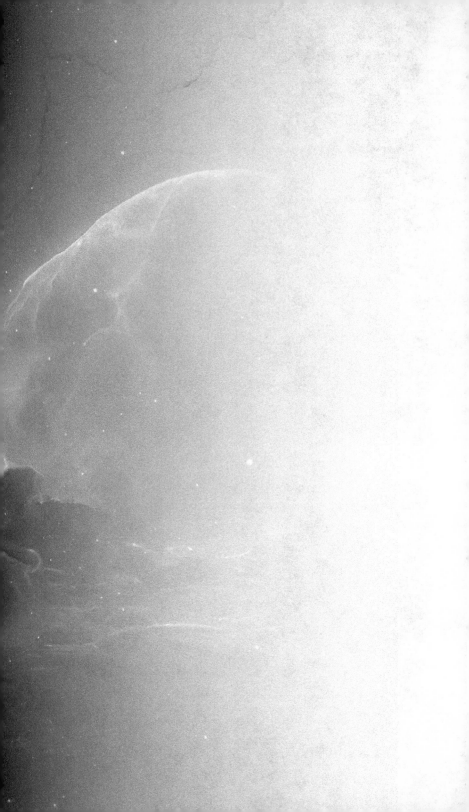

CHAPTER FORTY-FIVE

The Concord had been past the DMZ for two weeks. The ship had been at maximum power at one hundred lights. It was on course, but its destination was unknown, even to Kris Galloway. The team had been rapidly assembled with only a course given and no destination. As far as they could tell, they were headed into deep space where there were no planets or stars.

Kris Galloway's eyes were tired and sagging as he sat in the command chair. It was his first time back on the bridge in two days. They were headed into the unknown. It was as unsettling for him as it was for his crew. They looked to him for answers, but he didn't have any.

Kris wondered if the Citaris understood that humans, by nature, didn't like to travel to unspecified destinations. It was like being blindfolded and kidnapped. It was disconcerting. The psych teams on board had to extend their hours for traumatized crew members. Kris would have liked to go but he didn't think it would instill confidence. Instead, he ate his feelings and the result of that was changing his pants size by one inch.

Jennifer came to his side and crooked her neck toward the ready room. Kris silently nodded and got up from the command chair, leaving Logan in command.

The pair walked into the ready room and their gazes landed on the four Citari battleships that were escorting them. It was the rule since the last mission. They were to be escorted through Citari space as protection from the Gawayans.

Kris' eyes drifted to Jennifer and he instantly felt guilty. Jennifer had just married her wife Grace when they had to ship out. Kris offered her an out from the tour, but Jennifer was too loyal to take it. She was aware of the stakes of The Reason. She knew what she was doing would affect humankind for centuries.

"It'll be two weeks in a few hours," Jennifer stated.

"Yep, and not even a hint from the Citaris," Kris remarked, landing in his chair. "Two weeks of just staying on course and not a peep."

"They must be afraid of being scanned," Jennifer said.

"That's just it. I had Mariah and C study the warp bubble we're in. It's not like any other. It's cloaked."

"Cloaked?"

"Nobody knows where we are. We can't be tracked," Kris revealed.

"How many escorts do we have?" Kris asked.

"Four," Jennifer answered. Her eyes drifted to the viewport and clearly saw there were now six keeping pace with them. Logan got on the inter-ship to tell them, but Kris told him he was aware of the new additions to the fleet. Kris' knuckles landed on the edge of the viewport. Kris turned and sat on the edge. Jennifer joined him.

"I think our wait is nearly over," Kris surmised. He sensed the flashes of four more ships joining the warp bubble. "This is no escort, Number One. This is an armada." They counted twelve more flashes until it settled down. They were soon surrounded by twenty-two Citari battlecruisers.

The main door slid open, and C entered, her expression clearly concerned as she pointed back outside. She was about to open her mouth, but Kris already began speaking.

"We know," he said.

"Do you know what it's about?" C questioned, trying to mask her growing alarm.

"No, but I'm betting radio silence is about to end."

CHAPTER FORTY-SIX

Kris and C heard the crackling sound of a Citari transporting in. They glanced over his shoulder and found Vichon loping along beside them. Kris stopped and turned, offering his hand. Vichon took hold of his hand with a firmer grip than usual.

"Christina, I'm glad you are here. I have something for you." Vichon searched around in his cloak and pulled out and handed her the second emblem. C stared at it, speechless. "Now, Christina, could you excuse us?" C nodded, still staring at the emblem. Kris indicated they should find a private place to speak. There were a few empty quarters on the deck, and they stole into one of them. The room was naturally bare and hadn't been used since his first mission across the DMZ, but they grabbed some chairs and sat down. Kris smiled as he crossed his legs and ran his hand through his hair.

"So, we can finally talk?"

"Yes," Vichon answered. "I'm sorry to have kept you so deeply in the dark, but it was necessary. We are operating with the utmost secrecy. That was why even your government wasn't briefed."

"Loose lips," Kris said.

"How is that?"

"Old Earth saying. Never mind."

"Ah, I see. By now, I'm sure you have an idea of where you are," Vichon began.

"Yeah, but I haven't got a clue why you've brought us here," Kris said innocently.

"On my world, Gaway's treachery has created rising resentment. There is a feeling of guilt for your lost fleet, Galloway. There is blood on our hands. We may have been the victors, but we were not totally in the right," Vichon admitted.

"You couldn't have known that." Kris said.

"We should have. After all... we're, as you might say, the 'big dogs' of the galaxy. The Gawayan problem needs to be vanquished, Galloway."

"Vanquished? When the Citaris use words like that, it can only mean one thing. You've got battleships arriving, ten every hour, and the cloaked warp bubble is getting bigger. My people estimate that you've committed at least a third of your war fleet."

"They are accurate," Vichon confirmed plainly.

"Okay, but that doesn't answer why the U.S.S. Concord is smack dab in the middle. You signed off on us coming armed, but you can't want us to go into battle with you. You've got something else up your sleeve?" Kris pressed, suspicious.

Vichon's soulful yellow eyes drifted away from a small viewport over to Kris. Kris stared into them. Vichon stood and turned away.

"There's been too much. What do you call it? Intrigue. The Earthers in your day were the hooligans of the galaxy, yes?" Vichon said questioningly.

"That's fair."

"But the Gawayans are master manipulators. They have an endgame, if you will."

"Clearly."

"You stood in the way of part of it. Who's to know what else they are aiming for? Not only have they infiltrated Earth, but we've learned of ten other worlds where they're planting seeds of dissent." Vichon turned to Kris and stared at him starkly. "They are an existential threat to the galaxy itself. They have the darkest of values," Vichon warned.

"Not all of them, certainly," Kris scoffed.

Vichon leaned into him, his pallor pinkening. Kris stepped back a few steps, having never seen Vichon look so serious. "You don't understand what we did."

"I sure don't. Don't you think it's time to tell me?" Kris said, sitting on a sheetless bed.

"You deserve at least that. No more secrets. This, of course, was before my time. When Earth was discovered, it was at first greeted with joy. Finding fellow sentient life was an amazing scientific discovery. But we soon realized that humans were complicated. As I've explained, they had nearly gone extinct. This was over one hundred ninety-five thousand years ago. Weather shifts were reducing populations at alarming rates. We rescued five thousand souls to repopulate them."

"What did you do with those five thousand?" Kris asked.

"They were the first inhabitants of Gaway," Vichon revealed.

"The Gawayans are humans?" Kris probed incredulously.

"Yes. We first studied them and put them in control groups."

"Control groups?" Kris repeated, puzzled.

"Yes. But there's more. Humans run the gamut from the kind and thoughtful to the vicious and cruel. It was decided to separate the humans by groups. Some were intermingled evenly. Others were settled with only good, others only bad."

"So, you could study how they turned out?"

"Yes, but this began over one hundred ninety-five thousand years ago. It was refined up until the eighth century, when the project was concluded. I know you may think it morally questionable. But it was done. Twelve different colonies on twelve different systems were... planted. Of the ten, three came to self-extinction."

"Incredible," Kris said. "They were the cruel groups?"

Two, yes. One, no. Beyond that, two of the cruel groups survived and seven of the kind, thoughtful groups thrived, even to this day. You see Earth is and has always been a combination of groups and their subsets. We stopped the program but kept studying Earth until the end of World War II."

Kris stepped up to Vichon, who stared at him warily. "The Gawayans were your first try, and you made mistakes," Kris suggested.

"Yes. They were your human dark side genetically rolled up into one ball. They are our mistake, and we intend to fix it. We need your help," Vichon urged.

"Clearly, I'm no fan of the Gawayans, but I don't know how this will go over on Earth. You've scattered us across the galaxy..."

"The Council has voted to reunify humanity with its better parts. We want the truth to be told. Humanity is not a mere twenty billion now but closer to half a trillion people. Relatives across a deep, dark sea," Vichon revealed.

Kris sat down. The truth nearly took the air out of him. It was incomprehensible. Man was at every corner of the galaxy. They had been seeded. But Kris did a little math. There was still an unmentioned human world that Vichon was hesitant to discuss.

"Who are the other dark side humans?" Kris asked pointedly.

Vichon nodded and smiled. "The Gawayans of course. The other is distant. No threat to you."

"Who are they?" Kris insisted. The Citari stared at Kris for several moments. Kris stared back. Kris needed to know. He deserved answers. Vichon turned away from Kris and cleared his throat.

"They call themselves the Kanna," Vichon began. "They are morally ambiguous. We don't understand them. They are the only world we are still observing. That's why the planets must remain secret. Earth may know, but engagement must be secure before we can truly move forward."

"You can reach the Kanna?" Kris asked.

"Yes, but that is for another day. I've revealed much," Vichon said plainly. "Too much, in fact."

"I understand. But thank you for confiding." Kris offered his hand and the men shook. "Now, Vichon, do you mind telling me how the crew of the Concord fits into what we're doing right now?" Kris asked. Vichon turned back to Kris and leaned in closer. He poked Kris on his knee.

"We need you to travel to Gaway. Nothing more than that." Kris looked at him, stunned, and Vichon smiled broadly. "Do you have a writing instrument?" Vichon asked. Kris reached for a pen. "I need you to write this down," Vichon continued. Kris grabbed a piece of paper and stared at Vichon, poised to write.

CHAPTER FORTY-SEVEN

Mariah had been summoned to the chart room. It was the same one where she came up with the inspired plan to reach Eric Doneghan. It was still lightly populated. Half the corridor lights were off. She could hear her footsteps echoing as she approached the chart room and first saw Jennifer, who closed the door after her. She surveyed the faces. Kris, C, Logan, Amanda, and a few people from C's tactical team spread out.

"This is mysterious," Mariah mused quietly.

"Okay," Kris started. "Vichon paid me a little visit."

This grabbed everyone's attention. They had all been waiting for some developments over the last two weeks and finally there was news. Kris stood and addressed them, scratching his head.

"He wants us to go to Gaway. On our own," Kris announced.

"What? They'd shoot our asses off at the first scan of us," Jennifer objected firmly.

"That'd be true if we were flying the Concord," Kris admitted.

Amanda squirmed in her seat and leaned forward. "If we're not flying the Concord, what are we flying?"

"A Gawayan scout ship that the Citaris are providing for us," Kris said, then looked around for reactions.

"I don't like the sound of this," Jennifer said. "It feels a little cloak and dagger to me."

"It is."

"What are we supposed to do on this ship?" Logan asked.

"Travel to Gaway and wait for instructions," Kris replied, eyeing all of them. They all moved uncomfortably. It was news, and there were new questions. Why would the Citaris want them to infiltrate Gaway? What was the end game? At a certain point everyone was talking over each other until Kris told them to be silent.

"It doesn't take an A.I. designer to figure out that this is about war. It's about what the Gawayans were up to."

"We can't start a war," Jennifer insisted.

"I know, but we're cut off from Earth. We are tasked to go to Gaway. Just the people in this room. I get why it's us. We blend in. We look like them. There'd be no suspicions. But what we'd have to do there is a mystery."

"We don't speak the language," Logan pointed out.

"We've been given translator patches to be worn on our skin. We'll understand what they're saying and vice versa. The Citaris provided the technology. Mariah, that's your deal. Hand them out, please," Kris requested.

"Aye, sir," Mariah said quickly.

"Where is this scout ship?" Jennifer asked.

"It's three light years away. Mixed it up with a Citari destroyer. It's three days overdue back to Gaway. We'll say we had a system-wide failure and we just got it working only recently," Kris relayed.

"I don't think we should go in there without knowing the full intent. We need some details—we can't go in flying blind," Jennifer insisted.

"Number One is right," C agreed. "What if they want us to do something that we can't do?"

"Well, here's the final part that Vichon told me. We do this. Whatever it is. And The Reason has been satisfied. Our hostilities and our dark past with the Citaris will be wiped clean. And since that is our main mission, we go along. And we can move on to reunification with the lost colonies across the stars. The Citaris want that and I'm sure everyone in this room does too. We've jumped into the unknown before, but this time we're finishing something."

"But aren't the Gawayans like us?" C asked.

"Yes, but only on the outside."

The intercom rang out and an ensign informed Kris that a Citari warship was docking with the Concord. Kris stepped out of the chart room and headed down the lightly lit corridor. Kris slipped into his quarters and picked up an old-fashioned letter and scribbled something on it. He sealed it in an envelope. He headed out and made a lonely journey to docking bay three. He found a lone Citari waiting for him, wearing a pouch over his shoulder. The Citari glanced up him. Kris handed him the letter and the alien turned on its heel and reboarded the Citari scout ship, which undocked. Kris watched at a porthole window as the scout ship put some distance between them and then warped off on a course only known to Kris.

The letter arrived at the DMZ on the scout ship. The Citari retrieved the letter from his pouch and walked into a modest shuttle bay. He stared ahead at an unmanned pod and opened the top of it. He placed the letter inside and withdrew from the shuttle bay. After sealing the door, he decompressed the shuttle bay and engaged the pod. It raced out into the darkness of space on its course to Earth.

CHAPTER FORTY-EIGHT

The Concord circled the Gawayan scout ship. It was around the size of one of their shuttles, so there was room for it to fit in the bay. A Citari pilot flew the wayward ship in and landed it in an unoccupied corner. When the bay pressurized, Amanda was the first to reach the scout ship. The Citari pilot, Kella, bowed to Amanda. Amanda stuck out her hand and shook it.

"So, you're my flying instructor?" Amanda asked.

"Amanda, it is not hard. It was designed by humans, and you tend to come to the same conclusions."

"Let's hit it." Amanda and Kella started toward the scout ship. Kris and Logan walked around the ship, marveling at Kella's insight.

"Humans do come to the same engineering conclusions, even though they were separated by lights years," Kris said.

"When do we go?" Logan asked.

"Tomorrow. Kella has our course and destination," Kris responded. "I think you better get up there and learn this thing, too."

"You don't think the Citaris would wipe them out?" Logan wondered.

Kris scratched his head. "Well, they were willing to wipe us out because we wouldn't listen, and the Gawayans seem to be a lot more headstrong than us. Let's hope not. I think Vichon has an angle. He always has one. Now go on, get up there."

CHAPTER FORTY-NINE

The Citari pod slipped into Earth's solar system unnoticed. It made a slight course correction that sent it hurtling towards the final leg of its journey. The pod was picked up by Earth's defense command as it slung under the moon.

NEAR, the agency that tracked all objects big and small, came to the same conclusion: it was headed for the District of Columbia. It was traveling at such a rapid clip that Earth's defenses didn't have time to react.

The President was on the toilet, grimacing at an op-ed about his lame duck presidency. He snorted disdainfully at the writer, and thought he'd give him a call and let him know what he really thought about his opinion. The President glanced up from his paper, hearing the rumbling of heavy footsteps beating toward him. It was his secret service detail. Before he could say anything, he was yanked off the toilet and wrapped in a robe.

The President was silent as they hustled him to an elevator. The doors closed and he and his details sped down to a hardened safe room where they would wait for the all clear or possibly... rescue.

The pod broke through the thick grey clouds that were churning over Washington D.C. It slowed and landed on the East Lawn of the White House. It made no sound. It just sat there silently as a drone approached it. The camera then peered into the pod and zoomed in on its contents. It was a letter. The image was tightened. It was addressed to the President from Kris Galloway. In bold letters it stated: FOR HIS EYES ONLY.

Jane Aoki was the leader of the team dispatched to the East Lawn. She had been watching the drone picture on her pad. She told the others to hold back, and she moved in closer. She approached the pod. Jane reached in and plucked out the letter and ran a scanner over it. It was what it was. A letter sent by the Citari through Kris Galloway.

The President was being escorted back from the safe room. He reached his door and indicated for his secret service agents to hang back. He entered the Oval Office alone and could see the letter resting on the resolute desk. He closed the door and crossed to his chair and eased himself into it. He opened the letter and read. He sat back in his chair in the Oval Office, his face ashen. He folded the letter. He stood and paced around the room in silence. He stared down at his shoes, thinking, and then leaned against his desk supported by his knuckles. He flipped open the letter again, donning his glasses. He was speechless. He moved behind his desk and pulled out a slim black comm. He pressed a single button and held it up to his ear.

"Severen. It's the President. I need to see you now. I need you to come alone. No one needs to know where you're headed. Shake your detail, in fact."

Severen arrived at the White House twenty minutes later. He knocked on the Oval Office door and the President opened it and pulled him inside. Severen couldn't help but notice the letter dangling from the President's hand.

"Mr. President, how can I—"

"Read this." The Commander in Chief thrust the letter into his hand. Severen held it up and his mouth fell agape. It was from Galloway. The Citaris had identified every Gawayan agent on Earth and their accomplices. There were many Severen had suspected, but now the whole ring was in his hand.

"Glad your name wasn't on there."

"But some of my people are," Severen said, sliding onto the couch, his hand on his head. "What do you want me to do?"

"Round up the Gawayans and have justice work on the traitors. This remains an absolute secret."

"There's a couple of congressmen on here," Severen pointed out.

"Justice and the F.B.I. aren't implicated. They'll know what to do."

Severen stepped out of the oval and found and empty office. He scanned the letter and sent it to Leo Harvest. They had been working on the Gawayan problem for months. Severen's comm rang and it was Leo on the other end.

"So, what do we do sir?" Leo asked.

"Enact wildfire immediately. And in terms of the I.I. agents on the Gawayan payroll, terminate with extreme prejudice. Give it to Ramona."

"Yes, sir," Leo said and hung up. The operation was one that Severen had been planning, but he didn't have all the names. Leo would handle it, and he had to go directly to the Department of Justice and get the ball rolling to open investigations and arrest the traitors. The Gawayans would no longer be a thorn in his side.

He wondered what else Vichon told Galloway. The secrets were clearly coming out, and this had to only be the beginning.

CHAPTER FIFTY

manda slowed the Gawayan scout ship as it approached the Great Net. It was a force field that encircled the Gawayan solar system. It went layers deep. No Citari ship could cross this field. It truly was impenetrable. That's what Logan thought after he sat back from perusing his detailed scans. The power source had to be enormous.

Amanda stared down at the alien communication that popped up in Gawayan. It was clear they were being scanned for their registration number. They were authorized without her having to say a word. A pathway opened and Amanda guided them through.

As they dropped through the Great Net, each layer would close behind them. There were twenty-six, all counted, which ranged in intensity. They finally slipped through the last one, and Amanda changed course for Gaway.

The scout ship landed just outside the capitol city of Mecca. *Another ancient Earth name,* Kris thought to himself. He sat silently as Amanda landed them in what appeared to be an abandoned area. The crew was also silent. None of them were sure what they were getting themselves into. But they knew what their task was. Lower the Great Net. They knew what that meant. The Citaris would be free to reach Gaway. But they didn't know the play. In the end, the Earth and the Citaris attained their restitution.

Kris stepped out of the scout ship and smelled a hint of sulfur. He eyed the polluted skies and the purple sunset on the horizon. His lungs ached as Jennifer came up beside him, looking into her scanner. Without glancing up, Jennifer grimaced.

"The Gawayans aren't big on climate. The air pollution levels here are beyond anything recorded on Earth."

Kris coughed and wiped his brow. He took out a small water bottle from his belt and washed out his eyes. He stared ahead at Mecca. Its buildings thrust over two thousand feet above the clouds. But they weren't clouds. It was a fog of pollution rising up and swirling around the skyscrapers.

C stepped out of the ship, picking through a bag provided by the Citaris. She pulled out an air breather. "I guess this explains why the Citaris gave us these," C said.

Kris grabbed one. He placed it on. There was a pair of goggles that went with it. Kris slipped them on, too. They rest of the crew followed suit. "Where do we have to go, C?"

The team walked through the swirling clouds of pollution that embraced them. They occasionally saw other Gawayans. They were certainly human, but there was a darkness about them. Kris noted the man walking with two beautiful women on leashes. Kris tried not to react. He stared back at everyone else, giving them a silent order with his eyes not to react.

They turned a corner and found a dead body on the road. Gawayans seemed to not have a care as they walked around or even over the body. Kris could feel a sense of coldness. It was a city filled with cruelty. He hadn't seen much of their society, but he hoped he was looking at the exception and not the rule.

As the team continued, they saw a street argument that was settled with a stabbing. They witnessed a district where live sex acts were performed in store windows for paying customers. The performers all seemed drugged, damaged. This clearly wasn't a career choice.

It was a city were depravity reigned and violence was encouraged. Kris realized they should be careful about how to engage. They were in enemy territory and any Gawayan could be a threat.

They reached a saucer-like building. They stared at it. It was the command and control of the Great Net. The team entered a quiet lobby. There was no one to be seen. C tightened her grip on the bag slung over her shoulder. "Let's get this over with."

Just then, a woman appeared with twenty armed guards and surrounded them. Kris didn't dare reach for his disruptor pistol. She was a tall woman of South Asian extraction. She glided over to Kris and stood before him with a smirk planted on her face.

"Kris Galloway. You've come a long way."

"And you are?"

"Kahn. Head of Gawayan security. We scanned the scout ship and were puzzled why there were so many aboard a ship that only had two occupants when it set out. Now I have the pleasure of meeting the key players on the Concord."

"You've lived on Earth?" Kris asked.

"I was assigned there for fifteen years."

"Surprised you came back to this," Kris observed.

"We do what we want here, Mr. Galloway? We aren't bound by all the rules that Earth inflicts on itself," Kahn reminded him slyly.

"No laws?" Kris said.

"Few. Gaway is a planet ruled by natural instincts. Nothing else."

"Must've been exhausting for you, living on Earth," Kris fawned, glancing over at C who held her bag even more firmly.

Kahn noticed. She moved over to C and crossed her arms in front of her. "And what's in your little bag? A present from the Citaris, no doubt." Kahn grabbed for it, but C held on tight. Kahn yanked it away. She opened the bag and found a device. "A bomb? You were going to blow up the Great Net? You thought you could just come in and take out our defenses? The Citaris aren't very smart, and neither are you."

C began to slowly back away from Kahn. Kahn noticed her movement and became puzzled. C took five more steps back. Kahn raised her pistol, but the device clicked on and ignited. It didn't explode per se. It was an electromagnetic pulse weapon. The lights in the building went out, as did the Great Net. What Kahn didn't know was that Kris had put a fail-safe in the plan. C wore a transponder that, when separated from the pulse bomb, would trigger. Kahn had sealed their fate by merely taking it away from C.

"Come on," Kris beckoned.

The team ran back outside, and the guards tried to fire on them, but the pulse bomb had fried their weapons, too.

Mariah ran ahead of them and disappeared into the thick smog. Guards chased after them, but Kahn stayed behind and took the stairs down to operations, where she found the Great Net team in panic. The shields were down, and they had no protection. Kahn was stunned.

The scout ship raced away from Gaway at maximum speed. Mariah listened in as she could hear the Gawayans marshalling their forces. The ships were launching and rapidly gaining on them. They had to get behind the Citari line. Amanda pushed the small vessel over its limit, yet the Gawayan battle cruisers were catching up. Kris glanced down at the console and saw they had a mere five minutes until they would be overtaken. Kris tried to get ahold of the Citaris but there was no answer.

"Can you get anything more out of this thing?" Kris asked.

"I don't know what it can take. I'm at one hundred and five percent and we've got vibrations," Amanda reported.

"Take it to one hundred and ten," Kris instructed, staring at her eye to eye.

Amanda glanced at the readouts. The engines were overheating. The data coming in all looked bad. She was afraid if she followed his orders, it could blow the whole works. When a ship is making noises, she knew from experience, it had reached the breaking point. Amanda was about to say no when twenty-five Citari ships appeared around them.

"Belay that order," Kris stopped her. Kris watched fifteen of the ships fan out in front of him and disappear into the cold void. It gave him chills as he saw the silent explosion dancing across his view. Gawayan ships were being decimated. It was what he saw so many years ago when the Citaris were at war with Earth.

Mariah then reported that the Concord was trying to get in contact with them. Kris ordered Amanda to take the scout into their shuttle bay. Amanda swerved the ship around and headed them in.

Kris was in his command chair. Mariah was trying to reach Vichon but there was no answer. Kris stood as a witness to the battle. He knew the Gawayan fleet would be lost, but would Vichon stop there? There were three populated planets in the Gawayan system. This could easily turn from war to extermination. Kris didn't like what he saw on Gaway, but he didn't want any part of a genocide. But Kris felt he knew the Citaris. They wanted civilizations to survive. He didn't know Vichon's playbook, but he was certain Vichon wouldn't take it that far. They had come close to extermination on Earth, but the Gawayans were pulling strings.

The Gawayans fought the Citaris for the better part of a day until their fleet was just floating wreckage. The Citaris flew past the destruction as they headed back to Gaway. Kris could see bodies floating in space. Human bodies torn from their ships after sudden decompression. He could see a flailing man in a spacesuit clinging to a rocket engine bell. There'd be no rescue for him. Kris realized he had no say about the events that were happening around him. They were accomplices at first and now just witnesses.

Mariah sent messages to Vichon on every channel she could think of, but there was still no answer. She approached Kris as he sat glumly in his command chair. "Nothing, sir. I can't get hold of him."

"Right," Kris sighed.

"Where do you think this is going?" Jennifer asked.

"The Citaris want payback. I can't figure out what their endgame is."

"We're approaching Gaway," Logan announced.

"Shit," Kris said running his hand through his hair. "What's the population, Jennifer"

"Two billion on Gaway Prime. On Gaway Minor and its moon another billion." Kris stood up from his chair. "They can't do this," Kris snapped. He checked Jennifer's scans—all the Gawayan worlds had been encircled. Mariah told everyone to be quiet. A message was being sent to Earth by Vichon. She sat back in her chair with a stunned look. Kris eyed her and moved toward the post.

"What is it?" Kris asked.

"The Citaris just asked the Earth Directorate to send four ships to Gaway," Mariah informed him. "The Gawayans have surrendered."

"Why would they want our fleet here?"

"No idea." Mariah shook her head.

"I know they were going to return the Gawayan spies on Earth, but that doesn't take four starcruisers."

Mariah then listened to her comm and turned back to Kris. "I've got Vichon."

"Put him on," Kris said.

The Citari leader appeared on screen with a slight smile on his face. Kris stared at him blankly, wondering how he could be smiling after all the carnage. "Galloway, you've succeeded again."

"I guess so," Kris hesitated.

"By now you're aware the Gawayans have surrendered," Vichon remarked.

"Yes, I'm glad you didn't take it further."

"We're in agreement. The Gawayans are troublesome. They always will be. We feel they need to be managed... guided, if you will."

"They don't go for rules down there," Kris advised.

"Then you'll have to show them."

"Me?"

"You are the new governor of the Gawayan system," Vichon announced.

"Me? In charge of a system?"

"Well, just until the fleet arrives. Then Earth will manage the Gawayans and a new governor will be appointed."

Kris landed in his chair with a thud. The Citaris wanted total control of the Gawayans. What better way than to have humans manage the problem? It was a job he didn't want, but it was the final piece to The Reason and it certainly wasn't a request. Kris was being handed power he didn't relish, over a people that, by nature, were all of humanity's bad attributes rolled into one system. How would he manage this? He had no clue.

The Concord went into orbit around Gaway. He and his team flew down to Mecca and were escorted by four battalions of Citari slice fighters. Kris was led to Killion House, the home of the Great Leader who had now been deposed and executed by the Citaris. The house was six levels high. On the top level was one room that stretched to every corner of the structure. The Great Chair was there, and Kris was instructed to take it. Reluctantly, he approached the gunmetal grey chair and sat down. Vichon beamed in and strode over to Kris.

"Vichon, I really don't know about this. I'm a starship captain, not a supreme leader," Kris insisted.

"Those are the best leaders. The ones who don't crave power. And you don't. When this all started between us, you weren't sure if you could be a starship captain again. You turned out to be masterful," Vichon smiled.

"I've only seen an inch of Gaway..." Kris started and Vichon cut him off.

"And they are bad. I know. I think you'd refer to them as a rotten bunch. All true."

"You can't fix them overnight."

"We don't expect you to. We just want them contained. They need to stay within their boundaries. Forever." Vichon clasped Kris' hand warmly. "You have brought lasting peace, Kris. You will be remembered as the father of human reunification," Vichon said.

"So, we're no longer banned from contact?" Kris said.

"No... No ban, but you still must follow rules. Your president and the leaders of Earth have agreed to the terms laid out by the Citari Council. Spreading humanity across the galaxy was unwise on our part. It's time that was fixed."

"So, who's gonna fix that?"

"I have a man in mind." Vichon released his hand, stepped back, smiled, and beamed back up to his ship.

Kris glanced at his crew. C sauntered over to Kris. "So how do we do this?"

Kris ruled Gaway for thirty-six days until the Earth fleet arrived. Kris was relieved. He wanted to go home. He finally handed over power to some civil servant. He gathered his crew and sped home.

As Kris sat in his command chair, he gazed at his unit and smiled. They were a solid team, and they were friends. He didn't covet the chair; he had just grown comfortable in it.

Mariah would go back to NASA to do research. Jennifer would take back command of the Concord until Kris was specified for a mission. C and Logan became a couple a few months after they returned. Kris sold his business and became a consultant for NASA. He reevaluated his life. Why had he disappeared, becoming so anonymous? He thought at the time it was healthy. But, in fact, he was just running away. When he confided this to Mindy, she revealed to him she already knew. She told him he had been through too much. Kris, Mindy, and the kids moved back to Houston. Kris became a senior consultant and waited for the next call.

The End

Acknowledgments

Hannah Ryan
Amy Sriberg

Antioch University
Colette Freedman
Ross Brown

About the Author

Photo © Joseph Puhy

STEPHEN LANGFORD is a Massachusetts-born writer of television, film, and novels. His love for science fiction and horror inspired him to become a writer, sharing his stories with audiences around the world.

After receiving a B.S. in Film from Emerson College, Stephen moved from Boston to Los Angeles to work for Embassy Television. Starting as a writer's assistant, he moved up the ladder and was promoted to Staff Writer, eventually becoming a Writer/Producer for the smash-hit Warner Bros. situation comedy *Family Matters*, which he worked on for eight years! He later wrote screenplays for feature films including *Lovewrecked, Club Dead, Warm Blooded Killers,* and *Big Baby,* and directed four other films as well.

Recently, Stephen has come full circle to his beginnings by writing for the new AMC anthology horror series, *Creepshow,* based on the beloved classic 1982 movie by Stephen King and George Romero. Along with writing partner Paul Dini, they wrote three episodes of the show, including the first outerspace horror episode: "The Right Snuff."

In 2019, Stephen received his Master of Fine Arts in Writing and Contemporary Medium from Antioch University, which is where *The Stars Are My Salvation* was born.

Stephen is married to his wife, Sandy. They have two grown children, two dogs, and reside in Tarzana, California.

www.Stephen-Langford.com

We want to hear from you!
Please visit our website for more information about
new releases, author updates, special offers, and more!

www.StygianPress.com

CPSIA information can be obtained
at www.ICGtesting.com
Printed in the USA
BVHW040405260423
663035BV00002B/10